# Cards of Fate

### A.R. Kingston

Keen Quill Press
*Colorado Springs, CO*

Copyright © 2022 by A.R. Kingston

All rights reserved. No part of this publication may be reproduced, distributed or transmitted in any form or by any means, including photocopying, recording, or other electronic or mechanical methods, without the prior written permission of the publisher, except in the case of brief quotations embodied in critical reviews and certain other noncommercial uses permitted by copyright law. For permission requests, write to the publisher, addressed "Attention: Permissions Coordinator," at the address below.

A.R. Kingston /Keen Quill Press
2910 N Powers Blvd
#444
Colorado Springs, CO 80922
www.arkingston.co
www.keenquillpress.com

Publisher's Note: This is a work of fiction. Names, characters, places, and incidents are a product of the author's imagination. Locales and public names are sometimes used for atmospheric purposes. Any resemblance to actual people, living or dead, or to businesses, companies, events, institutions, or locales is completely coincidental.

Concept Art ©2022 @wafflecaramel

Ordering Information:
Quantity sales. Special discounts are available on quantity purchases by corporations, associations, and others. For details, contact the "Special Sales Department" at the address above.

Cards of Fate/ A.R. Kingston -- 1st ed.
ISBN 978-1-734-2400-7-8

Leopold and Morgana

*Grand Duke Leighton Charmant*

Princess Lafreya

*Abnaroth, the demon king*

*(For full image go to arkingston.com)*

# Contents

The Sun Emperor ............................................................. 1

The Devoth Priestess ...................................................... 15

The Full Moon ................................................................ 21

The Jester ....................................................................... 29

The Devil ........................................................................ 41

The Ace of Swords ......................................................... 55

The Three of Coins ........................................................ 65

The Seven of Coins ........................................................ 71

The Four of Swords ....................................................... 81

The Nine of Swords ....................................................... 89

The Three of Chalices ................................................... 97

The Five of Staves ........................................................ 107

The Three of Staves ..................................................... 113

The Three of Swords .................................................... 123

The Five of Chalices .................................................... 131

The Ace of Staves ......................................................... 135

The Ten of Swords ....................................................... 141

The Wheel of Life ........................................................ 151

The Nine of Staves ....................................................... 159

Judgment ...................................................................... 173

The Lovers ................................................................... 181

| | |
|---|---:|
| The Ace of Chalices | 191 |
| The Ace of Coins | 199 |
| The Six of Swords | 205 |
| The Five of Swords | 215 |
| The Two of Chalices | 221 |
| The Four of Staves | 235 |
| The Ten of Chalices | 243 |
| The Hanged Man | 251 |
| The Page of Swords | 257 |
| The Monk | 265 |
| The Star | 273 |
| The Enchantress | 281 |
| Strength | 291 |
| Ten of Coins | 299 |
| The Tower of Sorrow | 307 |
| Death | 325 |
| The Chariot of Fire | 341 |

CHAPTER 1

# The Sun Emperor

**S**trolling through the square of the capital city of Perdetia, Morgana de Laurent crinkled her nose and narrowed her pink eyes at the stench of burned flesh lingering in the air. Last night—much to the protest of Princess Lafreya—a druid burned there. The poor man had been discovered in one of the outer villages of the kingdom, and despite the old king being dead, the advisors of the old monarchy went ahead with the execution against protests from Lafreya, whose orders they were supposed to follow. The same stupid laws that still considered magic folk evil also prevented a woman from ruling the kingdom even though she was the first in line.

Shaking her head of aubergine hair, Morgana picked up her pace. It was just her luck that as a witch she would find herself in the one place on the continent of Dresbourn that still followed the rules of the Devoth, being known as the demon king. When the Devoth prince—one of many god-like creatures—was pulled from the Otherworld to usher forward a new dawn, he took it upon himself to eliminate anyone who wielded magic out of fear that those who were a product of Devoth–mortal relationships could put an end to him. The demon king's rule saw the death of many people like Morgana, and the survivors fled into the woods to hide from him. It was something she should have done—flee to a territory that abolished his two hundred years of terror—but something kept her in Perdetia despite the dangers she might face if her identity were discovered.

Almost running through the stone gate that separated the castle from the rest of the city, she burst through the double oak doors and hurried down the hall. She had to find Lafreya. She knew there was something her best friend needed to tell her, and her heart thundered from the anticipation. Skipping the steps, she headed for the princess's private study, barely able to contain her excitement. Stopping before the studded wood doors, she froze upon hearing a commotion on the other side and pressed her ear to the wood to hear the conversation better.

"We cannot allow you to marry that . . . that man."

*Of course,* thought Morgana, *I should have expected King Nathaniel's old advisors to oppose to the union between Lafreya and Grand Duke Charmant of Bragburg.*

After all, it was the Charmant family that opposed the demon king's rule from the start, and seeing as King Nathaniel always secretly supported the Devoth hold over the world, it should have been no surprise to Morgana that Nathaniel's advisors—who maintained some control over the kingdom—would try to prevent

Perdetia from abolishing the old laws. Gritting her teeth, Morgana held her breath and listened intently, wondering what her mild-mannered friend would do. Would she give up the love of her life, or would she stand up for herself and put the old relics in their place until Morgana could officially take over as her sole advisor?

"Too late!" Lafreya yelled shrilly. "I'm going to marry him whether you like it or not."

Poor Lafreya—she truly loved Leighton despite everything their relationship put her through. At first, even Morgana questioned their union. She reminded the princess, her best friend and cousin, that the Charmant line was cursed after the battle with the demon king, but Lafreya did not seem phased. It wasn't until she met the cursed duke herself that Morgana realized he and Lafreya were destined for one another—they each held a soul card. Everyone is born with a fate card, usually one from one of the four suites. Major arcana cards like Morgana's and Lafreya's were rare and only came into play occasionally, usually during a time of significant change. Last time someone held a major arcana card was right before the demon king was summoned into their word by a cult of Devoth followers—those who wished to unite the mortal world with the Otherworld—and every single holder of those cards perished in the first battle with the Devoth prince.

Before the days of the demon king, everyone knew what their card was, as it was standard practice to learn a child's destiny. These days, few people found out; they saw the ritual as archaic and dangerous, not to mention they preferred not to know what fate had in store for them. Most folks these days preferred to pretend that they were the masters of their own destiny, even if it wasn't entirely true. But their card would guide them on their journey, even if they were not aware of it. Morgana could not blame them—she herself wished not to know what her fate card was, or at least she wished to forget. It always loomed at the back of her mind, holding her back from the one thing she really wanted.

It wasn't hard to learn what card you held: All you needed was a deck, which you shuffled until you felt ready. Then you placed thirteen cards down on the table, closed your eyes, reached out, and grabbed one. The one you picked was your fate card. Anyone could do it, but most people simply refused. The only reason she knew hers was because her mother—a woman with a major arcana card of her own—was obsessed with knowing who held what card. The baroness brought her up to believe in the power of the fate cards, and as much as Morgana wished to forget, she couldn't break free of the hold they had on her. Eventually her life was to end in ruin, and only the Chariot of Fire—her soul card—could save her.

She balled up her fists and listened to the rest of the conversation taking place on the other side of the door.

"Think of the kingdom, Your Highness," one advisor protested. Morgana recognized the voice as that of the oldest of the three men King Nathaniel kept on staff. "Grand Duke Charmant is a cursed man. He carries a curse placed on his ancestor by his own wife when she prevented the demon king from killing him, and now all the descendants of the Charmants are doomed. Your intended will be dead in a few years' time, and worst yet, he will pass on his disease to any children you have with him. And may I remind you, a Perdetian heir cannot be cursed. We must maintain a pure blood line, and we must maintain order in Dresbourn."

Morgana had finally had enough of eavesdropping and flung

open the doors. "The princess said she intends to marry the duke. Last I checked, she's a free woman, and arranged marriages haven't been enforced for at least a century. Now, I know that you three still wish you could keep Nathaniel's wish and wed her to the man you see fit to carry on your archaic traditions. However, as her current advisor, I must protest and support my princess's decision to accept Grand Duke Charmant's proposal of marriage and the union of our two kingdoms."

"And what of his curse?" the oldest advisor, with a long white beard flowing over his potbelly, protested. "He will taint our entire line. Or do you not care what happens to our kingdom, Lady de Laurent?"

"Let me be frank here in asking"—Morgana glared at the old man— "so what if he does? I mean, you have a spare as the young prince. Worst-case scenario, you can squeeze an untainted line of royals out of him if need be and allow the princess to wed the man she chose."

"I blame you for this," the old man hissed. "If it wasn't for the de Laurents, we would not be in this predicament to begin with. You just wish to throw our kingdom into ruin and have the magic folk run wild, much like that druid we burned yesterday."

"That's right," a younger advisor with long salt-and-pepper hair butted in. "Why, I bet there are more like *him* hiding out among us, waiting to take over once that heathen becomes our king. The entire Charmant line should just die out, but I guess you don't feel the same."

At his words, Morgana cringed. She was one of the magic folks he spoke of, hiding in plain sight. She knew that the three old relics would see her dead the second they learned she was a witch—and not only because of their hatred for magic. The king and his advisors hated her entire family line and would have loved to see it end alongside Leighton's. King Nathaniel never did like her, or perhaps he simply did not love her mother, who was the cousin of the late queen. From what Morgana had gathered, the late king was once a kind man. He was the youngest brother to the emperor of Vekureth, and back when he first met the queen of Perdetia, he was said to be a gentle soul who wished to abolish all anti-magic laws. It wasn't until he became Perdetia's king that his demeanor and stance changed, and he revealed himself to be a staunch supporter of the demon king. Knowing what she was up against, Morgana smiled, much as she did when Lafreya and Leighton began sharing a bed together. Bracing for a fight, she met the advisor's gaze.

"Obviously, I do not feel the same way you do, gentlemen. Is that so wrong for me to have a different opinion from the rest of you?"

"It is when it threatens our way of life," the middle-aged man with shoulder-length gray hair butted in. "But I guess that is to be expected from the woman whose father is a druid and, dare I say, also her butler."

The last part of his statement made Morgana snort. She knew since she got to Perdetia that people suspected Stephan—her mother's butler and longtime lover—of being a druid and her father, but nothing could have been further from the truth. Her biological mother was a witch— much like her—who died when Morgana was only three. Stephan, the mortal butler, and Baroness Constance de Laurent found Morgana in the woods using magic to survive and took pity on her. The baroness and her lover took her in and raised her as their daughter despite what it meant for their reputation, and they allowed her to practice her magic within their estate—which was protected from King Nathaniel by ancient land rights. Realizing her identity as a witch was still safe from the people who threatened her wellbeing, she gave the old advisors a toothy grin and nodded her head.

"I guess you're right. And yet, there is still nothing you can legally do about it. After all, you are here to advise, not rule in her place. So I guess it's my job as Lafreya's current advisor to invite you gentlemen to shut it and move on. Although I recommend you practice calling Leighton Charmant your new king."

The oldest advisor glared at her. "What's in it for you, de Laurent? What do you have to gain from all of this?"

"Well, if I had to put my finger on it"—Morgana smirked—"I'd have to say it would be not having to hear your constant screeching once the grand duke is king. Once he's in charge, you three are out, and Lafreya gets to keep me as her sole advisor. And if I was a betting woman, I'd guess that is what you are most afraid of. Or am I wrong?"

"You . . ." The middle-aged advisor narrowed his eyes at her. "You *will* regret that, you harlot. The demon king won't allow the largest kingdom in Dresbourn to slip away from him. Our late king knew that. Mark my words, you and the princess are putting Perdetia at risk by agreeing to this ill-fated union with the grand duke."

"Indeed." The oldest man puffed out his chest. "We shall hold an emergency meeting about this. I shall not allow this union to happen."

Giving the princess a menacing glare, the oldest man waved his hand, and the other two advisors turned on their heels and followed him out the door as their robes swished angrily behind them. One glance at her best friend and Morgana knew the woman was on a verge of a breakdown. Her ruby hair was frazzled, and her forest-green eyes sparkled with the tears she was holding back at the thought of not being with Leighton. Shaking her head, Morgana lifted her hand in the air and flicked her wrist to magically pull the runner out from the advisors' feet when she heard them at the top of the stairs. What followed was a scream and the sound of the three old men rolling down the steps in unison. The pain shooting up her arm from using magic was a small price to pay to give her cousin some peace from the old advisors. Folding her arms over her chest, Morgana looked at Lafreya, who shook her head with a smile.

"Did you really need to do that, Morgana? I could have dealt with them later."

"Come now, we both know that couldn't be further from the truth. If those old coots cared even a smidgen of what you had to say, the town square wouldn't stink of a dead man this morning. We both know that you and Gabriel are just puppets to them. They'd try to use you both to rule as they see fit. And it's not like I killed them. I simply shut them up long enough for you to marry Leighton and phase them out."

"You, my dear cousin, are positively evil in the best way possible sometimes." Lafreya approached her and took hold of her hand. "Thank you—for standing up for me, and for always having my back when I need it."

"Don't mention it. You can thank me once you are married by abolishing those damaged laws which still see the death of anyone suspected of using magic."

"You know I will. I would have done so two years ago after my father died."

"I know. Not your fault that a woman, even one first in line, needs a penis to sit on the throne beside her before she can change the old regime's hold. It's a good thing you met Leighton a few weeks after your father's death, though, or you'd have been married off to the first available count. Plus, I've waited seventeen years for change. What's a few more months of hell?"

Lafreya let out a light giggle. Her bubbly personality contradicted the pragmatic one of her cousin. The two were polar opposites since they met, when the baroness introduced the two three-year-olds. But much as it was with Lafreya and Leighton, the difference in their demeanor only strengthened their relationship, with each of them bringing something new to the table. The girls were inseparable since the first day together, and when Lafreya learned a month later her adopted cousin was a witch, she vowed to do everything in her power to protect her from her father and the Devoth laws he kept imposing on their kingdoms. In turn, Morgana was there for her when her mother fell ill and died when the princess was ten. The two of them had been through a lot together over the last seventeen years, and Lafreya wished to ask her cousin a personal question now that she was engaged. She opened her mouth to speak when a stern knock on the door interrupted her. The princess sighed and looked at the doors across from her.

"Come in."

"Your Highness."

Morgana's head snapped back at the sound of his voice, and

her heart leaped into her throat as she watched the young blond knight bow to the princess. When he lifted his head up, his cerulean eyes locked on hers, and she felt her knees grow weak. Leopold Ellingham was a longtime friend of hers, though five years older. She first met him the same day she met Lafreya, and back then she didn't talk; she couldn't after she watched the demon king kill her mother. It was Leo who drew the words out of her, and she had loved him ever since. When he left for his first campaign seven years ago, he asked her to wait for him, and she did. It wasn't until he became the captain of the royal guard that she gave up on the notion of being with him, at least until the laws changed. Seeing him again in his armor and blue-and-gold surcoat made her blush, and she wondered what he was doing there.

"Speak, Captain," Lafreya demanded in a playful tone.

"Your highness." Leo bowed once again. "I have some unfortunate news to give you. It seems that the three advisors of the late king had a slight tumble down the stairs. I guess the runner slipped right out from under them. They have sustained some injuries. A few broken bones, but nothing too serious. Although I am afraid they will be laid up for a bit."

"Don't worry about it, Captain Ellingham. They were slated for retirement soon, anyway."

"I see. In that case"— he stole another glance at Morgana— "may I borrow your current advisor? There is something I wish to discuss with Lady de Laurent in private."

"Oh, well." She side-glanced her cousin with a grin. "I am not using her right now, so you may have her for as long as you want—if she will follow you, that is. Perhaps it is her you should be asking."

"Very well." Leo nodded and placed his arms behind his back. "Royal advisor, may have a word with you out in the hallway?"

"Certainly, Captain." She nodded at him. "Lead the way."

Following him, she caught a whiff of his scent, and the woody aroma made her blush. It always reminded her of a warm cup of hot buttered rum on a crisp winter's night. The scent made a warm heat sweep her cheeks as it always brought her comfort and made her heart flutter. Shutting the doors behind them, she turned and saw him standing at one of the stained-glass windows, looking over at the town square, and she could instantly tell something was bothering him. After knowing him for as long as she had, she could read his body language, and she came up behind him and placed a gentle hand on the cold steel covering his back.

"Were you there last night?" He turned his head to look at her. "You know, when—"

"When they roasted an innocent man at the stake?" she said. "Unfortunately I had no choice but to watch. Royal advisor's duty and all. I bet your men must be really proud of themselves for flushing such a dangerous soul out of hiding."

"Don't start with me, Morgie." He drew his brows together and gripped the windowsill harder. "You know I had no control over that. If it was up to me, we'd stop hunting innocent people who just happen to use magic and focus on what's important: fighting off the monsters the demon king dragged into our world to cause chaos."

Looking at his reddening face, Morgana shook her head. He always had a strong sense of justice she admired, and she knew being in his position couldn't be easy, not when it forced him to hunt and execute the innocent. She didn't know how many times he turned a blind eye to people who were probably just like her, but she knew it must have been plenty. As did Lafreya and Prince Gabriel. Leo must have fought hard to spare the man's life, but it was useless with the old advisors still running the place. The three old men still had far too much sway in protecting the old laws. Had she known what was going to happen, she would have made them take a tumble sooner, but she didn't get word of the burning until they were almost lighting the flames.

"I'm sorry, Leo." She placed her hand on his gauntlet. "I didn't mean it like that."

"I know." He stared out the window. "I just need you to know that I tried my damned hardest to get him off. I don't want you thinking of me as some monster."

"I don't think that. And I know you tried. We all did. I've never seen Lafreya that upset. I thought she was going to be sick from the spectacle."

"I figured that much. It's too bad that she can't change these laws until she marries that heartless bastard."

Morgana frowned. "He has a name, you know. It's Leighton, and he's not heartless. He's actually rather sweet once you get to know him."

Turning to look at her, Leo gave her a smirk, and she knew he must have been thinking the duke put her under some form of spell. She couldn't blame him for thinking the way he did; after all, he'd never met the grand duke. Leighton had always avoided visiting Perdetia's capitol, choosing instead to stay at the de Laurent estate when he came to see Lafreya. Leo—like many others—only saw Leighton in passing, and at first glance the man lived up to his reputation of being cold-hearted. Morgana herself was put off by the man's stoic façade at first. However, once she realized it was a mask he wore to hide his emotions, she grew to like him, and over his courtship with Lafreya she learned how to read his emotions by the tiny changes in his face.

"Trust me, Leo." She leaned on the windowsill beside him. "He's not how he seems. I assure you, Leighton is a decent man and the only one fit to sit on the throne beside Lafreya. Now"— she tilted her head to look up at him— "want to tell me why you really wished to speak to me? Surely public executions and Lafreya's betrothed were not on your mind when you asked me to join you here."

"Fine. You got me." Leo pushed himself off the window. "I was wondering if you had time to reconsider us being together. You know I love you, Morgie. I'll do anything to be with you. I'll give you anything you ask."

Hearing him ask her to be with him made her wince as the screams of the burning man and Leo's guilt over his death were fresh on her mind. She wanted nothing more than to be with him, but she knew that until the laws changed, that was not a possibility. If they discovered she was a witch, she knew she couldn't rely on her friends to protect her. She couldn't put Leo at risk because she knew what he would do if someone tried to kill her. As much as it pained her, she knew it was best to keep him away until she could tell him the truth without putting him and his position at risk.

"I'm sorry, Leo." She took hold of his hand and gave him a pained smile. "As I told you before, the timing is simply not right. I will be busy helping Lafreya plan her wedding. But I want you to ask after she is queen, and perhaps my response will be different."

"I see." Leo's face dropped, and Morgana's heart sank with his expression. "In that case, I shall let you be, as I have things to take care of. I guess I'll see you around."

Watching him leave with his head hung low, Morgana cursed the laws preventing them from being together, but she reminded herself that she kept him away for his own good. Leo would only have to wait three more months until Leighton was king and the laws were abolished.

She knew she'd have to tell her mother and Stephan about what happened to Nathaniel's advisors, and once again they would scold her. Since they took her in, her parents had warned her against using her magic inside the capitol, and once again, when it came to her friends, she couldn't help it. Blowing a stray strand of her wavy purple hair out of her face, she turned and headed the opposite way to her estate.

CHAPTER 2

# The Devoth Priestess

Zipping up Lafreya's cornflower blue dress, Morgana peeked over her friend's shoulder and looked at her reflection in the mirror. The week flew by without the other advisors to get in their way, and the two of them accomplished a lot in preparation for merging the two kingdoms. Now it was time for them to visit Bragburg and the grand duke and discuss how the merger would take place. Morgana knew Lafreya was looking forward to seeing Leighton again, but something didn't sit right with her. She had a strange vision during the night, a dream of chaos and panic followed by pitch-black darkness.

"Are you sure you want to make the trip today?" She buttoned the top button of her friend's dress. "Perhaps we should have Leighton come here instead. He should probably make his appearance in the capitol, which will soon be his as well as yours."

"What's wrong, Morgana?" Lafreya turned to regard her with a pout. "You're not actually worried about what those old men said about the demon king?"

"Of course I am. Perdetia is the only kingdom in this hemisphere which still follows the Devoth law of killing magic practitioners. Do you really think he will let it go without a fight?"

"Don't be silly. I heard he retreated to Iatan when he began losing control over the kingdoms here. Why, I bet he went back to the Otherworld by now."

"I can tell you that is not true. His link to his world was severed when he was brought here, which is why he wears his broken chain around his neck." Morgana stole a glance at the shadow in the corner, a parting gift the demon king left her after the encounter she had with him when she was three. "He's stuck here, in our world, and I bet he's still plotting. Devoth loves control and toying with the lives of mortals, and he is no different."

"Do you say this because you have this strange connection with him?"

"Maybe. I've always had this strange link to him"— Morgana swallowed and looked at the shadow figure slinking closer— "ever since he killed my mother and left me alive. But it's not my link to him this time which makes me worry. I just have this bad feeling about this. I think we should stay here."

"No way. I want to see Leighton. It's been over a week since we were together. Plus, I got you and Leopold's best men with me. I will be fine. It's only a two-hour carriage ride."

"I still don't understand why we can't take Leo with us. Is it not the duty of the captain to accompany the princess?"

"It is." Lafreya heaved out a sigh. "But Gabe said he'd feel better if I allowed him to keep Leo here. My brother is only sixteen, Morgana. He has no idea how to run a kingdom in my stead. Allow the poor kid to have someone he can trust by his side. We will be back tomorrow morning, and you will see that you were worried about nothing, as usual."

"Fine. But I still don't like this one bit." Morgana turned around. "I shall allow you to finish up while I wait for you in the carriage. Just hurry. The sooner we make it to Bragburg, the better I will feel."

Watching Morgana leave her room, Lafreya turned back to the mirror with a faint smile. Morgana always worried about every little thing, which was why she prevented herself from being with the one man she wanted. Morgana tended to overthink, and Lafreya was still hoping to cure her cousin of the tendency. Shaking her head, Lafreya pinned up her ruby hair, allowing a few loose strands to cascade down her shoulders. She was looking forward to being with Leighton again, and as she left her room, she spotted a familiar figure waiting for her in the corner. He was leaning against the wall in the shadows, but she recognized his blond hair and silhouette almost instantly.

"Captain Ellingham." She approached the young knight. "Is there something I can do for you this fine morning?"

"Your Highness." Leo pushed himself off the wall and looked down at her. He was an entire head taller than her and Morgana, and the princess had to tilt her head up to meet his gaze. "I have a favor I wish to ask you. Not as a soldier, but as a friend."

"Of course. Just make it quick. I don't want to keep the carriage waiting."

"Could . . ."—he rubbed the back of his head as he always did when he was nervous— "could you put in a good word for me with Morgana? She'll listen to you, of all people."

"Ah." Lafreya grinned. "You want me to convince my dear cousin to allow you to pursue her romantically."

"No, yes,"—he winced—"I mean, I just want you to feel her out and see where she stands. She knows I love her, but she keeps telling me the timing isn't right, and, well, I just want you to assure her she has nothing to worry about. I have plenty of money saved, if that's her concern. I can provide her with the life she's accustomed to. She has nothing to worry about there."

*Leo, you idiot.* Lafreya thought as she looked over at his flushed face. *How can you not see that she loves you as much as you love her? She has loved you since she first met you. All you must do is wait a few more months, and she'll be yours. Why do you turn stupid when it comes to her?*

"You know your money and status mean nothing to her, Leo. She is a de Laurent. Her mother has been sleeping with her butler since she was fifteen. She'd still have you if you were still a servant shoveling horse muck for that awful man who picked you from the orphanage to serve as his squire."

"Then why does she keep rejecting me? What else can I do to make her be with me?"

"Nothing." Lafreya shrugged. "I assure you, if Morgana says the timing isn't right, she means it. You know she is busy helping me plan the wedding. Perhaps she simply doesn't wish to neglect you in the process." Looking at his drawn face, she sighed. "But fine, Leo. I will talk to my cousin and convince her to give you a chance while the wedding preparations are happening. No promises, though. You know how stubborn she can be. Deal?"

"Deal." Leo smiled. "Thank you. That's all I ask. At the very least, find out if she feels the same way I do."

Lafreya rolled her eyes. "You should know by now that she does. But all right. I need to get going now, before your girl comes looking for me. She seems a lot more antsy than usual."

"Have a safe trip, Your Highness."

Waving her hand, Lafreya picked up her skirt and scurried down the hallway through the open doors where her gold-and-white carriage awaited her. A dozen soldiers sat on their white horses at the front while a dozen more flanked the rear. She reckoned that was enough to keep her safe, and she smiled and waved at Morgana, who was staring out the window at her, frowning. Jumping into the cabin, she plopped down on the gold velvet seat across from her cousin as the door shut behind her and stared at the pink eyes across from her. They would have two whole hours to discuss things, and she was certain she could convince Morgana to relax a little and allow Leo in on her little secret.

CHAPTER 3

# The Full Moon

Sitting across from the princess, Morgana studied her face and smiled. Somehow the idea of her marrying Leighton delighted her. While King Nathaniel was always nice to Morgana and treated her well—despite her being the daughter of the one woman he loathed—she never liked the man. Something about him always made her skin crawl. When he died in Vekureth helping his oldest brother fight off ogres and reaper hags, it devastated Lafreya, her hatred for him notwithstanding, and it was Morgana who had to pick up the pieces. So after her father died, she fell for the young duke of Bragburg. Morgana was naturally leery toward Leighton, given his curse, a parting memento of his ancestors' battle with the demon king. It wasn't until she met the man a day later that her fear subsided. He doted on Lafreya, and when Morgana was relieved to see her friend happy again, she vowed to help the duke break his curse before it turned him into a statue.

Studying Lafreya's expression caused Morgana to frown. Leighton was currently far from the young woman's mind. She and her cousin were only three months apart—with Morgana being the oldest—and after seventeen years, she could almost read the princess's thoughts. Watching her fidget in her seat, play with the fabric of her blue skirt, and chew on her bottom lip, Morgana knew instantly that the topic of conversation for the next two hours would be her. She hated discussing her personal life, and as she stole one glance at the shadow sitting beside her, she sighed. No one knew about the thing that followed her around, and she preferred to keep it that way, which was why she hated talking about herself—she feared letting the fact slip. Preparing herself for the inevitable, she smiled and leaned in, focusing her pink eyes on the green ones of her cousin.

"All right, what is it you wish to say to me? Might as well spit it out now."

"It's about Leopold."

"What about him?"

Morgana winced. Aside from her personal life, Leo was the other topic of conversation she hated to talk about. Everyone close to her knew how she felt about the young knight, and yet no one could figure out why she kept rejecting his advances. Half the time she herself didn't know. Sure, there was the fact that she was a witch and he the captain of the royal guard, but she knew his stance on things and that he'd never compromise her safety. Part of her didn't want him to give up the position he worked so hard to get. Part of her thought it would have been selfish of her to ask—but another part of her didn't care. There was also her fate card looming over her head, threatening to destroy her, but she couldn't blame her fate on the fear she faced, either. No, if she had to guess, her fear of Leo stemmed from the damage done to her over the years, damage that left her fearful of allowing him to hurt her—so instead she chose to hurt him. Across from her, Lafreya pouted, and Morgana held her breath, preparing for the conversation to follow.

"He loves you, you know." Lafreya stared at her. "Just now, before I left, he begged me to put in a good word for him with you. And"—she crossed her arms—"I know you love him. You've loved him since you first met. So isn't about time you let the poor man get close? He's only been chasing you for seven long years."

"And I expect you want me to tell him the truth about me?" Morgana leaned back in her seat. "Want me to tell your captain that your advisor is a witch? One of those evil magic-using creatures that the entire kingdom fears so much?"

"Do you think Leo would care if he knew the truth? You know his stance on our laws. Not to mention, I doubt he'd care if you were a hunchback with a crooked nose and a hairy mole."

"Last time I checked," Morgana said, narrowing her eyes, "we aren't exactly rounding up hunchbacks and burning them at the stake, now, are we? As princess, you couldn't do anything to save that poor man last week. You expect a mere captain to protect me if someone was to find out?"

"I expect him to do everything in his power to save you, even if that means becoming a fugitive. Both he and I would do what needs to be done to keep you safe."

"That right there is the problem. I don't want him to go out of his way for me. I'm not worth it."

"Why not?" Lafreya arched her brow. "Does this have to do with all the men you slept with? Because if that's the case, we both know Leo had plenty of women while he was on the road with my father."

"True." Morgana leaned her head on her hand. "But mine are far worse than his."

"Like Kasaru of X'aris? I hear you seduced the advisor so you could foster a deal between our two nations."

"Well, that rumor isn't entirely true." Morgana played with the loose purple chiffon sleeves of her dress. "We negotiated the deal first, and the sex was just the cherry on top. I mean, he was pretty good looking—tall, muscular, with delicious dark skin, a wicked smile, and a enormous cock to boot. He told me how much he liked my appearance because in his homeland it meant one was close to the magic world, and they worshiped people like me. Once he told me he'd like to explore the far reaches of my flesh"— she glanced up from her lap— "well, let's just say I couldn't resist finding out what the X'aris men had to offer, and boy, that was *a lot* to handle. But . . . no, Kasaru doesn't fit into the category of things I regret. He was a gentleman, and if it wasn't for Leo, I could have fallen for him."

"Well, he certainly fell for you, like everyone you've slept with. He even told me that if you ever change your mind, or if I'm willing to let you go, he'd gladly take you back to X'aris and make you his wife."

"Did he happen to mention that I'd be his fourth wife?" Morgana smirked. "I don't know about those X'aris women, but I don't like to share."

"Wait." Lafreya gasped. "It's that professor from the Westview Academy, isn't it? What was his name again? Giffard?"

Morgana grimaced. "Yes, Giffard it was."

"Seriously, are you *ever* going to tell me what actually happened between the two of you? I mean, you were only thirteen and that nasty old prune was well over fifty and smelled of moth balls and dogbane fungus. The memory of him still makes me sick."

"Nothing." Morgana shuddered at the thought of the old man. "Potions were not my strong suit, and I did what I had to do in order to pass, since I was not a princess like you."

Darting her eyes away, Morgana steadied her ragged breath as a sour taste formed in her mouth at the memory of what he did to her. There was no way she was going to tell Lafreya that he took advantage of her, forcing her to have sex with him while she was his student. Nor was she about to say that he was the first—and by far the worst—sexual experience in her life, or how broken he had left her and how that was partly why she rejected Leo. When she returned her gaze to the princess, she found her observing her with an arched brow.

"You still sticking to that story, years later?" Lafreya's hard gaze was piercing, almost as if she knew the truth. Their eyes locked on one another for a tense moment before the princess let out a loud huff and returned her gaze to the window. "Fine, I guess it's best to leave that pervert in the past where he belongs. But," she said, grinning, "do you remember how he wanted to marry you afterwards? He would not stop pestering the baroness for a month after the semester was over, wondering when he could wed you and take you home."

"Ugh, how could I forget?" Morgana rolled her eyes. "He was

so insistent it almost hurt. Granted, mother would never ever allow it. The mere idea of me being married to a man over twice my age repulsed her. Still"—Morgana exhaled— "fortune sure did smile upon me when he had that tragic accident in the potions lab that shriveled up his member."

"Oh, yes, I remember that. Wasn't he making an anti-birth potion when a vial of hobnail mushrooms exploded in his hand?"

"Sure did. Got all over his trousers, and by the time he got them off, it was too late."

"Last I heard, he quit his job after that incident and moved to a monastery, claiming it was an act of divine intervention and that he needed to repay for his sins." Lafreya squinted at Morgana. "Hey . . . wait a second. I don't suppose *you* had something to do with it, did you?"

"Who? Little old me?" Morgana glanced up at her friend with a devilish grin, batting her long, thick lashes. "I can neither confirm nor deny the crimes I stand accused of here today, Your Highness."

"That so? Welp, I guess it will remain unsolved for all eternity then." Lafreya smirked with a wink and reached out to place a hand on Morgana's knee. "But just because you have a past is no reason to deny yourself a future. I know you feel like damaged goods, but those of us who know you still see you as perfect as you once were."

Looking at Lafreya's warm smile made Morgana's heart ache. She knew there was a truth to what her cousin was saying, but it was not one she could accept. All she knew was how hollow she felt on the inside—a void no amount of sex could fill. Nodding her head, she smiled at the princess and opened her mouth to reply, but she never got the chance to speak as a loud explosion rocked their carriage. The interior cabin filled with blinding light, and her body rolled into the window as their carriage tipped over. Tumbling with the cabin, she wanted to cushion the blow, but her head hit the ceiling and then the side wall faster than she could act, and after a throbbing pain in her temple, Morgana's world briefly went black.

CHAPTER 4

# The Jester

Fighting off the shadows threatening to consume her psyche, Morgana winced and pushed herself up, her head still throbbing. Outside the crumpled carriage, the clanging of swords, screams of men, and rattling of bones filled the air. Shifting her aching body, she glanced up at the splintered wood of the carriage door caving in on them. Beside her, Lafreya lay unconscious in her brand-new cornflower blue dress, with a small trickle of blood running down her forehead, staining the satin sleeve her head rested upon. Muttering curses under her breath, Morgana leaned her back into the velvet-lined wall and kicked open what remained of the door.

Standing to steal a peek outside the overturned carriage, she spotted an army of at least fifty skeletons making quick work of the Perdetia knights sent to accompany them to Bragburg. To the side, the carriage driver lay dead by his horses. Morgana had only heard tales of the demon king's ability to raise the dead to do his bidding, and it would appear the foothills between Perdetia and Bragburg had more than a few dead bodies resting beneath the soil. Observing the force of bones attacking Leopold's men, she surmised they passed an ancient burial ground because the armor still clinging to the bones predated anything she knew. Their carriage had rolled straight into a trap without anyone knowing it.

Heaps of bodies piled up around the area before her, their navy blue and gold surcoats stained in the crimson blood pooling beneath them. Turning her head to her right, she could see the Bragburg duchy a stone's throw away, the faint outlines of the white brick towers with black roofs on the horizon teasing her. If she could get the duke to help, they might be able to escape this onslaught alive. Pricking her finger on the sharp piece of twisted metal peeling off the doorframe, she willed her blood to materialize into a chartreuse butterfly. Holding in a ragged breath, she whispered a message to the duke before sending her creation off to Bragburg, praying it would find Leighton in time.

"Morgana?"

Glancing down by her feet, she observed Lafreya stirring, scrutinizing herself for any injuries. But aside from the gash on her forehead, which oozed a steady flow of blood, the princess remained unharmed, though badly shaken by the ordeal. Morgana was about to breathe a sigh of relief when a thunderous clang rang out next to ear. Whirling around, she watched a helmeted skull bounce off the carriage as the last bit of men retreated toward Perdetia, leaving the skeletal army to advance upon them. If they got their hands on the princess, all hope of not having to hide her identity was gone. Not willing to sacrifice her chance at freedom or the safety of her best friend, she grabbed hold of Lafreya's shaking hand and yanked her up to her feet.

"Come on," she commanded in a stern tone, "we have to get out of here now."

"What's going on?" Lafreya brushed a tight ruby curl out of her face. "Morgana, what happened?"

"The demon king. We have to get you out of here."

Standing on the concave body of the cabin, Morgana lent her hand to Lafreya, pulling her up to stand beside her. As the princess huddled close to her, a skeletal hand reached for the two of them, and Morgana swung her foot toward it. Her toe hit the skull with a dull thwack, and the head rolled away from them as the rest of the body stumbled around, looking for where it went. Glancing around the field, she could see they were trapped where they stood. The bony soldiers surrounded them on all sides, getting closer. She couldn't kill the undead army, but as she caught a glimpse of the black regalia of Bragburg on the horizon, she figured she could slow down the onslaught enough until help arrived.

Spreading her feet on the side of the carriage for stability, she rolled up her sleeves and raised her arms in the air, bracing herself. She'd have to tap into her magic reserve—her mana, as it was known—and without offering a sacrifice like she did with the butterfly messenger, she'd have to sacrifice herself. Taking a deep breath, she flicked her wrist, drawing the magic from deep inside and focusing it into a gust of wind at a group of skeletons to their right. The energy left her body, hitting their attackers and sending their bones toppling in every direction. Almost immediately, a wave of burning hot pain spread through her body, making her knees wobble. Gritting her teeth, she took another deep breath and swallowed the bile creeping up her throat as her ears continued to ring. Turning to her left, she flicked her wrists again, toppling another group of soldiers, collapsing to one knee in the process. Her head throbbed, and every fiber of her body screamed in agony as she pushed herself up and readied herself for another round.

"Morgana"—Lafreya tugged on the chiffon overskirt of her emerald dress— "please, stop. You will exhaust yourself."

"That's probably true."

Morgana nodded her head, gritted her teeth, balled up her fists, and dug her nails into her palms. Everyone who used magic only had so much mana inside them. Once the reserve of magic energy was drained, they would have to wait for it to regenerate before they could use it again—a condition known as "the psipher" among magic folk. If the person used more mana than their body deemed safe, they would pass out with a fever until their body could recover from the loss of the energy tied to their life force. She had only done that once, and the results were devastating. But the approaching black Bragburg horses gave her hope that she could hold out a little longer, and she closed her eyes as she drew in another deep breath.

"Still, I can't let them get you. If the demon king takes you, all hope will be lost. Not just for me, but for everyone. Don't worry, I just need to hold out long enough for Leighton to arrive and help us, and as you can see, he's almost here."

Turning to her side, Morgana again glanced at the black horses and black-clad riders peeking over the horizon. They kicked up dust as they galloped toward them, and leading the charge was

Leighton, leaned over in his saddle, his horse pushing forward as hard as it could. Glancing about her, Morgana looked for an opening for Lafreya to run through the sea of bones and get away, but the skeletons had already regrouped and blocked them off from the Bragburg soldiers. She would have to fight a little longer if she wished to keep her friend from falling into the demon king's hands.

Morgana steadied herself for another onslaught when she noted the skeletal army breaking apart around them, the bones cascading to the sodden ground. Frowning, she spun around, wondering what happened, and noticed a large shadow wash over the ground, stopping to hover above them. Glancing up, she yelped as an enormous dragon of bleached bones floated over them, his jet-black, torn-up wings churning the surrounding dust. A thick black chain dangled off his neck, and as he looked down at them with his burning amber eyes, Morgana nearly fell over as a scream escaped her throat. The demon king himself had come to retrieve the princess, and as he landed by the carriage, nearly blowing them over, Morgana shoved Lafreya behind her, attempting to shelter the princess with her body.

"Step aside, witch." The dragon roared and breathed out a breath so stale it made Morgana gag. "I don't have anything against you—that, and you are no match for me. Now step aside, I'd hate to hurt you."

She knew he was telling the truth, of course. The demon king was powerful, far more than any witch still left alive and certainly far more than her. She didn't know why he wouldn't just kill her on the spot; she was a threat to his rule. But she was also not about to back down and surrender, not even to him. She had to protect her friend at any cost, no matter how much she trembled at the beast before her. Staring defiantly into the fire in the hollowed-out eye sockets, she swallowed the lump in her throat, growled, and let loose a ball of violet lightning from her palm, which fizzled out as it struck between his eyes.

Roaring with laughter at her feeble attempt, the dragon lifted its talons and released a steady stream of black electricity into her. Her body grew rigid as the current coursed through her, and her blood sizzled. But something told her he was holding back, sticking to his claim of not wanting to kill her. Letting out a blood-curdling scream, Morgana crumpled into a heap on the ground, and the dragon released her from his electrifying hold before he snatched the screaming princess in his claws and took off into the air. Lifting her pounding head, all she could do was watch helplessly as the demon king flew for the mountains, heading to the only thing that lay beyond: the Sea of Suldant.

"Damn it!" She yelled while reaching her hand toward the sky. "Lafreya . . . ."

Realizing she lost, Morgana allowed her arm to drop to the ground. Hanging her head in defeat, she sobbed at what had transpired. Grimacing from the pain, she pushed herself up to her knees and listened to the thundering of hooves approaching from behind. She heard Leighton scream Lafreya's name as his horse darted past her. The dragon was long gone, though, and the horse swung back around. Soon two black boots hit the ground beside her, and a gloved hand reached down toward her. She grabbed hold of his hand, which was cold and hard as stone from the curse he carried. Awash with guilt of letting the princess slip away from her, she allowed him to pull her up and glanced at his charcoal-gray eyes.

Leighton's thick black hair swayed with the breeze left in the dragon's wake sweeping across his collar, but his face remained almost unchanged. Anyone who met the duke assumed he was a cold, uncaring individual with no emotions to speak of. Morgana knew better, having gotten to know the man as he courted Lafreya, and she learned to spot the minute changes in his face and know what his mask concealed. Now she studied the slight downturned angle of his brows, the flicker in his eyes, the barely noticeable flare of his nostrils, and the tremor in his hands. Behind his unmoving expression was a brewing storm of terror and panic. The very thing he vowed to destroy now stole the one person he cared about the most. And Morgana allowed it—biting down on her quivering lip, she stared back into his eyes to watch them close and open as he took in a deep, ragged breath.

"Lady Morgana"—the duke steadied her body while she continued to sway— "are you all right?"

"Yes . . . I'll survive. Aside from the nice jolt the demon king just gave me, my psipher is acting up. You know how this condition is. I get weak from using too much mana, and my body hurts when I don't offer a sacrifice. But I should recover in about an hour or so."

She glanced up at the now empty horizon and stomped her foot with a scream. The demon king snatched away the last bit of hope from her. Dread chilled her to the core at the thought of what he would do with her friend and his reasons for kidnapping her. A sob blocked her throat at the thoughts rushing through her head, and tears pricked her eyes while she tightened her fists, piercing her palms with her sharp nails. Trembling with the hate and hysteria coursing through her body, she gripped her hair and screamed at the sky again before turning back to the duke, who continued to look at her with his brows gently drawn together.

"I'm sorry, Leighton. I couldn't save her." Her voice faltered. "I tried to stop him. I really did."

"Don't apologize." Leighton's voice cracked. "This is all my fault. She's gone because of me, and I was not even fast enough to get to you."

"Leighton, please don't—"

"Don't what?" He snapped. "Don't blame myself? How can I not? We both know the reason he took her was because of me. I should have known he'd never let Perdetia fall. He would never allow me, the bane of his existence, to be king and undo the hold he still had here. I should have stayed away from her. Now because of me, she'll—"

"Please don't say it. I can't bear to think about what he'll do to her. Not after I watched him slaughter my mother. And"—she sucked in a pained breath—"perhaps we still have a chance. If he wanted her dead, he would have killed her on the spot, not taken her. Maybe she's still alive."

"Are you suggesting we go after him?"

"We should have done so a long time ago. We should have done it back when I first agreed to help you break your curse. We should have been looking for his hiding place all along—before you even proposed to her. But we allowed him to make the first move, and now he left us with no choice but to go after him."

"You're right. We now no longer have a choice but to confront him." Leighton trailed his cold eyes in the direction the demon king fled. "Let us return to my estate and hunt this bastard down before he hurts a hair on my fiancé's head. I'm guessing he's headed for the place where he was summoned, in Iatan, and I have a friend there who may just know where that is."

Nodding her head, Morgana got ready to follow the duke away from the blood-soaked battlefield when the distant clopping of hooves caught her attention. She turned just in time to see a white stallion in glistening steel armor come to a halt before her, stomping its hooves on the ground as it snorted at her. Trailing her eyes up the blue surcoat—with the golden crest of a lion holding a sword—she winced as the high afternoon sun skated off the pauldrons before she was met with the stern cerulean eyes of the rider. His short golden hair glistened, tousled by the wind, blowing a few loose strands around on his forehead, and her heart jumped into her throat at the sight of him.

"Leopold," she stammered, "what . . . what are you doing here?"

"Where is Princess Lafreya?" He looked around frantically with a scowl. "What happened here?"

The sound of her friend's name made Morgana's flesh crawl, and her heart hammered in her chest. A pained breath caught in her lungs. Her eyes looked up to Leopold's, and she pondered how she would tell the captain of the royal guard that she allowed the princess to be kidnapped by the demon king. Before they left, she swore to protect Lafreya, and she failed miserably at predicting an attack, which should have been obvious after what Leighton had said. Sweeping her eyes downward, she clutched her skirt in her fists, not daring to see Leo's reaction.

"Kidnapped by the demon king, I'm afraid," she mumbled. "He laid a trap for us and used the bodies buried in these hills to attack us when we least expected it. Duke Charmant tried to stop him, but unfortunately he could not make it here in time before the king's dragon form snatched her from me and took off for the Sea of Suldant."

"Damn it," Leopold snarled. He looked down at Morgana, and his expression instantly softened. "What of you, Morgie? Were you injured in the assault?"

"No, not really." She shot Leighton a look to keep him silent because she didn't want Leo to know about her magic—or her recent battle with the Devoth. "I only got a few scrapes and bruises from when the carriage tipped over. I am more upset at allowing Lafreya to slip away from me."

"Can't say I blame you. If she'd just taken me with her, I wouldn't have let this happen. But in any case"—he leaned over his saddle and took hold of her wrist with the cold steel gauntlet on his arm and effortlessly pulled her up to sit in front of him—"you ride with me. I need to get you and the duke out of here before my men arrive."

"Why?" Pressed against the cool breast plate hidden under the blue fabric, Morgana felt her heart race, and she felt her face grow hot at the proximity of his body. "What's going on, Leo?"

"Prince Gabriel sent the royal guard after the two of you. He's claiming you and the grand duke are working together to kill the princess and overthrow Perdetia. If my men get here and find her gone"—he gritted his teeth— "well, let's just say that it will be the end of you both, and frankly I'd rather die than see any harm come to you, Morgana."

"What?" She looked up at him, wide-eyed. "Gabe said all that? But why? No, I . . ." She shook her head violently. "I don't believe it."

"I don't know what's going on here." Leighton nodded toward

the knights on the horizon behind her. "But we seem to be in big trouble. I know you trust Captain Ellingham, so perhaps it's best to run for now and sort through the rest later. There must be an explanation for why Gabriel turned against us. And frankly it's probably one neither of us will like."

Leaning to peek behind Leopold's shoulder, Morgana squealed when she spotted the royal guard closing the distance behind them, their swords drawn, splitting into three groups to block them off. Stifling another scream with her hand, she turned back to the grand duke, who looked just as bewildered as she was. Whatever was happening left them with no other option but to retreat to the safety of the Bragburg duchy where they could figure out how to save Lafreya and put an end to the madness surrounding them.

"All right," she said, bobbing her head. "Let's get out of here for now and figure out what to do next once we are safely away from Perdetia's wrath."

"Your Grace, think you can get us to your duchy with my men blocking the path?"

"Yes." Leighton leaped into the saddle of his black mare. "Follow me. It's a bit of a long way around, but this way we will avoid the guard. Once we're safe, we will figure out what to do next."

Turning his horse north, Leighton dug his heels into her sides and took off in the direction of Sunhill Grove, a sacred forest once belonging to the druids. With Perdetia and Bragburg being the central-most kingdoms, Morgana knew that the only thing that lay beyond was the Kingdom of Kalingrad, and beyond that a tundra that stretched as far the eye could see. When the druids still lived in these parts, the Sunhill Grove was where they performed their solstice rituals and brought offerings to the gods. Since the demon king's takeover and the destruction of magic beings, the forest had become an overgrown thicket of trees that most people avoided, as the fear of magic lingered.

Leopold looked at Morgana and instructed her to hold on tight before urging his horse to follow the duke. Wrapping her arms tightly around him, she stilled her racing heart and pulled herself closer as he took off, leaving a trail of dust behind him. They raced for the safety of the forest, with the royal guard close on their heels. Leopold spurred his horse to go faster while Morgana buried her face in his chest out of fear and tried to come up with any rational explanation of what was happening all around them.

CHAPTER 5

# The Devil

As the horses galloped through the sea of saw-toothed evergreens, Morgana pressed herself closer to Leopold. She wondered how the day veered so wildly off course. This was supposed to be a quick trip to Bragburg, a two-hour carriage ride they had made countless times. Now her best friend was kidnapped by the demon king, possibly murdered, and the prince was accusing her of treason. She pondered what had made Gabriel suspect her. They may have bickered occasionally, but she never thought he would turn against her; they were friends. The only explanation she could come up with was that either he was compromised or replaced by the demon king—and that it happened recently. Her mind was filled with rumors of the Devoth being able to take on the appearances of people they kill. He couldn't have taken Gabriel's, though, she realized—even a Devoth couldn't be in two places at one—so the prince in Perdetia must have been a puppet. But if he passed himself off as a mortal to gain access to the castle, she wondered who he could be—one of the king's advisors, perhaps, or maybe even one of the dignitaries who visited the castle in the last few days. In any case, it appeared as if he had been planning this for a while, and now they were caught up in his game.

Pondering their predicament, she caught a whiff of Leo's sensual scent, and a warm heat swept her cheeks as she recalled the last time they were that close together. It was right before King Nathaniel dragged him on his second campaign, the failed one to Vekureth. The two of them were alone together by the pond abutting her mother's estate. Giving in to her desires, she pulled him down on top of her and told him he could have her. Much to her surprise, he refused because he was leaving the next day and was afraid it would not be fair to ask her to wait for him again. She told him she'd wait for him regardless, but once he returned as a captain, she pushed all feelings for him aside, knowing full well how much he would struggle to choose between her and the promotion he had always hoped to get.

Lost between bitter memories and the conundrum of what happened to Lafreya and Gabriel, she clung to Leo until something wheezed past his hair. She peeked around to see a dozen royal guard knights behind them with weapons drawn. She realized they would not make it to safety without her help and lifted her wrist so Leo wouldn't notice it. Clenching her jaw as she twirled her finger, she forced a gentle kinetic energy through her finger, moving the loose soil below the hooves of the horse closest to them. As the ground shifted beneath it, the white beast stumbled and kneeled to the ground, throwing off her rider. Almost instantly a sharp pain accosted her head as if someone rammed a hot dagger into her brain. Tightening her grip around the captain, she gave her finger another flick, seizing the next horse's reigns and diverting its course, which slammed the knight into an overhanging tree branch. With every soldier she took down, the pain in her joints increased exponentially until her entire body felt as if it were on fire, and by the time their horse came to a stop, she was using all the energy she had simply to hang on.

Panting, she peeled herself away from Leo and glanced around the secluded area enclosed by monumental dark-gray monolith. Instantly she recognized the space for what it was: sacred ground where the only thing to grow was a few patches of green grass due to the pulse lines present within the confines of the circle. These pulse lines, as she recalled, were where veins of magic energies ran under the earth, and wherever they converged, the forces of magic were strongest. These places of converging pulse lines were often sacred places for those who used magic, and Sunhill Grove was one of them. Back when the druids still existed in these parts of Dresbourn, they held ceremonies in the grove, enclosed by their magic stones. Morgana's eyes scanned the glowing runes on the pillars, reading the spell designed to keep out anyone who was not pure of heart or who had ill intentions to other living things. The duke chose well; by stepping inside the grove, they would be protected from the knights who were out to take them in by force.

"We'll stop here for the night." Leighton's deep voice echoed throughout the clearing. "This old ceremonial ground of the druids is protected by runes. The royal guard will not be able to find us, not unless they mean us no harm, and I doubt any of them just want to have a friendly chat."

The duke jumped off his horse, tied it up to the post between two stones, and walked over to offer Morgana a hand down. Having exhausted herself on their ride, she gladly accepted and fell into his arms as her legs turned to jelly the moment they hit the ground. Lifting her up closer to him, Leighton took her chin in his hand, tilted her head up, and frowned. She realized he must have been staring at the streak of blood trickling from her nose, and she didn't blame him—she couldn't explain why it happened. It felt as if she was getting close to completely draining her mana, but she was not sure how it was possible. Most of it should have recovered before the guard caught up to them on the path, but she felt as if she was almost out of magic. Fortunately Leighton didn't press for an explanation because he knew she was keeping it a secret from Leo. He simply reached out his stiff hand and wiped the crimson rivulet from her face before gently letting go to allow her to steady herself on her feet.

"Are you going to be all right, Lady Morgana?" He held on to her waist while she continued to sway. "You seem to have only gotten worse since we left the carriage."

"I'll be fine." She pressed a finger to her throbbing temple. "I think I just need some time to recover from the chaos of today. I promise you, I'm not as frail as I look."

"I hope you're right. Lafreya would kill me if I let anything happen to you." Leighton shook his head and turned to glance at Leopold, who was giving him a look that could slice through steel. "So, what do you say, Captain? This place good enough for you, or do you wish to travel by the cloak of night?"

Still shooting daggers at the duke, Leo hopped off his horse and glanced about the desolate glade with his hands planted firmly on his hips. It had little to offer to them by way of resources, and unlike Morgana, he couldn't see the runes on the stones protecting them. Glancing back over at the man who still had his hand wrapped around Morgana's hip, he gritted his teeth. He hated to admit it, but he was jealous of the man because he knew Leighton was exactly the type who caught Morgana's fancy. He was rich, poised, well read—a man who knew more about monsters from his travels than anyone, and unlike Leo, the duke had a royal title. He had everything Leo didn't have but had coveted since he was little. If it weren't for the title of captain, he figured he wouldn't ever stand a chance with Morgana, even if everyone claimed otherwise. Heaving out a ragged breath as he watched Leighton, he took off his gauntlets and tossed them on the ground next to a rotted-out log before going to tie up his horse.

"I guess this will do," Leo muttered under his breath. "What should we do first, Your Grace?"

"First things first." Leighton led Morgana to the log and gingerly sat her on the ground. "We need to make a fire to keep us warm at night. There is plenty of scrub brush and firewood around the pillars. It should be enough to last us through the night. I shall leave the fire up to you." He looked up at Leo, who was still scowling at him. "You do know how to make a fire, don't you, Captain?"

Smirking at Leopold, Leighton realized picking a fight with the man who saved him wasn't the best idea, but he couldn't help it.

The thought of losing Lafreya tore him up. He didn't want to think about what happened to her or what the demon king's plans for her were. Whether the Devoth planned to kill her or wed her, the duke didn't want to know, and taking his frustration out on Leo helped ease the tension. He had never met the captain personally until now, having seen him only from a distance as he lingered around Morgana's estate every time he came to visit. A year ago, he promised Lafreya he would help get the captain and the witch together, but now he couldn't resist giving the man as hard a time as he himself was having. Leaning against a pillar, he watched Leo glare back at him silently, delighted by the emotions he drew from the knight.

"What kind of an idiot do you take me for, Your Grace?" Leopold retorted with a sharp edge to his voice. "I didn't become the captain of the royal guard because of my looks, you know. Of course I know how to make a fire. And what of you, Your Grace? What are you going to do?"

"I'll go find us something to eat. I know the surroundings better than you. The woods beyond the dell are filled with berries, and since I know how to find my way back, I'll gather some and return. You stay here, Captain, and get that fire going. Oh"—he turned toward the knight—"be sure to keep an eye on Lady Morgana. I am not pleased with her condition in the least, even if she says she's all right."

"I assure you, Your Grace," Leo sneered, "you don't have to tell me to look after her. I'm more concerned about her than you are."

Sniggering at the emotions he drew from the knight, he walked out of the ceremonial ground to leave the two be. While he searched the forest, his mind raced with possibilities of what was happening to his fiancé, but he dared not consider the worst. He knew there was a possibility she was already dead or that the demon king was having his way with her. Deep down, however, he knew she was still alive. She had to be, given that their fate cards were a perfect match for one another. She was the Golden Empress, and he was the Hanged Man. Their cards were soul cards; they always belonged together. That's how major arcana cards work. Still, the fear of her being tortured ate away at him, and he did his best to push those thoughts aside. An aged breath hissed through his clenched teeth, and he walked further into the woods, trying to focus on something other than Lafreya.

Watching Leighton leave, Leo let out a soft grumble. He didn't much like nobles, to begin with—ever since he was taken from the orphanage by a mean knight and put into servitude—and Leighton seemed less concerned with finding the princess and more focused on getting his hands on Morgana. Jealousy took hold of him in its ugly grip, and he had to remind himself that Morgana would never have the duke, not while he was Lafreya's. That was one thing he loved about Morgana: she never went after anyone Lafreya liked, and there was no way she would start now. Stilling his ragged nerves, he removed his pauldrons, breast plate, and faulds, and began gathering the wood that littered the grove into a pile. Every now and then, he'd steal a glance over his shoulder, catching her gaze on him, causing his heart to hammer to the point of pain. Sucking in in a steady breath, he peered straight at her before letting his thoughts pour out of him, hoping she could shine some light on their situation.

"Tell me honestly, Morgie. What is going on with you and the duke? Why would Prince Gabriel be out to hunt the two of you down?"

"There is nothing between me and Leighton. You should know this. He's a friend, nothing more, nothing less."

"That's not what I'm asking." He heaved out a sigh. "I need to know why the prince is insisting I bring you in as a traitor. I know the two of you like to bicker, but I didn't think he'd want you dead. How do you explain what's happening now?"

"Clearly Gabe was compromised by the demon king. How he managed that is unclear. In that aspect, your guess is as good as mine."

With a nod of his head, Leo stood and went back to gathering firewood and dry grass for kindling before fishing around his saddle bag for a flint. Her explanation made sense because he knew her, and that was the reason he ran with her. He knew she'd never betray a friend—the demon king must have replaced the prince. He struck the flint with his dagger and watched the fire crackle to life, filling the area with a warm amber glow. Glancing up at the woman beside him, he wondered if it was simply the fading light above them or if she'd gotten paler in the short time it took him to make the fire. Her skin took on the appearance of bleached parchment. He timidly reached out to touch her cheek but retracted his hand the moment he heard a tree branch snapping a short distance away. Twisting his head, he saw Leighton holding a bag of berries, which he tossed on the ground.

Morgana sat on the ground with her legs pressed to her chest and her chin resting in the crook, and watched the duke distribute the food among them. Her eyes trailed to Leo sitting by the firelight and landed on the gold-laced cobalt grip of his sword, its pummel decorated with a large star sapphire. The Heartseaker—the mystical blade belonging to the captain of the royal guard—was breathtaking. Legend had it, a druid blacksmith crafted the sword from the finest material available and infused it with magic. The blade would strike down any foe, but it would not harm the innocent. Leo wore it for the past two years, but when Morgana questioned him, hoping to learn more about it, he refused to answer her, saying he would rather forget about the blade and how he got it. The man who wore it before him was Leo's mentor, and Morgana didn't blame him for not wishing to revisit the old captain's death, not even for her.

While she nibbled her food, she continued to ponder the blade's supposed mythical properties and wondered if it would be of help to them in saving Lafreya. If anything could kill a Devoth, the Heartseaker was sure to be it. Morgana opened her mouth to ask Leo what he thought, but her head suddenly throbbed, and she placed a finger to her temple to stop the world from spinning. Never had she been in that much pain from using magic, and certainly never for that long. Mana regenerates quick, and she should have been fine after several hours of not using magic, yet she still felt as if her powers were draining. Not wishing to think the worst, she convinced herself she simply used too much magic in a short time, then she continued to push food down her throat until her stomach churned and she had to get up and run behind the nearest pillar to empty it of its contents.

*Look at yourself—trembling and getting sick from using a little too much magic. How do you expect to save your friend when you can't even hold your food down? The demon king will destroy you like he did your mother.*

Still leaning over, dry heaving onto the ground, she gripped the pillar with her trembling hand and looked in the direction of the all-too-familiar menacing voice laughing at her. The shadow couldn't cross the magic barrier created by the pillars, but it could linger close by and whisper its hate-filled words to her. She wanted to scream at the shadow, but the sound of heavy boots coming up behind her made her bite her tongue. This was not something even her parents knew about, and Leo already had enough to worry about with Lafreya being gone. He didn't need to know about her personal issues.

"Morgie?" He placed a gentle hand on her shoulder, giving it a firm squeeze. "Are you feeling all right?"

"I'm fine." She turned to him and forced a smile. "I think the stress of the day is finally getting to me."

"Want me to hold your hair while you throw up?"

*Well, look at that. Isn't the captain just the nicest guy you can find? I bet your daddy was just as sweet . . . until he had enough of you and left your mother to be slaughtered by the demon king. I bet the captain will abandon you too, especially after he learns what you are.*

Morgana darted her eyes at the shadow sitting outside the protective circle, grinning with an open maw at her. She didn't remember much of her father. All she knew was that she loved him and that they spent a lot of time together. Partial memories of him remained: the way they walked in the woods, the way he kissed her at night, and how she used to sit on his lap while he read her a book or told her stories of the Otherworld. But when it came to his face, she couldn't piece anything together. After he just disappeared one day, he became a phantom to her, and in his wake he left a hole in her soul. The encounter with the professor added to the void, and now she feared rejection so much that she couldn't even fully embrace the one man she wanted. Looking back at Leopold gazing down at her, she shook her head, wondering why he continued to chase her when he could have better.

"What do you see in me, Leo?"

"The woman I want to spend the rest of my life with."

She looked at his radiant smile. "Well, I guess that makes you crazy."

"If I'm crazy"—he brought her hand to his lips— "I'm just crazy about you. Now, let us return to the fire. You look exhausted, and I want you to sit down and try to relax. Allow me to worry about finding the princess in your stead."

Gripping his warm hand, she nodded and walked beside him back over to the campsite. Before the flames dancing under the starlight, Leighton stood with his back turned to them, mixing something up in a wood cup, stopping briefly to glance at them. Curling up the corners of his lips, he returned to what he was doing in silence. Letting go of Leopold's hand, Morgana settled down in her spot by the log and tipped her head to the side, signaling for him to join her. He did so without saying a word. The two of them sat in the surrounding stillness, staring into the amber flames until the duke approached, crouching beside her.

"Here you go," he said, handing her the cup, which was filled with a caustic green liquid. "Drink it. You keep looking worse by the minute, and this should at least help make you feel better."

"What's this?"

"A potion of glowing morel, bloodgrass, and wyvern thorn. It will help restore your"—he paused to think how he should phrase the next part to keep the captain from catching on to her true nature—"strength."

"But I can't take this." She peered into the cup of swirling goo. "You need these herbs to slow down the progression of your crystallization curse."

"I'll be fine, Morgana." Leighton placed his gloved hand over hers. "We both know it doesn't matter how much I try to slow it down. This gift from the demon king to my ancestors will claim me soon enough. Plus, I always have plenty of herbs on hand, so drink and feel better."

"Thank you."

Putting the cup to her lips, she took a swig of the bitter medicine, allowing the liquid to glide down her throat. As unpleasant as the potion was, it served its purpose at alleviating her upset stomach and easing the stiffness in her joints, allowing her to relax for a bit. She handed the cup back to Leighton and watched him walk back to his spot and sit and stare at Leo. The two continued to look at one another as if sizing each other up, until the duke shifted his weight closer, draped his arms over his knees, and peered more intently at the knight.

"Spit it out, Captain. I can see something is on your mind. I get it, you don't trust me. Can't say I blame you, since I never allowed you to get to know me. But it seems we are stuck together, so why not be frank about what's bothering you instead of letting it eat you alive?"

"I was simply wondering," Leo said, reclining and tilting his head to the star-studded sky. "Why Lafreya? I gather the demon king wants to prevent your union because he doesn't want to give up Perdetia. But why go after her? Why not kill you directly?"

"Because he can't." Morgana placed her hand on his knee. "When the demon king tried to kill the first Duke Charmant, the duke's sorceress wife drew energy from the pulse lines around Bragburg to spare his life. The duke and his son were cursed to carry the crystallization plague as a result, but because of the earth energy attached to them, the demon king can't kill a Charmant, not unless they happen to be in the place the cult summoned him. His power is strongest there."

"I see." Leo looked at Leighton. "So I guess he's telling you to follow him. What's your plan now, Your Grace? Obviously you'll take the bait and go after him. I know I would if he took Morgana. But I also know my men better than anyone. They won't give up their search for us. So where do we go from here? How do we get to your duchy and get Lafreya back?"

"Simple. We go through Kalingrad. As you know, Bragburg shares a border with them, as well as Perdetia. If we go through the Black Forest and over the Taiga River, we will end up close to my estate. From there my healers can look at Morgana, and I can seek help from a friend over in Iatan. If anyone can help us find Lafreya, it's him."

"Very well." Leo cradled his chin. "I suppose that's as good a plan as any. In such case, I recommend we get some sleep so we can leave before the sun comes up in the morning. That way, we have a better chance of making it to the bridge to Kalingrad unnoticed by the Guard."

"I concur." The duke laid down on the ground by his log. "Especially you, Morgana. You need to get some rest so you can recover. Have a good night . . . Captain."

"Likewise, Your Grace."

Stealing another glance at Morgana, Leopold recalled the last time they were together like that, alone in the still of the night. It had to have been around ten years ago, when she fell asleep in the stables waiting for him to finish his chores. He remembered how he lay beside her in the hay, pulling her body into his, how she shifted her head to lie on his shoulder. He never expected to fall in love with her, but when he realized he had, he knew he needed to be more than just a foot soldier to have her. She deserved more than he could offer. Now she was closer than ever, yet he could see her slipping away from him. Her skin grew paler under the light of the moon, and he knew it wasn't stress or the bump on her head causing it. He'd have to find her help—and soon.

Dragging in a deep breath, he scolded himself for not allowing himself to have her when she asked. He covered her up with his surcoat, watching her body relax from the warmth, and his breath caught in his lungs at how fragile she looked. Lying down beside her, he reached out to hold her clammy hand, and she murmured his name in her sleep, dousing his body in scorching heat. She always talked in her sleep when he was near, and this always twisted his insides in knots. Closing his eyes, he allowed sleep to drag him away. The last thing he saw was her face slipping away from him into a pleasant slumber. His dreams filled with a happy longing for a life that could be—once the ordeal with the missing princess was over.

CHAPTER 6

# The Ace of Swords

**S**hifting on the dew-kissed grass of the clearing, Morgana's body stiffened with internal flames that refused to be quenched even as a light morning breeze caressed her skin. She knew something was wrong. The pain radiating through her core was not from using magic; this was something far worse. If she could make it to Bragburg, the healers there could treat her, but that was still a day or two away. She'd have to put up with the spasms until then. Forcing herself to sit up and open her heavy eyelids, she swallowed the acid sitting in her throat and glanced about the grounds for her companions. The men were not far from her, getting their horses ready. She reckoned they must have gotten up a while ago and let her sleep, and she cleared her throat to get their attention. Turning his head to face her, Leo's radiant smile warmed up the barren clearing, making her heart flip.

"Morgie, you're finally awake. Are you feeling any better?"

"Yes." She forced herself to smile. "Almost back to normal."

"I'm glad to hear that." He offered her a hand up. "I was beginning to worry about you. Duke Charmant insisted we get going right away, but I felt bad waking you." He continued to hold her palm, stroking the back of it with his thumb. "Will you ride with me?"

"I'd like that." She slanted her lips at him. "Let us get going. The sooner we get back to Bragburg, the sooner we find Lafreya."

Fighting the heavy, stabbing pain in her legs and the disconnection between her limbs and brain, she followed him over to the white horse, allowing him to lift her up to sit in the saddle with him. She placed her arms around him, drawing their bodies together, and he spurred his horse on, leaving the safety of the sacred ground behind them. The animal must have sensed her pain because it moved slowly, taking care to avoid any obstacle along the grooved pine forest road that might serve to hurt her further. Above them birds chirped, and ethereal specks of light filtered from the trees above.

As Morgana gripped Leo, her chest tightened, and the air caught in her lungs as apprehension filled her. Having some oracle powers, she could foresee the future on rare occasions, and faint visions flooded in behind her eyes, but they were unclear. The only thing she could make out was Leopold's shocked face, the clanging of metal, and the pitch-black darkness that followed. Turning around to look at the woods fading into the background, she didn't see a thing, not even a hint of soldiers pursuing them. She turned her head back and spotted the canyon separating them from Kalingrad up ahead, and her heart sank into her feet. The bridge ahead lay broken on either side of the gorge, cutting them off from safety.

"Damn it." Leo halted his horse right before the steep drop. "What do we do now, Your Grace? We can't exactly go back the way we came, not unless we wish to fight all the way to Bragburg."

The duke rode up beside them. "Lady Morgana, I hate to ask this of you, but . . . do you think you can fix this?"

"Yes," she said. Then she clenched her jaw tight before jumping from the horse. "Stand aside and keep watch. This shouldn't take long for me to mend."

Facing the chasm separating them from the safety of Kalingrad, she rolled up her sleeves, took a deep, pained breath, and lifted her arms. The ache in her joints was still barely tolerable, but she squeezed her eyes tight, moved her fingers, and manipulated the broken rope and wood in the air. Her bones stiffened and cracked with every twitch, and a scorching pain twisted in her side, making her nauseous. Forcing her eyes open, she watched the bridge slowly rise, one painful plank at a time, and realized it was going to take longer than anticipated. She was still far too weak to make it happen any faster.

"M-Morgana?" Leo sat on his horse, slack-jawed, his eyes wide. "You're . . . you're a—"

"A witch, Leo." She turned to glare at him, nearly dropping the parts she raised. "Now do you understand why I told you the timing wasn't right for me to be with you? There is no us until Leighton and Lafreya wed."

"Then the pains you keep randomly getting aren't a mysterious illness like Lafreya always claimed, they are the result of—"

*Cards of Fate* ✣ 57

"The psipher," she interrupted again. "Yes. It's a mana-induced syndrome that all witches must suffer. It's the price we all pay for using magic without a sacrifice."

The revelation took the air out of Leopold's lungs, and he gripped his reins to keep himself from falling out of his saddle. Four years ago, when he left for his second campaign to Vekureth, their party camped in the cursed mountains beyond Bragburg called the Notch of Bones, which divided Dresbourn in half. There he encountered a shadelych—a creature who crossed over from the Otherworld to invade mortals' dreams and feed on their fears as it feeds nightmares to its victims. When Leo met the thing in his dreams, it showed him a choice he'd have to make between the woman he loved and his career, and then it showed him her death.

Back then, he dismissed the nightmare, not believing anything the monster had to show him. He didn't think there was any reason for him to choose between Morgana and being a knight. Now he understood what the creature meant, and his heart slammed in his chest as he recalled the vivid dream. In his mind, there was no contest between Morgana and his career, he'd always pick her no matter what. The thing that bothered him was the last part of the vision—her death. He could live with her being a witch, but he couldn't stand the thought of losing her, and now it seemed like a real possibility, and it was one he couldn't live with.

Picking up his jaw, he swallowed and looked at her in silence. All he could do was blink at her. The words he wanted to say were lodged in his throat, and she shook her head, frowning, before returning to raising the bridge, seemingly unwilling to talk to him further. He went to dismount his horse and approach her when the sound of voices clamoring from the tree line caught his attention. There at the other end of the dirt road stood four white horses with the blue-and-gold-clad men of the royal guard, getting ready to charge the three of them while Morgana was not even halfway done.

"Shit," Morgana muttered. "Just my cursed luck. Oh, well. Do you gentlemen think you can distract them long enough for me to fix this bridge? It shouldn't be much longer, another five minutes or so."

"Leave it to us." The duke spun his black horse around to face the guardsmen. "Come on, Captain"—he smirked at the man beside him— "you still going to help us escape, or will you turn on us and side with your men now that you know the truth?"

"If you think I'd turn on my girl, you're dead wrong. Witch or no witch, I'll stand beside her." Leo scoffed, reared his horse to face his soldiers and drew his sword, the gold wings of the cross guard framing his hand. "All I ask is that you try not to hurt them. They are still my men, after all."

"You have my word, Captain. I won't cause them any injury they won't recover from. Now, why don't you take the two on the right while I deal with the two on the left?"

With a sly smile, the duke unsheathed his sword and galloped toward the advancing group of soldiers with Leo not far behind him. Using the pummel of his sword, he knocked a guard off his horse before twisting the blade around to perry a sword coming at him from the side. Hearing metal clashing in the distance, Morgana turned her attention back to the bridge, which was refusing to budge any further. Digging her heels into the loose soil, she gritted her teeth and raised her hands higher. For some reason, the task was requiring a lot more mana than she expected. She felt herself getting weaker. All her strength was sapped from her body. Realizing this was more than a simple case of the psipher, she tilted her head to the sky and focused all her remaining energy into her fingers, manipulating the planks higher into the air.

Crackling waves of pain shot up from her feet and into her arms as the wood straightened and the hemp fibers wove together, becoming whole. Her body grew heavy, and she could no longer feel her legs, and a blinding darkness rose behind her eyes. Knowing that the men didn't stand a chance without the bridge, she lifted her arms higher. Drawing the last of her strength, she let out a pained scream, sending a magic shockwave through the area, forcing all the mana she had left into mending the bridge and allowing her friends to get to safety. She didn't care that she may die. Saving Leighton and Leo was the only thing she cared about because they could still get Lafreya back without her. With her head spinning, she felt her legs give out, drawing her to the ground as the last fibers melded. By the time she hit the gravel, she felt nothing but the welcoming icy darkness swallowing her up and dragging her away, holding her hostage somewhere on the precipices between life and death.

"Morgie!" Leo flew from his saddle, ran to her, and scooped her limp body into his arms, the dream from four years ago fresh in his mind. "Morgie, wake up." He shook her, but she did not flinch, her head lolling from side to side. "What's . . . what's wrong with her?" He turned to face the duke. "Why is she like this?"

"I don't know." Leighton spun his horse around and galloped

past the guards scrambling to their feet. "Come on, Captain, let's grab the lady and go. We need to get over that bridge before they catch up to us. We can hide on the other side, and then we can figure out what's wrong with Morgana."

Leighton dismounted, then lifted Morgana to allow Leo to get on his horse before he placed her slack body beside him. Cradling her close to him, Leopold gripped the reigns with one hand, waited for the duke to climb back into his saddle, and squeezed his horse's sides to move him forward. Without hesitation, the stallion galloped across the bridge with Leighton's mare close behind. Skidding to a stop on the other side of the bridge, he spun the steed around and watched the duke leap off his horse and draw his sword, aiming it at the ropes.

"What are you doing?"

"Trust me, Captain."

The duke glanced back over at the soldiers already halfway across the bridge and struck one of the four cables holding the planks, breaking it. The wood platform tittered and swayed, spooking the horses, who halted in their tracks and reared in protest. The men were still trying to advance, so he raised his arm to the rope on the opposite end, threatening to break it as well. Realizing what he was going to do, the men turned their horses around and retreated to the other side, allowing Leighton to sever the rest of the strands, cutting off the guards' access to Kalingrad and giving them a chance to escape.

"Thank you, Your Grace," Leo said, "for not killing them."

"I'm a man of my word, Captain," Leighton said, then climbed back on his horse. "Now, follow me. I know a safe place where we can camp for the night and take care of Morgana before setting off for Bragburg in the morning. I have my own lady to worry about."

Stealing a glance at the woman flopped over in his arms, Leo huffed, then followed the duke into the woods pulsing with darkness. Rain-slicked moss and loose stone covered the damp forest floor between the twisted birch trees, and with the shadows pooling around them, it made it difficult for the horses to walk. The cluster of black and white trees made it almost impossible to see in the fading sunlight, and the steeds lost footing more than once. It was fortunate that most of Dresbourn was covered in woods, but at the same time, the cover of foliage came with its own drawbacks. In the faint light, his eyes drifted to Morgana, and he almost fell out of his saddle when he noticed she looked almost like a corpse. Darting his head up, he spotted a clearing up ahead and figured it would be as good a place as any to examine her.

"Your Grace!" he yelled from his horse, his voice catching in his throat. "Stop here. It's Morgana. I . . . I'm not sure she's still with us."

Drawing his brows together, Leighton dismounted his horse and came over to take Morgana from Leo, and her body hung limp in his arms. He laid her down on the dried grass, crouched beside her, and took her wrist in his hand. Leo jumped from his saddle, stood behind the duke, and observed her wrist dangling lifelessly in his hand. Cold sweat dripped down his back, and his whole body trembled at seeing her like that. At that moment, she looked closer to the world of the dead than that of the living.

"Is . . . is she . . ."

"She's still alive"—Leighton tilted his head to look behind him— "Though barely. She must have used up almost all her mana to fix that bridge."

"What does that mean? Is that bad?"

"Very bad. Magic folk survive on mana. If they use too much mana, they get sick, and if they go over their reserves, they can die. But it appears Morgana still has enough mana left to keep her hanging on."

"Does this mean she'll recover?"

"I don't know." Leighton gave him a grave look. "I know mana recovers over time, but I don't know if it can recover if too much is used. Best you can do right now is just keep her warm while I get a fire going. I promise you, once we get to Bragburg, I will do everything in my power to save her."

Swallowing the dread welling up inside him, Leopold placed her head down in his lap and stroked her hair, which was moist with sweat. He could feel her shivering, and once more he recalled the dream the shadelych fed him. The last half of the dream continued to haunt him, and he considered what he could do to help her hang on, but nothing came to mind. Wrapping her in his arms, he watched Leighton light a fire and sit down beside him. In his grip, her body continued to convulse, and she murmured something under her breath that he couldn't hear. Looking down at her lying unconscious in his lap, he swallowed hard, realizing how close they were to fulfilling the last part of the shadelych's nightmare, and his thoughts went to a dark place as time slipped away like sand in an hourglass.

CHAPTER 7

# The Three of Coins

Watching Morgana's head resting in his lap, Leopold heaved out a sigh and tilted his head back. Her breath had gotten more ragged, and she barely flinched in the hours they sat on the ground. He had only seen her pass out once before, back when they first met. He had foolishly taken the girls up the inner battlement with him when he was tasked with inspecting it. He slipped and fell off, and a miracle saved him from instant death, but he later learned that Morgana fainted from fright. He realized now what must have happened, although he had no way of asking her to confirm his suspicions. But even back then she was only out for a day, so perhaps, he thought, all she needed was a bit more time to recover.

"Come on, Morgie, wake up." He combed his fingers through

her hair. "Wake up. You and I have a lot to talk about. Don't think I'll let you off the hook this easily."

"She'll pull through, Captain." Leighton put down the stick he had been whittling and looked up. "If she's still hanging on, there is still hope she'll survive this . . . whatever *this* is."

"How can you be so sure? From what I've gathered, witches don't normally pass out from using magic."

"It's true. But"—Leighton smiled at him— "Morgana is tough. She'll hang on purely out of spite."

"You're probably right, Your Grace." Leo nodded and looked back at Morgana, running the back of his finger over her frigid cheek. "She should have just told me what she was. I would have made sure she'd stay safe."

"Oh, she knew that. Believe me, she did. She simply didn't wish to compromise your position by having you choose between being captain and being with her. Everything she did was to protect you."

Leopold's eyes shifted to the black-clad duke sitting beside him, leaning on his knees. He knew the man was telling the truth—the shadelych showed him that much. Still, he wished she'd have trusted him enough to make that choice on his own instead of making it for him. Of course, she would have told him once Leighton was king, but that seemed like a remote possibility after what happened to the princess. Knowing their future was uncertain, he groaned and stared at the moon shimmering above him in the striated clouds.

"So, Your Grace, how long have you been aware of her secret?"

"Lafreya told me when she introduced the two of us. She didn't want to keep secrets between us, and she saw no reason to hide Morgana's identity from a man whose ancestors went to war with the demon king."

"And how long has the princess known? How long has everyone been keeping me in the dark?"

"Lafreya knew all her life. She has spent years protecting her cousin." Leighton cast Leo a soft gaze. "They only kept you in the dark because they thought being a knight was important to you. They did it for you."

"They didn't need to do that. They should have trusted me enough to decide what was best for myself. If only I had known what Morgana was, I would have done everything to protect her. I would have made sure none of this ever happened."

"It's not too late to save her, lover boy," said a small, faint voice from behind him. "Or should I say, *Captain*?"

"Who . . ." Leo spun around in his spot, looking for the source of the sound. "Who said that?"

"Me, Captain," the voice hissed.

Leaping out of the shadows, a small hairless black cat landed in his lap and swatted his face with its paw, causing him to fall back with a yelp. The animal's dark peach fuzz almost blended into the darkness of the night, with only its chartreuse eyes to indicate its position as it sat near Morgana's shoulder and glared at him inquisitively. Having never seen anything as unusual as the strange beast before him, Leopold blinked at the cat, who slowly twitched its large, bat-like ears without another word. Seemingly having enough of his gawking, it let out a soft hiss and swatted at his face once more, shocking him back to reality.

"What's wrong, soldier?" it rumbled. "Cat got your tongue?"

"A talking cat?" Leo gasped at the animal, who continued to chuckle at him. "Are you a witch too? Can witches do that?" He turned to Leighton. "Shift into animals, that is?"

"I'm not, and they can't." The feline pawed his face and narrowed its eyes at him. "Name's Grimalkin, and what I am is Baba Yaga's familiar. You are probably haven't heard of her since you're not from around here, but she is a well-renowned and powerful witch in these parts. She's been alive since before the witch hunts started and ended throughout Dresbourn. Some Kalingradians these days seek her out for cures to their ailments and to extend their life. Earlier this evening, she had a telepathic contact from an anonymous source who informed her of your"—the cat looked at Morgana—"um, predicament. She couldn't let a young woman die, so she sent me here to fetch you. And I have to say, I'm glad I came. Your witch isn't looking too well and may not make it until sunrise without intervention."

"Does this mean you can help us?" Leo jolted in his spot, and the cat jumped to the ground by his feet. "Can you make Morgana feel better?"

"I don't know." Grimalkin sniffed the unconscious woman on his lap. "Maybe. At the very least, my master thinks she can still save your girl's life. So go on, grab her and follow me, but hurry. I'm afraid she doesn't have much time left."

Nodding jerkily, Leopold scooped Morgana into his arms and followed the cat through the dense forest, with the duke guiding their horses behind him. The darkness clotted around them like Yuletide pudding, and they could barely make out the cat, who would intermittently turn to allow them to catch up to its glistening eyeballs. Occasionally an ethereal spray of moonlight slipped through the trees and caught on Morgana's hair, making it glow with a deep lavender hue. He pressed her closer to his body, praying she would survive as they continued to edge down a path chocked by the trees. Stealing a glance at her pale face, a thought trickled into the back of his head, and he looked up at the creature slinking in front of him.

"Does Morgana have a familiar too?"

"I don't know, Captain." The cat turned its head to look at him. "Does your lover keep a talking cat, rat, or bird?"

"She's not my lover," Leo mumbled. "And she doesn't have a talking animal. She doesn't keep any pets that I know of."

"First off, I'm not a pet," Grimalkin grumbled. "I'm an assistant from the Otherworld. Second, that means your lover doesn't have one. Not all witches keep familiars, especially not ones brazen enough to live in a city—and Perdetia of all the cursed places. Your lover is either incredibly brave or incredibly stupid."

"I keep telling you, she's not my lover."

"If that's the case, you are doing something wrong, soldier. I could smell the lust from a mile away."

"On whom," Leo scoffed, "me or her?"

"On both of you." The cat stopped and sat down next to a wall of trees. "I can hear her heart pounding even now, with her so close to death. And yours isn't much better. Why, I bet she'd confess how much she loves you if she wasn't almost dead."

"Funny, you might be the first cat to say that, but you are certainly not the first one to believe that Morgana holds strong feeling for me."

"That's because she does. You must be in denial—or dense, if you can't see it."

"Whatever you say, cat. Why'd you stop, anyway?"

"Just waiting for the door to open."

Leo was about to ask what door the cat was talking about

when the trees before him began to creak and moan and part ways, opening a passage that wasn't there before. His body grew taut as he stared in disbelief, then noticed the cat vanishing into the clearing beyond. Fighting down the unease, he gripped Morgana tighter and took a timid step past the trees, wondering what he would encounter on the other side.

CHAPTER 8

# The Seven of Coins

Afer wandering into the overgrown clearing of knee-high grass, Leo stiffened and took a few steps back. The yellowed weeds swallowed up his boots, and he looked up, growing cold to the marrow. Towering a good ten feet above him stood a time-worn log cabin, walking about on a pair of chicken legs. The weathered timber was solid and sturdy, with not so much as a door or window to break up its surface. The only sign of life inside the forbidden structure was the thick plumes of white smoke puffing up from the chimney at the far end of the roof. Taking another uneasy step back, Leo shook his head and looked down at the small black cat weaving in and out of his feet.

"What in the world is this place?"

The beast rolled its eyes. "Baba Yaga's house, of course. What did you think this was, pretty boy, an inn?"

"Perfect. Just perfect," he grumbled. "And how are we supposed to get in? Do you think the three of us can shimmy down the chimney?"

"You know," Grimalkin said, licking its paw and rubbing it over its pruned face. "I knew Perdetia knights lived a sheltered life, but you, my friend—you appear to have turned stupid in the process. Alas, I guess it can't be helped since magic is so foreign to you. Just stand back and watch. I promise it won't be a letdown."

Taking a step forward, Grimalkin cleared its throat and let out a loud yowl, which sliced through the smothering silence. Hearing the animal's shrill cry, the cabin turned around and tilted down as if to observe them. At first it simply stood there, leaning over further, the roof thatch tickling Leo's forehead. Then, as if being satisfied with what it saw, the cabin lifted, hopped around, and slowly lowered itself to the ground, the chicken feet vanishing beneath the stacked timbers. Rooted to the ground, Leopold watched in awe as the wood shifted and windows and a door formed on the once solid surface. Before long, amber light fanned from the dust-filmed glass, and a rickety door swung open to welcome them inside.

"Gentlemen"—the cat turned its head to look at them—"follow me. You may leave your horses to run free. They won't be able to escape."

Sweeping his gaze about the clearing, Leo noted the trees had moved together, twisting their trunks to form an impenetrable wall. Exchanging a glance with Leighton, he shook off his fear and followed the beast into the dusty, cobweb-filled interior of the log cabin. To his right, a fire crackled in a brick hearth, chipped from years of neglect. Beside it sat a rotting wood bucket large enough to fit a man, upon which leaned a birch twig broom that had seen better days and was clearly no longer used for cleaning. His eyes continued to trace a path along the wall, which was decorated with strings of dried mushrooms and herbs, to a cloth-covered table where a stout, gray-haired woman in a brown sack dress worked at a spinning wheel.

Grimalkin let out a haunting meow, and the woman turned around to greet them with her milky eyes. Nodding her head, she gave the men a snaggle-toothed smile, waving for them to come closer. Still transfixed by the large, hairy mole on her chin, Leo took a step forward, cradling Morgana tighter to his chest, approaching their host. Cackling, the woman jumped from her seat and hobbled over to meet him on her wobbly, bowed-out legs. Wiping her liver-spot-covered hands on her apron, she took one look into his arms and ran her knobby fingers along Morgana's clammy skin.

"Oh, yes, yes. I see the problem." She licked her thin, cracked lips, pulled at her wispy hair, and rubbed her crooked nose. "Go lay your friend down by the fire, boy, and let me take a good look at her."

"That's just great," Leo whispered in Leighton's ear, looking again at her white eyes, "the old hag is as blind as a bat. How is she supposed to help us?"

"You, Captain"—the woman tottered closer and began to whack Leo with a wooden spoon hidden in her apron—"have a lot to learn about us witches if you ever hope to be with one."

"Ouch." Leo ducked his head into his armor, desperate to defend himself from her continued thwacks. "Stop that," he protested. "All right. I'm sorry. I'm sorry. I didn't mean to offend you."

"You know, just because I can't see with my eyes"—she tucked the spoon back into her apron pocket—"don't mean I can't see at all. For example, I can see you are rather handsome, and I understand why your lady friend likes you so much. I can also tell your black-clad friend is radiating a deadly curse and that his left hand is almost useless as it's almost turned to stone." She turned to Leighton. "You know, I was there when your ancestor came down with the curse—I even knew the woman who saved him from turning into a statue on the spot. Good man he was. Despite knowing he would die in a few years, he still vowed to take down that Devoth prince. I'm glad to see his legacy lives on in you." She smiled at the duke, then turned her head to Leo with a frown. "As for the woman you are clutching so tightly to your chest, boy, afraid that she will slip away from you, I can tell she is fading, and fast. So you want my help or not?"

"Yes. Of course," Leopold stammered. "I won't question you again. Please"—he set eyes on Morgana with a twinge in his heart—"just save her."

"Then do as you're told, boy, and never question things you can't comprehend ever again."

Nodding his head, Leopold shot Leighton a glance, who simply pointed behind him at a makeshift hay bed, which had gathered by the fire in the short time they had been talking. Tightening his grip on Morgana, he walked over and gently placed her on the cluster of straw, then took a few steps back to allow Baba Yaga some access. Without a word, the old woman shoved him aside and waddled over to the witch on the floor to begin her examination. Leo watched as she massaged her with her knotted fingers and bobbed her head as she went. Occasionally she'd lick her cracked lips and lean over to smell Morgana, clicking her tongue. Finally, after what seemed like an eternity, she stopped, leaped up, and hopped from one leg to the other, cackling.

"Well, I have good news for you boys." She continued to laugh. "It's like the source told me. There is a mana tick attached behind her ear. It's a simple fix."

"A *what* now?" Leo glanced over at Leighton, who lifted his shoulders in response.

"A mana tick." Baba Yaga pulled back Morgana's aubergine hair to reveal a pulsating blue and green ball with tiny black legs protruding from the crease behind her ear. "It feeds on the energy all us magic folk use—our mana, as we call it. We only have so much inside us. Every time this poor dear used her magic, the nasty little bugger got fatter, and she grew weaker. They can kill us, you know, for we can't live without mana, and these parasites can suck us dry. Good thing I got contacted when I did. Otherwise your lady friend might not have made it through the night with how plump this one has gotten. Why, I bet she hardly has any mana left in her and is only hanging on because of you, Captain."

"Me?" Leo jolted back. "Why me?"

"And you have the nerve to call me blind when your eyes can't see the obvious," she retorted sharply. "But no matter that now. We need to get this thing off."

"Do you know how long it's been attached to her for?" The duke cradled his chin. "Is there a way to know?"

"Hmm, I don't know." She pinched the round body with her fingers and twisted the tick off, holding it to her nose. "Hard to tell with these critters. It depends on how much magic she has been using. But at least a day or two, if I had to take a guess."

Leighton pressed a fist over his lips and scowled. "Then this guy must have been planted on her before or during the carriage accident."

"Which means," Leo added, "you and Lafreya are not the only ones to know Morgana is a witch. Someone else knows too."

"Someone like the demon king, and it seems he wished to kill her. I guess with the people no longer burning witches, and Morgana's identity kept a secret, he took matters in his own hands. Question is, why? How is Morgana a threat to him?" Leighton continued to frown. "Well, this certainly complicates things for us. It's not an obstacle I was expecting to tackle."

"Indeed . . . but we can figure it out later. Right now I'm more concerned about Morgana." Leo shifted his eyes back to the old woman. "Will she be all right now that the tick is off her? Will her mana come back?"

"Oh, don't you worry, my boy. Your lady friend will recover in a day's time. Actually, she'll be good to go after a good night's sleep." Grabbing a vial of clear rose liquid, she squeezed the tick, popping its contents into the mixture. The potion bubbled, swirled, and changed to a solid basil green, which Leo could have easily mistaken for sludge at first glance. "Now, come on over here and help me give her this potion to restore the mana she lost. After that, we can let the girl sleep while I treat you to a good meal, and you can rest here for the night."

Obeying her command, Leo inched over to Morgana, lifted her head up into his lap, and gingerly parted her lips with his thumb. Grinning at him, Baba Yaga crouched down and poured the potion in the space he provided, rubbing her under the chin to force her to swallow. No sooner had the potion gone down did the color instantly return to her skin, which grew warmer under his touch. He felt her shift on his lap, and he smiled. His soul grew light knowing that she would not die. She was going to be all right after all, just like the old witch promised.

"All right, boys, follow me."

"That's really nice of you to offer us lodging," Leighton objected, "but we really ought to get going. You see, it's imperative we get back to Bragburg and—"

"Find your fiancé. Oh, I know, my cursed duke. I know what you seek, and I can tell you that your princess is all right. The demon king will not hurt her. You are the actual target in this scheme, and you don't dangle a dead worm on a lure when you seek to catch a fish."

"How can you be so sure that he won't harm her?"

Baba Yaga traced her milky eyes over the faded outline of the duke forming in her mind. She couldn't tell him it was the Devoth prince himself who had contacted her earlier that night and informed her of the young witch getting ready to die in her woods. Asking her to save the girl wasn't the only thing he did; he also begged her to keep her at the cabin and allow the duke to come to him. She was willing to help him save the witch—it would not have been right to allow an innocent to die—but she wouldn't separate the group, not with the fate lines linking them together. Whatever the demon king's plan was, it didn't involve the witch or the princess. He wanted the cursed duke of Bragburg, nothing more.

"I know a lot of things, boy, none of which I can tell you because I cannot risk swaying your fate. What I can tell you is that it's *you* he is after, but he can't kill you unless you are in his domain. Going after your fiancé was a calculated risk to draw you to him. I assure you, Your Grace, your princess will remain alive . . . for now. Come, have some food. You wouldn't want to be dragging your unconscious friend through the woods at this hour, regardless."

"Very well. We shall spend the night here and leave in the morning." The duke nodded at Leo. "You coming to eat, Captain?"

"Yes. Just . . . give me a moment. I want to be alone with her for a bit."

"Fine. But don't take too long. I doubt our host will take kindly to you not joining us."

Giving the duke a single nod, Leopold watched him stride across the room and sit at the table before he returned his attention to Morgana. Her luminous porcelain skin had a tinge of pink to it, her chest rose in even strokes, and there was even a hint of a smile on her lips. Watching her sleeping again lifted the ominous weight of dread that had hung over him since he learned she was a witch. His heart slammed painfully in his chest at the thought that he almost lost her. His visions from the Notch of Bones once again creeped up in his mind, making his blood run cold. Heaving out the breath of stale air he'd been holding in, he placed her back down in the straw and took off his surcoat to cover her up.

"Even if we can't save Lafreya, I won't ever let anything happen to you again. I'll keep you safe for as long as I live." He leaned over to whisper in her ear, stroking her hair. "I promise you this, you and your secret are safe with me."

Planting a soft kiss on her forehead, he stood and left her to rest, then strolled over to join Leighton and Baba Yaga at the table. He pulled out a rickety wood chair, plopped down on its uneven surface, and watched the old woman dancing about the cramped kitchenet, plating food and boiling water in a rusty cast-iron kettle. He wasn't in the mood for refreshments, but as she slid over a plate and a chipped porcelain cup filled to the brim with herbal tea, he smiled and accepted her hospitality, even though his thoughts continued to wander elsewhere, focusing on the woman sleeping behind him, wondering if he would be able to spare her of the fate he saw in his vision from years prior.

CHAPTER 9

# The Four of Swords

Picking at his food, Leopold stole a glance over his shoulder at the woman sleeping on the bed of hay with the hairless black cat curled up next to her feet. A thorn twisted in his heart at the thought of everything she'd gone through alone, keeping her identity a secret in the one place where it could have cost her, her life. Staring at Morgana, he knew exactly what he had to do next, since finding the princess and restoring order wasn't a guarantee. If the worst came to pass, he'd leave Perdetia and his post behind to be with her. He'd even move to Bragburg if he had to. He'd run with her to the furthest reaches of the earth to escape the demon king and never regret his decision as long as she was his.

Baba Yaga watched Leopold stare off into space before fixating on the tawny liquid in his cup. She shook her head. Her earlier encounter with the demon king left her shaken at the uncertain future. For some reason, the Devoth prince wanted the young witch in her cabin alive, but she couldn't figure out why. The woman on her floor was obscured in a cloud of darkness; her future was muddled, and several fate lines converged upon her. Determining Morgana's fate would be impossible, but she could still get some answers from the men, whose fate lines linked directly to the young woman. Reaching into her apron pocket, she pulled out a faded deck of navy-blue cards. Shuffling them in her hands, she knew the fortune of the two men would not be enough to reveal the Devoth's intentions, but they would be enough to shed some light on the mystery she faced. Clearing the phlegm in her throat, she trailed her milky eyes over to her guests.

"Say, boys," she began, mixing the cards, "it's been so long since I've had company here. Do you want me to read you your fortunes? I can tell you about your past, your present, and what your future has in store for you. What do you say to that?"

When Leo's eyes snapped up to the frayed edges of the cards with celestial designs, a shudder raked down his spine. He knew what they were; he'd seen them once before at Baroness de Laurent's estate, when she'd shown him his fate card. Illegal as they were where he lived, he refused to sell the woman out for practicing the forbidden art of fortunetelling. The baroness was the first noble to treat him like an equal, and he always appreciated her hospitality. Still, drawing his fate card and knowing what it meant for him was one thing, but knowing the future was another thing all together—one he wasn't a fan of. Finding himself in the company of fate cards again, his heart tightened, and his stomach cramped. He didn't wish to know his future. The prospect of it made beads of sweat form on his face. Chewing his lips, he rapped his fingers on the faded tabletop before looking up at the old woman's face with a scowl.

"Surely you don't expect me to believe some cards can predict my future?" he scoffed. "They are just cards, after all. Child's playthings. Any other purpose they may serve is purely superstition for those who are desperate to believe."

"What's wrong, Captain?" Leighton jeered, drawing three cards from the deck. "Are you afraid to hear that Morgana will never crawl into bed with you?"

"No," he snapped. "That's not it at all."

"Uh huh." The duke smirked. "In that case, what do you have to lose?"

Glaring at the man sitting beside him, Leopold thought about how much he'd love to wipe that nasty grin off his face with one punch. He was really starting to dislike the cursed duke of Bragburg—not for being a snobby noble, but for seeing right through him. The duke was correct, of course. He feared what the cards might tell him, loathed the possibility of never being with her despite everything they'd been through. Most of all, he feared that the cards would confirm what the shadelych showed him: her death. There was no way he'd admit any of it to Leighton, who sat across from him, legs crossed, with a playful smirk on his face. Seeing little choice in the matter, Leo swallowed his pride, drew three cards from the deck, and placed them face down on the table before him.

"Good, good. I'm glad you're willing to trust me." The witch cackled. "Now then, I shall read the duke's fortune first, and then

I will get to you, my dear Captain."

Taking the cards from Leightons's hand, she laid them out in a neat row on the table between them. Cracking her fingers, she reached out and flipped over the leftmost card. Its faded face revealed a bearded man in a brown cloak holding up a lantern. Giving her chapped lips another lick, Baba Yaga leaned and hovered over the card, holding her hand over it as if her palms could see what her eyes could not. She nodded her head silently, darting her eyes up to regard the duke with a glazed-over stare.

"The Monk card," she hummed, "and its upside down, my poor boy. This tells me your past has been a lonely one. You've never had any friends growing up. Orphaned at a young age, you had to shoulder the responsibilities of running your province on your own. As result, you withdrew from society. You buried yourself in books and assisted allies in fighting monsters, waiting to meet your end. That is, until a certain princess came along to change your mind, and a young witch told you there was a cure for your . . . condition."

Without saying a word, Leighton nodded at her, tucking his left arm under the table. Watching him, Leopold raised a brow at the man's stolid demeanor and wondered if he had any emotions at all. Then he wondered what the princess saw in the cold-blooded man to begin with. Perhaps it was the advanced weaponry they had—a result of Bragburg defiance toward the demon king—or perhaps he had a bit more to offer than that. Recalling his conversation with Morgana a week prior, he glanced over at the old woman, who flipped over another card, then fell back with a gasp in her chair. On its face, a horned figure in a cloak of black clouds greeted him with an unnerving smirk.

"The Devil," she wheezed. "I'm afraid you're in danger, Your Grace. I sense deception all around you. Something isn't right here, and I can't tell you what it is. My advice is to be careful from here on out. Bad things are coming, and fast."

Without flinching, the duke cradled his chin in his right hand, leaning over in his chair, studying the card with a soft hum. Baba Yaga huffed out her moldy breath, and he waved his hand to her, signaling for her to flip over the last card as he sat back with his arms folded across his chest, his expression unchanging. Leo watched it turn over, studying the image of a skeleton riding a pale horse, and wondered if this meant the duke was going to die. Rumor had it his curse would claim him in a few years, and surely this was a sign of the end for him. Scratching his head, he leaned back and waited to hear what it meant, his own cards clutched tightly in his sweaty hands.

"Death. The end is near. What form that end will take for you, I cannot say, but your journey will be over soon." She nodded at Leighton with a grim smile before turning to Leo, who was slumped in his chair. "Now . . . your turn, Captain." She grabbed hold if his cards, pried them out of his hand, and laid them on the table. "I have no doubt it will be another major arcana spread. I knew the three of you were special the second you walked through my door."

Leo watched her wrinkled hand reach for the first card in the spread, the air catching in his lungs. Sweat beaded up on the back of his neck, and his armor turned into an oven. For a split moment, he was taken over by the urge to stop her. His arm reached for the cards before he stopped, and then he pulled it back. Reclining, with stale air burning in his lungs, he felt his flesh prick while he watched the card turn over. He wanted to look away but couldn't, and instead stared at a man dressed in a black-and-red cassock, wearing a red miter on his head and holding a *globus cruciger* in his right hand.

"The Bishop. I should have guessed," she hummed with a widening grin. "You and tradition have been at war with one another for years, have you not?"

"It's true." Leo nodded. "I've always had a problem with Perdetia laws, especially the burnings in the town square. At the same time, I've been climbing up the ranks of the royal guard and charged with preserving the very traditions I can't stand."

"You'll be the change you seek—that I have no doubt of. There is something about you I like. Now, allow me to see what you are going through now."

As her hand reached for the middle card, Leo's arm shot out and stopped it. His heart leaped into his throat and his pulse quickened. She tilted her head at him with a raised brow, and he closed his eyes, let go of her hand, and nodded. He was finally ready to see what it was going to be. Rolling her eyes, the witch flipped it over and chortled. On its face sat a six-spoked wheel rolling along a lush landscape, helped by a pair of cherubs.

"Ah yes, the Wheel of Life." She clapped her hands. "You are going through a phase of life which sees tremendous change. I can't tell you whether the change is good or bad—*that* I can't see—but my advice for you would be to stick to your gut. It will serve you well in the upcoming days."

His heart hammered behind his sternum, and he turned his head to look at Morgana, who continued to turn his world upside down. For her, he'd take on the whole kingdom of Perdetia if he had to.

When he turned back around, he found the last card flipped and the witch tapping her knotted finger on it, grinning wide. Beside him, Leighton covered his face to conceal a snicker. The card on the table had two naked people on its face, engaged in a passionate act.

"What . . . what's so funny?"

"You got the Lovers. You will end up with the girl you wish to be with, but whether or not you get to keep her will be up to you. I see a dark cloud looming over her head. She will have some difficult decisions to make in the future, and you will need to be stronger than the storm if you wish for your love to survive."

"What . . . what is that even supposed to mean?"

"As I said, that's for you to decide. I can't tell you what to do. Doing so would not be right. The future, after all, is yours to shape. Now, why not get some rest, boys? You still have a long journey ahead of you, and I need you to get up early to get me fish to replace what I shall give you for your journey."

"We really won't have time to fish." Leighton's brows drew together. "We simply won't take anything from you."

"You will if you wake up early enough." The witch narrowed her eyes. "It won't take but an hour of your time, and as I said, your princess isn't in any danger. She is no good dead; the demon king needs her alive to lure you in. He needs to kill you before he can proceed with trying to conquer the world again. After all, it was your ancestor that put an end to his plans in the first place. He won't make the same mistake twice. You need to die first. You'll have plenty of time to rescue your girl. Trust me."

"Fine." Leighton's jaw tightened. Shooting up from his chair, he glared at the old woman. "Wake me up first thing in the morning.

I'll get you your fish, and then we'll leave."

Leo was taken aback by the duke's reaction. He thought it was the first genuine display of emotion he'd seen from the man he perceived as heartless and uncaring. He watched him storm over to the fireplace where two more beds had formed, then got up to join him. The duke left the spot closest to Morgana open, and Leo settled beside her while the surrounding candles extinguished one at a time. In the perfect darkness, Leopold rolled over, draping his arm around Morgana, and his name fell from her lips.

Heat spread through his body at hearing her voice, and he cradled her tighter. The first time he held her like that, she was only five. She had run away from home thinking everyone hated her, and, worried about her safety, Leo went after her, eventually locating her in the woods. When he found her, she was cowering from a Tormentor, a monster born from the emotions of those dying from hunger, who feeds on the life force of the living. He had only been training for two years, but he knew she was in trouble, and he drew his sword and engaged it in a fight, forcing the creature away from her. It was a difficult battle, but he gladly fought it for her, knowing that if he lost, the creature would devour her soul. Once the monster was dead, there was no way for them to get out until morning. It was too dark and rainy, and the path was unclear. They spent the night together instead, keeping each other warm as they cuddled between the roots of a nearby tree. He remembered how perfectly she fit in the nook of his body then, and he thought of how even now she settled in that space as if she belonged there. Closing his eyes, he inhaled her scent, stiffening, and recalled the last card from his spread, and he wondered what storm the old hag was talking about.

CHAPTER 10

# The Nine of Swords

While the duke and Leo were having their fortunes read, Morgana was hopelessly lost in the vivid realm of dreams—and hers were far from pleasant. Wandering through a desolate landscape awash with dense blooming shadows and trees groaning in the distance, she glanced about for any signs of life, but none were to be found. An artic gale whipped past her half-naked body, chilling her to the marrow and dousing her in a sheet of ice. Wrapping her arms around herself, she pushed forward as the road before her stretched into the distance.

She did not know how long she had walked—the tides of time seemed to have stopped in the bleak space—but as the veil of blackness lifted and her surroundings shifted, she found herself in a tattered dress standing barefoot among the ruins of a smoldering kingdom. The cracked soles of her feet bled, and she glanced about at the corpses in the streets amid the folded roofs and charred timbers. A broken-up cart lay to her side, and baskets scattered their produce at her feet. She recognized the place almost instantly. This was all that was left of Perdetia's capitol after what she assumed was the demon king's second assault on the place.

Her heart dropped like a brick. She wanted to run and check on Leo, Lafreya, and her mother to make sure they were not killed, but something cemented her in place. Somewhere in the distance, the mewing of a baby filled her ear, and she spun around, hoping to pinpoint the source of the sound. At first she found nothing, only the smell of burnt hair and cold silence. She would have thought she was crazy, but she heard the infant calling again, more demanding this time, its shrill cries echoing around her. Scanning between the crumbled stones of the nearby abbey and the charred remains of cottages, she spotted a black tower on a hill beyond the castle. She knew the tower was not in Perdetia—she'd seen it in her dreams many times before. And she knew avoiding it was best, but the urgent cries seemed to be coming from there, and she was unable to let an innocent child suffer.

Taking a timid step forward, she wondered what the tower was, and then she stopped. Something inside her prevented her from moving. Some arcane fear kept her rooted in place. But as the wailing got louder, she forced herself to move, sprinting toward the menacing column of dark brick. The closer she got to the foreboding structure, the more the weather changed, and a torrential rain came down in sheets upon her, sizzling on the cracked cobblestone road leading up toward the hill. Running through the dense carpet of fog on the eroding soil, she stilled her breath until she reached her destination. As she stood before the rotted, moss-covered door, the wind whipped her hair, and lightning split the moonless sky, followed by a peel of thunder. Her flesh tingled at the thought of what was on the other side, and she found it difficult to breathe.

Pushing down the hard rock in her throat, she clenched her jaw and reached for the door, flinging it open with bated breath. The dank interior was free of light. Shadows leaped on the wall, and the only sound was the whimpering of a child coming from the uppermost floor. Pushing through her paralytic fear, Morgana drew in a sharp breath and stepped inside. Inching her way up the winding, crooked stone steps, she used the rough walls for guidance as darkness engulfed her. Instinct pulled her. A deep-seated urge to protect the child pushed her further up the tower until she stood at the top landing, looking at a studded wood door framed in human bones.

From the inner chamber, the crying stopped, and Morgana's heart sank to her feet, her stomach knotted with fear. Standing as still as death, she pressed her ear to the wood and was greeted with a smothering silence. She wanted to turn around and run, but the sensation of something warm, wet, and sticky on her feet drew her attention to the floor. A damp maroon puddle was clotting on the stones, slowly seeping out from under the door, and inching for the stairs at a crawl. Fighting the nausea, she flung the door open, and a horrid odor of decay hit her almost instantly. The compartment on the other side stood eerily still.

Shuffling into the gloom-enfolded space, she glanced out the sole slit window at the lightning illuminating the room in bursts of eerie blue light. At the far end of the chamber, a wood bassinet, decorated in carved ivory, swayed next to a torn-up bed upon which lay the Heartseaker—she recognized the glowing serrated blade and regalia of the royal guard. She ran for the crib but found it empty, aside from cobwebs gathering in the corners. It was clear no one had used the room in a long time. She plopped down on the bed and glanced at the moss-covered ceiling. Rain dripped on her head from the hole above, and she wanted to scream to break the silence.

"There you are." A familiar soft, husky voice came from the doorway. "I thought I'd find you here."

"Leo?"

Turning toward the doors, she spotted his smiling face as he stood there with outstretched arms, calling her to him. She jumped to her feet and ran, hoping to embrace him, but she stopped when she spotted a lingering shadow with amber eyes standing behind him. The yell caught in her throat, and Leo looked at her, his expression of bewilderment instantly contorting into a horrifying grimace as a curved black blade burst through his armor, sending a fine crimson mist all over her face. Clutching his chest, he gasped for breath before falling to the ground, his blood-soaked hand reaching for her. Behind him, the all-too-familiar eyes of the demon king burned in the darkness.

"No . . ." She fell back with tears burning her eyes. "Please, no."

"I'm sorry, Morgana, but I cannot allow you to be with that man. He is not worthy of you."

The amorphous figure in the door took a step forward, and a flash of lightning illuminated its beautiful features as it morphed and took the shape of the man who visited her dreams regularly.

The man, around thirty-five, with ashen skin, glowing amber eyes, and long white hair, stood before her, grinning, his pointed canines glistening with the sparks from outside. The black horns on his head rose and curled behind him, and a black chain dangled from the metal choker around his neck. A part of her wanted to run away from him and scream. She loathed him for what he did to her mother. But a part deep down inside did not fear him; it wanted to get close. She longed to be near the Devoth prince.

"What do you want from me?"

"I've come here to warn you, darling." He kneeled beside her. "Stay away from the duke. Remain where you are. The last thing I want to do is hurt you."

"Why would I abandon my friends?" she snarled. "Why would I listen to anything you have to say? I hate you for everything you took from me."

"Very well, little one." The demon king stood up. "In that case, allow me to show you your potential future."

Lifting his arm into the air, he summoned the bolts of lightning to cascade from the sky and strike the blackened tower. The foundation gave way beneath her, sucking Leo's body into the abysmal pit, and the tower crumbled to the ground. Falling from the tower among the stone, she looked up to see the demon king floating above on his leathery black wings. Instinctively she reached for his hand, but before she knew it, she hit the sodden ground. Feeling her body jolt in her sleep, she startled herself awake. Shaking off the nightmare, she opened her heavy lids to the rays of sun filtering in through the window. A small sigh of relief escaped her lungs. It was only a dream. As she moved her hand along the sheets, she felt something moist beside her and froze.

Flinging back the covers, she let loose a soul-shattering scream as she gazed at the body on the blood-streaked sheets. Leopold's lifeless body lay beside her, a dagger protruding from his chest. It was his dagger—the same one she had given him on his thirteenth birthday, which he had kept on him ever since. Shuddering, she looked over the red foam bubbling on his lips. His lifeless blue eyes stared up at the ceiling, and the gummy blood pooled under his body. With no breath left to cry, Morgana glanced over at her bloodied hands and fell off the bed, shaking her head in disbelief.

*Do you like what we've done to him?* Her own voice giggled behind her. *Doesn't he look better this way?*

She jolted her head to her side, her eyes widening, pulse racing. There was what she could only describe as her doppelgänger. The thing before her had all her features: the same lines of her face, same curves of her body, and the same waves of her hair. Except this version of her was made of moving shadows, fading in and out while her physical form twisted within them.

"What . . . what are you really? And what did you do to Leo?"

*Me?* The figure replied. *I'm you. I'm everything you wish to hide and suppress. I am the part you fear to face, for you know what we are capable of.* The shadow tittered. *As for your lover . . . well, we killed him after we caught him sleeping around with the village whore.*

"No." Morgana shook her head. "Leo isn't like that. He wouldn't cheat, and . . . and I would never do anything to hurt him."

*Oh, but he is, and we did. We caught him in bed with another, and we took his dagger off his belt and drove it into his chest while he slept.* The shadow tilted her head, her gaping maw widening into a wicked grin. *But what did you expect, Morgana? You are pathetic. Damaged. You think a man like him could love someone like you? Think he'd like sleeping with someone who at thirteen got taken advantage of by a fifty-six-year-old man and preceded to bed half the men in Dresbourn as a result? You should have known he'd cheat on you. After all, they all leave, eventually.* The smile on her face spread from ear to ear. *And just think, this isn't even our best work. You should see what we did to the child you had with him.*

"You didn't." Morgana swallowed the bitterness in her mouth. "You wouldn't. I wouldn't . . ."

*You sure about that?*

"Why? Why do you torture me? What do you want?"

*Listen to the demon king. Stay where you are. Leave the cursed duke to his fate.*

"No, I—" Morgana glared at the shadow. "I would never betray a friend. And this . . . this nightmare isn't my future. It's just one likely scenario."

*Oh?* the shadow hissed. *You wish to see more, do you? Then allow me to show you more.*

Morgana did not wish to see more; she knew the demon king was toying with her. Since her mother's death, the Devoth prince had visited her in her dreams, watching her from the shadows. Occasionally he would interact with her, but never before had he tortured her with visions of possible futures. Refusing to give in to him, she sat on the floor, placed her face in her knees, and attempted to force herself awake.

CHAPTER 11

# The Three of Chalices

As the sun came up in the morning, the cabin shifted and allowed the windows to reappear on its surface, illuminating the dusty interior in a faint mist of light. Feeling someone shaking him awake, Leopold forced open his eyelids, still heavy with sleep, and saw Leighton crouching beside him, motioning toward the door and telling him it was time to fish. His eyes lingered on the woman still sleeping beside him, and he was reluctant to leave her side, but they needed supplies to make it back to Bragburg, and they promised the old woman they would go fishing in the morning. Nodding at the duke, Leo got up and put on his armor before following the sleek black cat out of the cabin.

In the clearing, the trees moved, allowing them a path through the tangled trunks. The men walked after Grimalkin, who led them to a velvety blue lake beyond, which glistened in the sun. Trout splashed in crystal-blue waters, rippling its otherwise glass-like surface. Watching the cat stretch and curl up on a sun-washed rock, Leopold settled down in the grass and cast his rod into the water, wordlessly waiting for the duke to sit down beside him.

For a while, they sat together in silence on the grassy bank, casting their rods into the lake, waiting for the fish to bite. Leo looked up at the sun still cresting its way over the dark blue waters, its rays sparkling upon the gentle waves in the distance. The sight reminded him of Morgana and how they used to sit by the pond near Perdetia in their youth, making his heart ache. He wanted her to be there by his side, to share the moment. Her near death still weighed heavily on his mind. Letting out a soft groan, he closed his eyes and dropped his head toward the ground between his legs, an act that did not go unnoticed by his companion, who sat watching him with a frown.

"So . . . Captain"—Leighton planted his rod in the ground and leaned back in the grass on his elbows—"what's the real deal with you and Lady Morgana?"

"What do you mean?"

"Well, you are clearly in love with her. Not only is it written on your face, but I've seen the way you act around her—not just here, but when you visited her estate all those times when I was there."

"And what if I am?" Leo scoffed. "You got some vested interest in my love life, Your Grace, that I am not aware of?"

"No, no interest. I'm just curious because I know how she feels about you. She told me that much. And I know she only rebuffs you because you are the captain of the guard. So I guess what I want to know is why didn't you make your move sooner—before things got complicated between you?"

"Where should I start?"

"The beginning seems like a good place."

"Very well. I first met Morgana when she was three. Her mother had just adopted her, and Lafreya was showing her around. I was only a squire at the time and an orphan like her. The knight I worked for insisted I accompany them for safety reasons. Back then she didn't talk—she couldn't. Her first words were to me a month later, which made me feel . . . special. With our difference in status, I didn't think there would ever be much between us, but then I got an anonymous sponsor, who paid for me to become a knight. The gap between us closed a little, and I began spending all my free time with her. She always knew how to make me feel important, like I was the only person in room with her. Then, when she was thirteen, I finally realized I was in love with her. It was tournament day, and I told her I'd win it, for her, wishing to impress her."

"And did you win?"

"No," Leo snorted, tossing a stone at the lake. "I got knocked down on my third match and sustained a nice injury in the process. Morgana, of course, snuck into my hospital room in the middle of the night to lie next to me and comfort me. Losing was an embarrassment, but she didn't care. She told me the only thing that mattered to her was that I was alive. I left for my first campaign a few days later, and she got up before the sun to see me off. Seeing her there made something take over me, made me brazen. I kissed her for the first time that day and told her I loved her. I asked her to wait for me and not to forget me while I was away."

"How did she respond to that?"

"I'll never forget it. She touched her lips and whispered, 'Always

". . . and never.'"

"All right, so what the hell happened? Why didn't you get together with her when you returned? You were not captain back then, and you could have still walked away at that point."

"Life, Your Grace." Leo heaved out a sigh and gazed at the horizon. "Life happened. While I was out slaying monsters, a professor at her academy was busy taking advantage of her. Ah"—he clenched his fists—"what am I saying? That bastard raped her repeatedly for an entire year while I was too far away to protect her. I wanted to kill him, would have killed him when I got back, but it seems an otherworldly force took care of it for me. As for me, well, I was out getting experience with all sorts of ladies on the road. I didn't want to, but the other guys insisted, saying I'd never please the woman of my choice if I didn't learn how. I still hate myself for it, but as Morgana said, you can't change the fact that they happened."

"Ah, I see." Leighton shifted on the grass. "So that is what she means when she says she is unworthy of a man's love. I hope you at least told her that you did not feel that way."

"Of course I did. I told her that nothing would make her imperfect in my eyes, and we slowly began growing close together again. Once again, there was hope. Then the king dragged me out on another campaign, which saw not only his death but that of my captain, who with his dying breath put me in charge. At the time, I didn't even realize that it was the very position I've been aiming for that drove a wedge between us. Now I think it's far too late to change anything other than how I feel about her."

"I doubt that very much, Captain. I know how much she loves you. I know she didn't want to tell you she was a witch until the laws were abolished, but now that you know, I think you may stand a chance. Want me to speak with her and find out?"

"I . . . I don't know." He stared blankly at the sun sparkling on the lake. "I'll get back to you on that. Just give me some time to mull it over."

The duke nodded in silence and Leo glanced up at the sun, drawing in a deep, painful breath as he considered his options. He already asked Lafreya to put in a good word for him, and she promised she'd do her best, but she was currently missing, and he had no way of knowing how that conversation went—or if it even happened. The duke's offer, however, was tempting, especially since he seemed to be on good terms with Morgana, better than he himself. But Leo didn't know the duke well. The man always avoided the capital when he visited the princess he claimed to love, choosing instead to hide out at the de Laurent estate. If Leo was going to consider getting help from him, he'd first have to figure out if he could trust him. Glancing over at the man basking in the sun beside him, he cleared his throat and met Leighton's stony gaze.

"Can I ask you something, Your Grace? About you, that is."

"Sure. What is it about me you wish to know?"

"Is it true what they say about you? About your sickness?"

"I'm afraid so." Leighton's voice dropped, and he shifted his gaze to the lake, his brows creasing his forehead. "For the last two and a half centuries, my family line has been plagued with the crystallization curse. As you know, Bragburg was the only place not to adopt the demon king's rule, and we suffered gravely for it. He tried to turn Duke Edmund into a statue, but the duke's wife cast a spell, binding him to the earth. It prevented the instant death, but it cursed us to turn to stone slowly. Ever since that day, my family line carried this curse. From birth, our bones begin to turn into glass, and the disease slowly spreads to the blood, skin, and other organs until we turn into crystal statues on our thirtieth birthday. As you can see"—Leighton removed the black glove from his left hand and showed Leo his ashen skin, catching the sun's ray on its semi-polished surface—"this hand is almost done turning. I can barely move my fingers. Seven more years and I'm a dead man, unless I find a way to break the curse."

"Then is what that old witch told you true? You really were orphaned at a young age, like Morgana and I?"

"Afraid so. My mother died a week after I was born from childbed fever, and nine years later my father turned into a statue, leaving me in charge of the whole duchy."

"Does this mean your engagement to Lafreya is out of pure necessity to produce an heir?"

"Funny"—Leighton leaned forward and looked at Leo—"your girl asked me the same thing once. So I shall tell you what I told her: No, not at all. If you want to know the truth, I could have married years ago to one of the ladies my advisors lined up for me. I might have even remained single if I never met the princess during standard trade negotiations. Back then, I didn't think highly of anyone from Perdetia. I assumed you were all the same. I figured the princess would be a lot like her father—brash and ruthless, wishing to reestablish the practice of witch-hunting through the rest of Dresbourn. Then I walked into the room to find this little redhead, and she took me off guard as she gave me a warm smile. She turned out to be the opposite of what I expected—warm, kind, gentle, and radiating this glow that warmed the room. At first I thought she was pulling the same trick on me that Nathaniel pulled on the late queen of Perdetia, but the more we talked, the more my opinion changed.

"I admired Lafreya and her desire to change the laws of the land and become a better ruler in her father's stead. I realized the two of us had more in common than I could have imagined, and I quickly fell for her despite knowing who her father was. After that day, I began pursuing her romantically, and she was more than happy to accept my advances. As you can imagine, my advisors were not pleased with me getting involved with a long-standing enemy of Bragburg. After all, my ancestor was the one to push back against the demon king first, and Perdetia was always on the Devoth's side. But from that moment forward, there was no other woman for me. Now, well, now she's gone because I was not there to save her and being with me put her in danger to begin with."

"It wasn't your fault. You had no way of knowing what the demon king was planning."

"No, but I should have guessed. I should have realized being with me put her at risk. Perdetia was the last holdout—the largest, most central kingdom in Dresbourn with the most political sway. It was his only way to maintain control. He took her to get to me."

"We will get her back for you . . . for all of us."

"I sure hope so, because frankly I don't think I can live without her."

"I know exactly how you feel." A smile cracked over Leo's lips. "And I am pleased to know you actually care for her as much as she seems to care for you."

"I'm glad to hear you say that." Leighton sat up, glanced over at the lake, and let out a light chuckle. "Say, Captain, did we just become friends?"

"I wouldn't push it that far, Your Grace." Leo gave the duke a childish grin. "But I definitely hate you a lot less now. I guess you are more human than I first gave you credit for."

Laughing at the remark, Leighton patted him on the back and returned to fishing. It satisfied Leo that the duke was in love with the princess and that Morgana was simply a friendly face to him. He still wasn't sure if he could trust the man to talk to her on his behalf, but he was starting to see the merit of befriending him, even if there was still something about the man's smugness and lack of emotions that he didn't quite like. But as they continued to fish and strike up friendly conversation, he grew at ease with the duke almost to the point of accepting his offer. Despite what Perdetians thought, Bragburg was a safe haven for people like Morgana, and that made it all right in his book.

"All right." Leighton rose. "Our hour is up. Let's go get Morgana and get on the road. We wasted enough time doing the old woman's bidding, now it's time to get my lady back."

Seeing no need to argue with reason, Leopold grabbed the fish and woke the cat up. Begrudgingly it stretched, rumbled, and guided them back to the cabin. With each passing step, Leo's heart pounded harder, and he wondered if Morgana was awake yet. He had so much he wished to tell her, and he wanted to assure her that he didn't care about what she was and that he still hoped there was a future to be had between them. No longer able to contain his excitement, he handed the basket over to the duke and ran the rest of the way to the cabin, wishing to see her face and embrace her in his arms, where he could feel her warm body against his. She still had a lot of questions to answer, but he couldn't wait to see where this new road would take them and how their cards would play out.

CHAPTER 12

# The Five of Staves

While the men were out fishing, back at the cabin Morgana was startling herself awake from her dreams of blood, death, and endless horror. Jolting up with a yelp in her makeshift bed of straw, she clutched her chest, panted, and glanced around the unfamiliar surroundings. A kaleidoscope of light fell by her feet from the window of the musty wood cabin, and she probed the ghosts of her memory for the last thing she could recall, but she felt like she was waking up with a bad hangover. Last she remembered, she was raising up the broken bridge leading to Kalingrad, telling Leo she was a witch, and the next thing she remembered was the dark realm of dreams—no recollection of how she got from the dirt road to the cabin. She looked for someone to ask and found her host sitting on a chair by a spinning wheel, working the yarn between her gnarled fingers.

"Excuse me . . ." She shifted in her spot to face the stout old woman in the corner. "Where am I?"

"My chicken-legged cabin in the middle of the Black Forest, of course." The woman looked up and smiled at her with her crooked smile. "Did you have a good night's rest, my young witch?"

"You're . . ." Morgana gasped. "You're Baba Yaga?"

"That's right, my lovely." The witch stood up and hobbled over closer to her. "But don't you worry, I don't eat young maidens or anything those old books you read say I do. Not to mention, I wouldn't snack on my own kind even if I did like the flesh of youthful souls."

"I know that." Morgana frowned. "I was just not expecting to run into you, of all people, out here—wherever here is."

"I'm just teasing you. And if you must know, you are in the heart of the Black Forest, right outside Kalingrad's outermost village of Rostov. Here you are safe from those nasty royal guard men who are hunting you and your friends because it is protected by magic radiating from the pulse lines beneath."

"How did I get here? The last thing I remember is passing out after I put the bridge back together. And what did you do to make me better? I feel as good as new suddenly."

"Oh, I didn't do much. You see, you've been attacked by a mana tick, dear. The little bugger had been on you for at least a day. Sucked you almost dry, did it. All I did was remove him and give you back what he stole. But if your lover didn't bring you to me when he did, you might have died. You should thank him once he returns from the fishing trip I sent him on."

"My lover? Do you mean Leopold?" Morgana flushed and

glanced away from the old witch. "He's . . . he's not my lover."

"And why not? There is certainly a lifetime of love between you."

"Things are . . ." She held back the tears, priming her sinuses. "Well, they are complicated between us."

"Lies." Baba Yaga walked closer to Morgana. "Sweet, beautiful lies. The only things complicated between the two of you is how difficult you make it for that poor boy to get close. I can smell the lust of dozens of men on your flesh, so clearly you don't shy away from physical contact. So go on, tell me the truth. Why do you bed every man except for the one who is worthy of sharing your bed?"

"I do it to fix something inside of me—something deep and painful, a part of me that was broken a long time ago."

"Dear child, you can't heal a wound by opening up fresh ones. Even you ought to know this."

"Just because I know better doesn't mean I have control over it. As the Tower of Sorrow, I am good at creating chaos all around me. One of these days, I will be my own ruin."

"Oh ho. We finally get to the root of the problem. This ruin you speak of. Is that what that devil on your back tells you will happen?"

"I guess you've got the gift of sight if you can see her sitting here beside me."

"Took you long enough to figure it out," the old woman cackled. "May I give you a word of advice, my dear girl?"

"Sure. I'd welcome any guidance you can offer."

"Stop listening to it. It is true that there is a dark, ominous cloud hanging over your head. You have a difficult and painful choice ahead of you, one which will cut deep. But no matter what you decide, it will be far from your ruin. Trust the good voice inside you, not the dark pest following you around."

Morgana wanted to ask the old crone what choice she'd need to make, but before she had the chance to open her mouth, the door to the cabin burst open and hit the wall with a loud crack, making her jump to her feet, afraid the demon king had found her. Much to her relief, it was only Leo standing on the other side, cemented frozen in his spot, with a stupid grin forming on his face. Behind him walked in a hairless black cat and Leighton, who dropped a basket on the ground and put his arm around Leo's shoulder, glancing over her. Seeing them together made her stomach flutter. It was a stark change from the previous evening. She waved to greet them, continuing to observe the strange contrast in their relationship.

"Morgana." Leo beamed from ear to ear. "You're awake. Does this mean you are feeling better?"

"Yes." She walked over closer to him and took hold of his hand. "And from what I hear, I have you to thank for it."

"Oh, that"—he rubbed the back of his head—"that was nothing. You know I'd do anything to protect you."

"I know. It's the part of you I find so charming." She smiled at him, and his cheeks turned a light shade of pink. "I also see that you and Leighton have warmed up to each other. What happened in the short time I was out?"

"We may have settled some of our differences along the way."

"Did you, now?" She stole a glance at the duke with a raised brow. "Is this true, Your Grace?"

"Yeah, guess so." Leighton shrugged, hanging up their rods. "We talked things out, man to man, and learned we have a lot in common. Guess we are well on our way to becoming fast friends."

He locked his eyes on the old woman. "Now we really should get going. I'd like to make it back to Bragburg and find my fiancé. Are we free to go?"

"You certainly are, my cursed friend." She shuffled over and grabbed the basket of fish. "Just let me fetch you the food I've prepared, and I will send you on your way. You'll see your princess in no time at all."

Hobbling over, Baba Yaga grabbed the basket from the floor and strolled into her kitchen with the black cat in tow. She grabbed a sack on the counter and strolled back over to Leighton. Handing him the parcel, she licked her chapped lips and looked at him. She still wanted to know why the demon king didn't wish to have the young woman with him, but she figured she would learn the truth soon enough, without alerting the trio to her connection with the Devoth.

"All right, my dears, looks like this is where we part ways. Once you get on your horses, face to your left, go forward, and wait for the trees to part ways. Ride down the path laid out for you, and it will bring you down to the banks of the Taiga River. You should make it there by nightfall. There should still be an old boat sitting there, lest the trolls stole it. You take that boat and ride the current downstream until you reach a sandy shore. This will drop you off close to the Bragburg border. It should be a short horse ride from there, and you should make it without any trouble. Hopefully you will get your princess back and return alive. I hope we shall meet again someday. There are a lot of questions I still have for you."

The trio thanked their host and left the cabin, which stood back up on its chicken legs and wiped the windows and door from its surface. Leopold once again offered Morgana a spot in his saddle, and she sat in front of him, resting her head on his chest, savoring his aroma while her cheeks burned from being so close to him. As promised, the trees parted and a single path appeared, leading them out of the magic clearing, which kept them safe. Setting off down the road, their horse followed behind Leighton's, and she observed the fireflies fluttering by, twinkling around their heads. Occasionally Leo would glance down at her with a soft smile, and she had to look away because she could barely keep herself from blushing.

The long, narrow road gave her plenty of time to think about the conversation she had with Baba Yaga, and occasionally she allowed her thought to wander to Leo. Her mind bounced between her feelings for Leo, Lafreya's fate, and the warning about the choice she would have to make. She worried about what happened to her friend and what that meant for the rest of them, but her mother's voice rang clear in her head: "the Golden Empress was blessed with a long life." Surely that meant Lafreya was unharmed and that they'd be able to save her. She knew a major arcana card only came into existence during a time of significant change, and she prayed that the change would be a good one and that the world wouldn't fall again. Fidgeting in the saddle, Morgana heard the bubbling of water in the distance. They were near their destination. She peeled herself away from Leo to watch a marshy bank come into view with a sigh. In a moment, they'd have to part, but for the time being, she held on to him in the silence that was always theirs.

CHAPTER 13

# The Three of Staves

Leo pulled on the reins to halt his horse and glanced about the clearing washed with maroon and sienna as the sun sank behind the trees. Lowering Morgana to the ground first, he hopped off to stand beside her, then continued to scan the swampy bank. Tall, bald cypress and gnarled gum trees rose from the deep, murky waters, their branches draped in strands of curly, sage-green moss, framing the shores of the bog. The winding river stretched down into the distance with no end in sight. Walking up beside him, Leighton grumbled under his breath. The duke saw the same problem.

"I guess Baba Yaga wasn't kidding that the only way to get to Bragburg from here is via the river. But the promised boat is nowhere to be found." Leighton placed his hands on his hips with a scowl. "You have any ideas as to what we do now, Leopold? I'll take any suggestion you give me."

"Well"—he scanned the area, which was filled with vines and logs scattered around the soggy bank—"we can always build a raft with what we have around us. It won't be pretty, but it should hold up until we get to the other side."

The duke nodded. "All right. Let's start gathering the supplies and get building. If we all work together, we can have this thing done by the time it gets dark, and we can leave first thing in the morning. Why don't you get the fire going, Captain, while I start gathering the logs?"

"Sounds good to me. Morgana, you can sit with the horses for now."

"No. I'm not useless. I'll go gather the vines scattered around the bank."

Leopold watched Morgana walk away and begin pulling the vines away from the trees, while Leighton left to gather logs large enough to work for a raft, leaving him alone in the small clearing. Crouching on his haunches, he began to work on the fire, but his eyes strayed to watch the woman with an armful of ivy, and he smiled. There was something different about her that night. She looked as if something weighed heavily on her, and there was a dark shadow on her face. But as she turned to smile at him, his heart thundered in his chest, and he had a hard time keeping his eyes off her, even as his flame roared to life, obscuring her silhouette in its warm glow.

Leopold rose to his feet, peeled off his armor, and located Leighton to help him gather the logs and assemble them in a tidy line by the bank. Morgana brought over the vines, and the three set off tying the logs together as the shadows of twilight encroached on them. They were making quick work of the binding, and by the time night cloaked the bank in its gloom, they were almost done. Excusing herself, Morgana left the men be, walking over to sit on a hollowed-out log by the water's edge.

Tying his knot, Leo stole a glance over his shoulder. The moon bathed her in its pale light, and a raspy breath escaped his lips. He continued to watch her aubergine hair shimmering with a lavender glow, and he felt as if he was being pulled to her by a hypnotic song. She always had that effect on him, ever since the day they first met at the stables, where he was shoveling hay. Shaking off the urge to rush to her side as he always did, he returned to the vine when he felt something nudge his ribcage. He spotted Leighton tilting his head to Morgana with a faint smile.

He frowned at the duke. "What?"

"She seems like she is in an amicable mood tonight," the duke whispered. "You should go talk to her. Let me finish up here."

"Are you sure?"

"Yes. I'm not a cripple, you know. It's only a few more knots. I think I can manage. Go on. Before I change my mind. And Leo"—Leighton looked up at him, smirking—"good luck."

Leopold stood up and walked over to where she was sitting, glancing up at the unblinking stars in the sky. His breath caught in his throat as the pearly luminance of the moon filtered in through the striated clouds and washed her in its silvery light. At that moment, she looked more unattainable than ever, and he stood there, unable to breathe, afraid of disrupting her meditative silence until something small stung the back of his head. Twisting his neck to look behind him, he saw Leighton waving him on with a puckered brow. Turning back to Morgana, he swallowed his fear and cleared his throat, and she turned to regard him with a warm smile.

"May I join you?"

As she looked into Leopold's radiant blue eyes, Morgana's cheeks warmed at the unspoken words in them and dared not break the perfect silence. Bobbing her head, she pointed to the spot next to her, and he walked around the log to sit beside her. With no metal plating between them, she felt his heat closer than ever, and her pulse raced at how close he was. After all these years, he still elicited such a reaction from her, and she turned her face back up toward the sky before she did something she might regret. The moon floated above her head like a waxen, cream rose in a sea of black, and it reminded her of the first time they met. The space between them shrunk, and Leo reached out his hand to brush a stray strand of hair behind her ear. She turned and looked up at his face frosted by the moonlight.

"What are you doing here all by yourself?" He spoke softly, his hand lingering on her cheek. "Do I bore you that much?"

"Stop it, Leo, you know that's not true." She rolled her eyes and gazed back up toward the sky. "I just came here to look at the stars and ponder our fate. I enjoy doing that sometimes. Not only does it remind me of our childhood, but they are so beautiful, mysterious, and far out of my reach. Looking at them helps me gather my thoughts and calm my soul. Some nights, I like to just sit and look at them, pondering what they would tell us if we could only ask."

"You know," Leo said, placing his hand on top of hers, "sometimes I wonder the same thing about you."

*Look at that. Our captain finally wants to get some answers. It's about time. So what are you going to do? Plan to tell him the truth?*

"Go on, then." Morgana ignored the shadow at her side, her eyes clipping to Leo's with a radiant smile. "Ask me anything you want. I promise to answer honestly."

"In that case"—he inhaled sharply and squeezed her hand—"tell me how long you've known you're a witch."

"I've known my entire life. My birth mother was one as well. I'm assuming my father was one too, but I can't be sure since my memories of him are hazy at best. After the demon king killed my mother, I used my magic to survive in the wild until my new parents found me and took me in."

"And what of them? Do your parents know what you are?"

He cringed as the last words left his lips, realizing he probably should not have referred to them as her parents. While everyone in Perdetia knew about the baroness's years-long love affair with her butler—Stephan—who was long suspected of being Morgana's father, no one actually referred to him as anything more than a servant. He shouldn't have brought it up, but Morgana did not seem phased by him implying Stephan was her father. She smiled at Leo instead, making his pulse drum in his ears.

"Of course. They found me while I was using magic to light a fire. Mother was the one who told me to hide who I was while in Perdetia and allowed me to hone my skills in the privacy of our home, where the king couldn't touch me. Guess I got lucky that old land laws made her estate fall outside of Perdetia's control."

Pursing his lips, Leopold nodded once and turned his face up to look at the sky with a blank expression. She kept her eyes on him, chewing her lips, realizing that was a lot for him to process, and yet he never once let go of her hand. Its warmth still radiated through her body, and she watched him with bated breath, waiting for him to speak or acknowledge her in some other way. Time seemed to have stopped. A stony silence fell around them like a shadow that robbed her of her breath until he finally turned to look at her. She expected to find contempt on his face but was instead greeted by his affectionate smile, his eyes sparkling in the deepening gloom.

"So, the eyes and hair." He reached out to stroke her head. "Is it true what the people say? That the closer you are to the Otherworld, the more likely you are to be born with the rare colors?"

"Yes, it's true. Perdetians were right to fear me. As you know, magic folk are genetically predisposed to it. This is why the king of Perdetia had his amber eyes, as it was said a sorceress was his grandmother—and why Lafreya has her rare hair. Since I'm a witch, I have both. I doubt the people knew what I was, though. I think they just figured my magic ancestry came from Stephan, who they think is a druid."

"All right." He grinned. "I can accept that explanation. But I have a few more questions to ask you. If you don't mind, that is."

"I did say you could ask me anything you want. So go ahead, get it off your chest. I bet you'll feel better afterwards."

He searched her face, trying to come up with the right words to say. "Well, you say you feel pain and get sick whenever you use magic, right?"

"The psipher, yes, but I don't always feel pain or get sick. You see, witches need to make a sacrifice to use magic. Sometimes we will prick or cut ourselves to offer up that sacrifice, but when we are using magic covertly, we draw the power from the world around us, and therefore we pay with our bodies. That's what the psipher is—a sacrifice for the use of magic all around us."

"Okay, and do you remember that time about a month after your parents adopted you? It was when you passed out on the inner battlement and were out for a few days with a fever. Your mother barely let me in to see you, blaming me for what happened."

"Yes. If I recall correctly, it was the day you fell off said battlement because the stones you were leaning against were not put in properly. They finally gave out that day, and you went with them."

"Right, I was talking to you and Lafreya just before I fell. I can still remember how loudly you screamed when the stones toppled. But that day I didn't hit the ground and die—because a cart full of hay broke loose and rolled down the hill right below me, catching me in the nick of time."

*Oh, you are a smart one, Leopold. Go on, tell her exactly what you think happened that day. Let's see if our witch answers you honestly, like she said she would.*

"You got very lucky that day."

"Yes, but"—he looked at her with a piercing gaze—"was it luck, or was it you using your magic to save me?"

"Fine. You caught me." She grinned at him. "I saved you that day, and the reason I passed out and had a fever for that long was because I used more magic than my small body could handle."

"I figured that much. I was just testing you," he said. "Does this mean that on the day you, Lafreya, and I were out in that meadow, when you were ten, and that Minotaur attacked us, it was you who sent that boulder rolling down the hill as I was fighting him off?"

"It was. That's why my hands suddenly locked up."

"How about my first jousting tournament, when I turned eighteen? I remember you watching in the stands, cheering me on. I recall I promised you I'd win." He probed her with his keen gaze. "My third opponent that day knocked me off my horse, and his lance broke, splintering in the process. I had a few pieces of wood stuck in my shoulder, and the doctor told me I got very lucky it wasn't much worse. I was told you had to retreat suddenly right after because you felt faint, and to this day Sir Hanning swears his lance slipped at the last minute, as if some otherworldly force was yanking on it."

"Well, you see . . . that would probably be because his lance did slip off your armor at the last minute. Right as you mounted your horse for that match, I was hit by a vision of it hitting you in the chest, splintering, and the shards going into your neck, killing you instantly. I couldn't bear the thought of losing you, so I decided to deflect it before it hit. I wish I could have prevented it from contacting you in the first place, but Hanning was fighting me the whole time and I had to use a lot of magic simply to have it not kill you. Which is also why I felt faint and had to run off. Although I had Lafreya make sure you survived, first."

"So . . . all these years I thought I was the luckiest guy on the planet, it was simply your magic keeping me alive?"

"Afraid so."

"Then this thing you gave me before I left for my first campaign a few days later." He reached under his black leather jerkin and pulled out a circular pendant with a serpent coiled around a sword. "What is this for?"

"That . . ."

She reached out to touch the charm, recalling how she got it. When she first came to Perdetia and met Leo, he showed her around the town, leading her to an abandoned well. He told her the story of the town legend surrounding the structure. It was said that an ancient spirit dwelled there who would grant each citizen one wish, so long as their intentions were pure. Being a witch, Morgana saw the creature's aura radiating out from beyond the darkness. Even back then, she knew her wish would be about Leo, but she held on to it until he was leaving for his first campaign. Knowing she couldn't protect him in battle, she asked the well spirit to do so in her stead, and it granted her the charm he now wore around his neck, keeping him safe.

"I didn't make it, if that's what you're asking. But it is meant to protect you in battle when I couldn't be there to watch over you."

"Why do it at all?" He locked his eyes on hers, his eyebrows slightly raised. "Why did you keep me alive?"

"Because"—she bit her lip and reached out to touch his cheek with the tips of her fingers—"I care about you, Leo—a lot. You are one of the few people I consider important to me, and I must protect those people at all costs, even if it kills me. I can't watch another person I care for die."

Leo beamed. "In that case, I was right about one thing."

"And what can that be?"

"I *am* the luckiest man on the planet because you consider me to be important to you."

Leaning over, Leo pulled her into a tight embrace, sucking the air out of her lungs and making her forget everything for a moment. Surrendering to his pull, she wrapped her arms around him, drawing her body close to his, and pressed her head on his chest. With nothing but cloth between them, she felt his body temperature rise and listened to the quickening thumping of the heart in his chest. Her cheeks brightened, and she wished the moment could last forever. But as he pulled away, she let him go and got up off the log, offering him her hand so they could rejoin the duke by the fire.

As Leo looked up at her radiating smile and outstretched hand, his heart skipped a beat, and he placed his palm in hers, tightening his grip on her silky skin. She pulled him to his feet and tugged him along to rejoin Leighton, who was waiting for them, smiling. They ate a small dinner and settled in for the night, and Morgana lay beside Leo. Placing his face in her hair, which still had the scent of vanilla, he closed his eyes and thought that the ice caps between them melted a bit that night. And that gave him hope for the future despite the storm the old witch warned him about. He didn't fall asleep at first. He simply recalled the moment they shared as a smile spread across his lips.

CHAPTER 14

# The Three of Swords

With the break of dawn, they pushed the raft into the water, got the horses on, and set off down the leisurely current of the river. The men insisted on steering their craft with the logs they found on shore, leaving Morgana to sit between the horses, who lay on the logs with their hooves tucked to their sides. Occasionally Leo's stallion would lean in and nuzzle her hair, making her giggle, and she'd rub his velvety soft snout, causing him to snort in delight. The beast and her were familiar; Leo had gotten him at the age of fourteen and raised him to be his faithful companion. But Morgana and the horse had seen little of each other for the better part of the last two years because she had been trying her best to avoid the captain, and it seemed like the horse missed her.

Running her fingers through its snow-white mane, she gave the horse a kiss on the forehead, then crawled to the edge of the raft. Peering at her murky reflection, she frowned when she spotted a dark splotch lingering behind her, observing her with its hate-filled eyes. The shadow said nothing at first. It simply slinked closer and sat down beside her, glancing at its own reflection in the waters of the river.

*You want to get close to him, don't you? You wish to be with him. But is that wise, given how your own father walked out on you? All men are the same. Leopold will leave you too.*

Gripping the edge of the raft, Morgana gritted her teeth in silence at what the thing was telling her. It was true that her father vanished one day, right before her mother died, but she doubted that he simply walked out on them. She recalled her father as a man who doted on her and whom she greatly admired, and she still missed him terribly. A man like that would never abandon his family, and Morgana long suspected that the demon king had something to do with it. Most likely, the Devoth prince killed her father right before he killed her mother—and yet the beast left her alive. She still didn't know why she was spared, nor did she care. She burned with a new hatred for the man who stole everything from her and continued to rob her by going after her friends. Turning away from the shadow, she glared at the water and thought of what she would do to the demon king once she found him.

The journey was slow, giving her plenty of time to think. They could only move as fast as the current, which was not in a hurry. Morgana sat by the horses, watching the men guide their raft down the river, growing more agitated the closer they got. Something felt *off* to her, and she was filled with a strange suspicion that something bad was going to happen once they reached Bragburg.

Fiddling with the hem of her skirt, Morgana waited for something to happen as she watched the river closely, and by the time she saw a distant bend in the river, the sun had already dipped behind the twisted, moss-covered trees. As she took in a deep breath, her nostrils suddenly filled with the putrid stench of raw sewage, making her choke on her spit. Knowing what was waiting for them by the shore, she jumped to her feet to warn her companions, but she was too late. A massive figure came into view in the fading twilight.

At first the twelve-foot-tall hairy creature paid no attention to their raft while it rummaged around in the water looking for food. But upon hearing the creaking of the logs, it lifted its head and turned its massive body of algae-covered brown fur to face them. Its singular molten eye squinted at them while its large bulbus nose sniffed the air, grumbling. Stomping closer to them, it opened its fang-filled mouth and let out an earth-shattering roar, filling the air with a caustic smell that assaulted the sinuses.

"What is that thing?" Leo yelled. "It stinks worse than the plague pits of Synia."

"River troll looking for dinner." Leighton dug his stick into the silt beneath, attempting to push them away. "We need to get out of here."

Digging his stick into the loose soil of the riverbed, Leo attempted to help push their raft back against the current, but it was of no use. The troll had already spotted them and was now reaching for a boulder that lay beside his feet. It raised the massive stone above its head and lobbed it in their direction. Morgana barely had time to summon an invisible shield before it hit and split their raft into shards, sending them flying in every direction. She hit the muddy water, and a shiver gripped her spine as the water's icy grip stung her skin. Pushing herself off the bottom, she burst through the surface and gasped for breath, trying to remove the tightness in her chest until she could wade out to where the water was only waist deep.

Her gaze swept across the river in search of her companions, and she spotted the frenzied horses stumbling their way to the bank. Fear gripped their eyes. The troll jerked its head toward the animals, probably wishing to make a meal of them, but the men splashing in the water drew its attention. At one end, Leighton swam closer to the swamp creature, and Leo stood in the shallow end, coughing as the frigid water continued to lap his chest. Morgana's last-minute shield spell kept everyone alive, at least for the time being. They still had the troll to deal with, and he didn't seem content to simply let them go.

"Leopold." Leighton stood behind the troll. "You flank his left while I get his right. Let's take down this nasty beast before it makes a meal out of us."

Nodding, Leo unsheathed the Heartseaker and aimed it at the troll, which responded with an ear-piercing roar. The beast swiped its talons at the knight, but he turned his body and deflected the blow with his blade, giving the duke a chance to slice at its legs. Letting out a shrill roar, the troll spun his massive frame around and struck the water with his enormous fists, sending Leighton toppling back into the mud. Taking the opportunity, Leopold drove his sword into the beast's side, piercing his flesh, and it arched its back, flailing around, trying to get the blade out.

Soaked to the bone, Morgana watched the fight until the troll broke free and spun around, striking Leo in the face with the back of its hand. Seeing him fall over bleeding from the nose, she grew hot, and her eyes flashed with a deadly fire. There was not much she could do. As she discovered when she was five, magic wasn't very effective against monsters. Still, there was a way she could use her powers to help. The monster picked up another boulder and aimed it at Leo, who was struggling to stand up in the deeper water. She grabbed a nearby pricker bush, jabbed a thorn in her finger, and waited for the bead of blood to form on her finger. Her lips curled, and she lifted her arm in the air, pointing her finger at the troll, holding the boulder over him.

Frozen in his spot, the monster turned his head and regarded her with its single eye. Its arms wobbled from the weight of the stone held above its head until its strength gave out, and the boulder came down, instantly killing it. Still gritting her teeth, Morgana panted and looked over at Leo, who was staggering to his feet. Knowing he was relatively unharmed, she allowed herself to relax, and her arm dropped to her side, her blood melting with the murky water. Both men frowned at her, and she simply shrugged in response.

"Morgana." Leopold finally sheathed his sword and ran over to her. "Are you all right? Did you get hurt?"

Seeing Leo bleeding from the nose, she rolled her eyes; it was typical of him to worry more about her than about himself. She reached out a finger, wiped off the blood, and smeared it between her fingers before regarding him with a hard stare.

"I'm fine. He didn't even get close to me. It's you I'm worried about. He hit you pretty hard."

"What, this?" He wiped away a fresh stream of blood and laughed. "It's nothing. I've been wailed on harder before. I'll get this taken care of as soon as we settle down."

"Promise?"

"I give you my word," he said, winking. "Let's get out of this frigid water first and find our horses, then I'll get the fire going." Leo looked over his shoulder at the black-clad duke grabbing a pack out of the river. "You coming, Your Grace?"

"I'll join you in a minute, Captain," Leighton called back. "Allow me to finish fishing our stuff out first."

Morgana hobbled out of the river and searched the area for the horses while Leo gathered the timbers and Leighton fished the rest of their belongings out of the water. It didn't take long to find the beasts; they were huddled together in the forest a short distance away from the bank. Upon seeing her approach, Leo's horse neighed and trotted over to nuzzle her hair. She stroked his face, took hold of his reins, and led him out, with the mare following behind them. After securing the animals to a nearby tree, she rummaged around in one of the saddle bags and pulled out a small med kit, tossing it to Leo.

She flicked her wrist, and her magic roared the timbers to life, engulfing the area in warmth. Sitting near the flames, she stretched out her arms and allowed the heat to thaw out her goose-fleshed skin. The moist dress clinging to her skin began to dry, and she relaxed once the shivering stopped. Sitting by the fire in silence, she watched the men dry their clothes and warm up until Leo got up and headed for the woods.

"Where are you going?" she asked.

He turned to smile at her. "I just want some time alone to think. Don't you worry about me. I'll be back soon."

He walked through the part in the trees and vanished out of sight. She became filled with deep longing to run after him, but she resisted the urge and warmed her hands by the flames. She wished to know what he wanted to think about, but then again, she had a lot of things on her mind as well. The conversation at Baba Yaga's cabin left her shaken, and she couldn't help but think about the choice she'd have to make and what it might be—or which of her friends it had to do with.

CHAPTER 15

# The Five of Chalices

The night's silence was broken up only by the crackling of the amber flames, and Morgana's mind drifted to Lafreya. Somewhere, her friend was dealing with the demon king, and there was no way of knowing what he was doing to her. Her heart raced at the thought of the choices she needed to make, and her body shuddered with fear. Her shoulders trembled uncontrollably, and tears welled up in her eyes. There was too much death and pain around her as it was, and she was not sure she'd be able to handle more of it. Just as she thought she was about to break down and cry, a stony hand wrapped around her. Pulling her close, Leighton laid her head on his shoulder and rubbed her arm.

"What's wrong, Morgana? What's on your mind?"

"I was just thinking of Lafreya." Her voice cracked. "I was thinking of what she was going through and how I wish I was with her—or better yet, how I could take her place."

"Morgana." Leighton held her tighter. "Don't say that. We'll get her back. You know we will. I won't allow her to slip away from me. She's the only thing that matters to me, and I won't rest until she's back where she belongs. Stop blaming yourself and stop convincing yourself you're cursed. This is the demon king's doing, not yours. There was nothing you could have done."

She pulled away and looked up at him. "Not true. I could have insisted that we stay in Perdetia. I *knew* something was wrong. I felt it in my bones. If we never made the trip, he would have never got his hands on her."

"Even if you chained yourself to the door, do you think Lafreya would have listened?"

"No. She was too eager to see you and get the wedding plans underway."

"See? No need to blame yourself. If anything, I am as much at fault for this as you are. Let's just focus on what we can do now, which is finding her and bringing her back."

"All right, let's do that. I just hope we can find her before he does something horrible to her. That monster took enough from me already, and I can't let him have my best friend."

Sniffling, Morgana pressed her knees to her chest and continued to stare at the flickering flames, pondering her friend's fate. The demon king already took her parents from her, haunted her dreams, and left her with a shadow that followed her around, and she didn't want to think about what he still had left to take from her. The evening hours slipped away, and as the shadows set around them, she looked up and furrowed her brow. Suddenly, she remembered Leo had retreated into the woods and promised to return, but it had been several hours without him. A fresh fear crept along her spine. She recalled the demon king's warning from her dream and shuddered, thinking that perhaps the Devoth had gotten him too.

"Say, Leighton, where do you think Leo wandered off to?"

"I don't know." The duke furrowed his brow. "I figured he went to think about you, but it has been a while, hasn't it?"

"It has been hours, and he said he wouldn't take long. Do you think he got lost?"

"It's either that or he got eaten by another river troll." Leighton stood up. "I should go check and see if I can find him."

"No"—Morgana grabbed hold of his wrist and stood to join him—"I'll go look for him. You should stay here in case he returns."

"Are you sure? What if you get lost?"

"I won't, and even if I do, I'll use my magic to find my way back."

Leighton nodded. "All right. But don't take too long or I will go looking for you. I can't lose you and the captain too."

"I won't, I promise. But you yell if he comes back without me, okay?"

"Will do."

Leighton waved her off, and with a tight knot in her stomach, Morgana turned in the direction Leo went. Walking through the rags of mist gathered at the twisted roots of the cypress trees, she had no clue which direction he went in. Guided by pure instinct, she knew that if she continued to walk, she'd go right to him. Her patience paid off when she spotted a break in the trees, then tiptoed to the nearest trunk and peeked out from behind it at the clearing beyond. There on the opposite end stood Leo, arms crossed, leaning against a large tree, lost in thought. Her heart fluttered at the sight of his drawn face, glancing up at the stars, seemingly oblivious to her presence. She wanted to run to him, but her legs turned to rubber, making it impossible to move, and she stood in her hiding spot, watching him, as pools of moonlight hung in the mist.

CHAPTER 16

# The Ace of Staves

Remaining in her hiding spot, Morgana watched Leo staring up at the star-speckled sky while the slice of silver moonlight illuminated his features. His stony face appeared deep in thought, and her breath slowed as she observed him in the weighty silence that fell around them like a thick blanket. Wrapped in shadows, she thought of turning back, but he turned around toward her with a frown, his arms still folded over his chest, and he peeled himself back from his tree to look at the spot concealing her presence as if he sensed her eyes upon him.

"You can show yourself. I know you're there." He relaxed, and she slinked out of the gloom, keeping her head down, walking to stand before him. "What's wrong, Morgie? What are you doing wandering the woods after the sun went down?"

"I . . ." her vocal cords gnarled. "I came looking for you because you've been gone a while. I thought he got you too like he got Lafreya, and I—" She choked on her sob, no longer able to contain her emotions. "I—"

"Whoa, hey." Leo wrapped his arms around her, pulling her in as her body shuddered with her tears. "It's all right," he said, holding her tighter, rubbing her back. "Let it all out. There is no need to be strong around me."

"Oh, Leo." Morgana pulled away and peered at his face. "I thought I lost you too. I thought he robbed me of you as well."

"You won't ever lose me, Morgie. I promise you that much. I'm a stubborn fool, and I'm not one to give up so easily—at least, not when it comes to you. I'll fight death itself if it means being with you."

"You know I'm bound to end up in hell, right?" She turned her head away from him. "I just don't want you to end up there with me."

"Are you saying that because you are a witch?"

"No. I'm saying that because the demon king has this strange hold on me, and I don't think he is going to let me go without a fight."

Looking at her tear-streaked face, he shook his head. She had always believed she was bound to the Devoth prince—ever since she was young. He recalled when she was eight and they were in her mother's greenhouse talking, and she first told him she felt connected to the demon king. He had asked her why she felt that way, and she said she thought that her fate card almost assured it and that she dreamed of him most nights. He didn't believe in fate cards then, and while his opinion of them had changed over the years, he still didn't think their predictions were set in stone. He also knew she wasn't destined to end up with the demon king, and he knew he held her soul card—the one destined to be with her. But it was pointless to tell her that. Morgana never listened to reason—not until she came to the same conclusion herself. Instead of arguing with her, he smiled warmly at her, leaned in closer, and wiped her tear away with his thumb.

"What if I don't care? What if I want to walk into hell with you and bathe in the flames at your side? What if I'm willing to fight the demon king if he stands in the way of us being together?"

"Then will you tell me what we do if we can't save Lafreya? Tell me what you plan to do if the world around us falls? What will the captain of the royal guard do with a witch when there is no longer a princess protecting her?"

"He will leave the guard and protect the witch himself. He will run with her to the furthest reaches of the earth where the demon king won't find them. That captain would do everything in his powers to protect her, even take on all the Devoth and monsters of the Otherworld if it meant keeping her safe. But you know what, Morgie?" He gently took hold of her chin and tilted her head up to look at him. "It would never come to that—because that very captain will put the princess back on the throne so the woman he loves can live in Perdetia without fear."

*Empty promises. Run away from him while you still have the chance. The demon king warned you. You should listen before you end up hurt.*

Ignoring the demon, Morgana wrapped her arms around his waist and placed her head on his chest, pulling their bodies together. Putting his arms around her, Leo pressed her closer and leaned his face on her head, inhaling her sweetness. The shadow in the woods vanished, growling, leaving them to stand alone in their silent embrace as the night fell around them like a wool cover. Lost in their private space with only the chirruping of crickets for company, Morgana felt her skin tingle with his touch, and she grew warm to the core with desire for him.

She wished the moment would last forever, then a snapping of a branch behind them split the night's calm. Leo's body stiffened and his head perked up at the faint footsteps blooming in the woods. He pulled Morgana away, pushing her behind his body. Drawing his sword, he pointed it at the woods and waited for an attack. But the attack never came; it was only the black-clad duke who emerged from the tree line. Grumbling under his breath, Leopold sheathed his blade and stood glaring at the man who interrupted them.

"I'm sorry." Leighton smirked as he studied the pair. "I didn't mean to interrupt you, but it was getting late, and I worried about you. I thought another troll ate you, so I decided to look for you." Leaning against a tree, he crossed his arms with a teasing grin. "I know you probably wish to remain here alone, but the woods are not safe at night. How about we go back to the campfire and rest instead? This way we can make it to Bragburg first thing in the morning and formulate a plan to get Lafreya back."

"Fair enough," Leo said. "I guess the sooner we find Princess Lafreya, the sooner we can all get on with our lives." Turning to look behind him, he took hold of Morgana's hand. "Sleep close to me tonight, please. I'll feel better if I know you are safely within my reach."

"All right. I'll stay as close as you'd like."

"Good. And one more thing, Morgie." He smiled at her. "When we get to the gates of hell, be sure not to stand me up."

"I wouldn't dream of it, Captain."

Squeezing his hand, she allowed him to lead her through the woods, back to the welcoming fire. Settling down by the crackling flames, she laid Leo's head on her lap and watched him fall asleep smiling. But sleep refused to claim her. Staring at the luminescent moon, she combed her fingers through his hair and breathed in the sodden air as the pressure in her chest mounted. Her fate card still lingered at the back of her mind, filling her to the core with a deathly chill. Thoughts of the choice loomed over her, and dark visions of death flickered behind her eyes.

As she watched the man sleeping soundly in her lap, her heart tightened, and she found it difficult to breathe. She wished to be with him, but as desperately as she pined for him, she feared the unknown, which lingered at the back of her thoughts, threatening her. Occasionally she would have visions of him, covered in blood and with a look of horror on his face, and that was enough to scare her halfway to death. Plagued by her unrelenting thoughts, she continued to sit and think until the faded light of dawn broke up the darkness and bathed the clearing in a deep bronze haze. Heaving in frustration, she sat and waited for the men to awake.

CHAPTER 17

# The Ten of Swords

Once the men awoke, the three of them began preparing for the quick trip to the Bragburg duchy. Leopold had asked her if she had slept well. She didn't want him to worry over her, so she lied, saying she slept great, despite the gray moons beneath her eyes showing otherwise. He frowned, clearly not believing her but knowing better than to argue with her, then placed her on his horse before getting in the saddle to sit behind her. Putting his hands around her, he tightened his grip on his reins and spurred his horse to follow Leighton through the sparse forest.

Sycamore trees were scattered about the gravel path, and light easily filtered through the gaps in the canopy, making the twisted road easy to see. Morgana listened to the hooves of the horses rapping on the ground until the air grew stagnant and she couldn't get enough air in her lungs to breathe. Her stomach cramped with fear at an unseen danger, and even the animals protested, choosing instead to rear and remain in their spots. Even as the men regained control and the horses trotted forward reluctantly, something didn't sit right with Morgana. Fear saturated every fiber of her body, poisoning her to the marrow. Flesh pricked at her nape, and disaster visited her in a blurry vision of fire and blood.

Not even the black spires of Bragburg alleviated her worry. Her gut told her the place was no longer safe. She wished to tell Leo to turn back, but he spurred his horse to a gallop as soon as the sprawling white estate appeared through the oak trees. Racing for the safety of the border, they left a trail of dust in their wake, and Morgana looked up toward the gray clouds melting across the city, holding out hope that they would make it there unharmed. All hope, however fleeting, was dashed the moment she spotted the sea of white horses on the horizon. Riders draped in blue-and-gold cloth were waiting for them before the gates of the duchy.

It appeared the entire army of Perdetia had come to greet them, and leading the charge was a regal white Clydesdale on which perched a redheaded woman in a blue riding gown. Her icy green eyes glinted, and her lips curled into a sneer at the sight of them. One look at her, and Morgana's heart sank into her stomach. Fear rippled up her spine one vertebra at a time, until it hit her like a ton of bricks: no matter what anyone else saw, the woman glaring at them vacantly was not her longtime friend. She was an impostor.

"Lafreya"—Leighton beamed and jumped off his horse to greet her—"you're safe!"

"No thanks to you, Grand Duke Charmant," the woman snarled. Her arctic voice boomed through the valley as she peeled back her lips. "After all, you conspired with that witch"—she pointed at Morgana—"to overthrow Perdetia and plunge us into chaos. Did you think I wouldn't catch on to your plan? Did you two believe I would allow you to threaten our way of life?"

"I . . ." The duke fell back. His face was filled with confusion and betrayal. "I beg your pardon?"

"Save your act for someone who cares, Your Grace. I know you knew Morgana was a witch. She told you that much when you met because she knew of your family's stance on Perdetia's policy. That is why you spent so much time with her, going so far as staying at her estate, perhaps even in her bed. That's how you two conspired to kidnap me, kill me, and bring down my kingdom when it was at its weakest. You were planning on lifting our ban on witchcraft, putting the lives of my people at risk." She spit her words out like venom, and Leighton looked at her glass-eyed. "Now, I should kill you right here for your evil plot, but unfortunately we are in your dukedom, where our laws don't apply. Not to mention, killing you would cause a war, which I have no energy to fight, so I shall let you go so long as you stay away from me and my kingdom—and our engagement is off. As for you, Morgana"—she turned to the couple—"it's the pyre for you. Captain Ellingham, arrest that witch, and bring her to me. I shall forgive you for falling under her spell. I know you didn't know what she was, or how she bewitched you. Therefore I'm giving you this chance to redeem yourself by helping me get rid of her for good."

"Your Highness?"

Morgana placed a hand on his shoulder, leaning to whisper in his ear. "Do it, Leo. Please, just do as you're told." Then she turned to the princess. "I won't fight you. I'll come willingly."

"But, Morgana," he protested through clenched teeth, "you

can't expect me to let them take you. You heard what she said. They'll kill you like they did the druid. We both know that."

*Listen to him and run. Save yourself. You are no good dead. Sacrifice these men and save your hide.*

"Stop being stupid and do it," Morgana said flatly. "She has the entire army of Perdetia with her, and there are only three of us. Even with my magic, we can't take them all, and she'll just kill you too for resisting. Spare yourself and arrest me now. You figure out how to save me later if that is what you wish. But for now just obey your orders. I beg you."

"No!" Leighton shouted, drawing his sword and stepping between them and Lafreya. "Lady Morgana, I won't allow this. They can't take you. Not while you are on my soil. I can have my men out here in a few minutes to remove these trespassers. Please, allow me to call them, and you can seek asylum with me."

"Stop it, Leighton." Morgana pressed herself to his ear. "This is not a battle you want to fight. That's not the real Lafreya, she's a body double created by the demon king. That is him speaking to us, not her. We don't stand a chance against this version. So go, retreat to your estate, and let them take me. Save the real Lafreya, no matter what. Don't worry about me. They won't kill me until morning. And a lot can happen in that time."

"How do you know that's not really her and that she hasn't been playing you this whole time? Playing all of us?"

"Because the real Lafreya would never betray you. She loves you. And I can prove it." Morgana shot a glance at the princess. "Do you see that stone around her neck?"

"Yes." Leighton assessed the tear-dropped cobalt jewel dangling off a black velvet ribbon. "She has never taken it off—at least, not since I have known her."

"That's because I gave her that necklace as a gift when we went off to the academy. It's supposed to be an Arial's tear. A magical gem that appears blue to you normal folks, but to those of us who use magic, it glows an iridescent green. But this one . . . this one is just a plain sapphire. It's a copy, just like the woman wearing it."

"Damn it." The duke sheathed his sword and stepped aside, gritting his teeth. "Fine, but I sure hope you know what you're doing."

"Yeah. Me too." Swallowing hard, Morgana stretched out her arms and turned to Leo. "Go ahead, Captain, take me in. I won't resist. The charges she accuses me of are true. I bewitched you and made you follow me. I also conspired to overthrow Perdetia. I am lifting the spell now. You are free of me."

Grinding his teeth, Leo clenched his fists until the knuckles beneath his gauntlets turned white and walked over to the pale Clydesdale. Smirking from atop her horse, the fake Lafreya handed him the magic-dampening thalanium handcuffs, which were tarnished by years of rust. It took all the willpower Leo had to not cut her down, and he swallowed his hatred as he walked over to Morgana, eyeing her with a puckered brow. She didn't flinch—she simply nodded once and stretched out her hands, allowing him to cuff her while he mouthed a silent apology. Beside them, Leighton looked on with a grimace, unable to help them.

"Good job, Captain." Lafreya let out a melodic laugh. "Now, bring the traitor to me, and let us ride back to Perdetia. Tomorrow morning, we shall have us a witch-burning."

Leopold faltered, and Morgana urged him with her eyes to comply. He pursed his lips, took in a deep breath, and walked over to Lafreya with his head hung low. His shaking hand raised the chains of the cuffs, offering them to the woman, who yanked on them to bring the witch closer. Leering down at her prisoner, the princess secured her to her horse, then leaned in.

"You know, I didn't take you for the self-sacrificing type. But I guess"—Lafreya shot a glance at Leo—"for him, you are willing to do just about anything. Too bad."

Sneering, Morgana tilted her head up and spit in Lafreya's face, hitting her between the eyes. The princess wiped her forehead, then cracked the witch across the face with the back of her hand. Beside them, Leopold lunged from his spot, hand on the hilt of his sword, ready to spring into action, but Morgana shot him a glance telling him to stand back, wiping the metallic blood from her split lip. His face turned an unflattering shade of red. She knew his sense of justice would cause him problems, and she refused to let him cause a scene when she was unable to help him, powerless as she was in the thalanium cuffs. Lafreya straightened on her horse and glared at him standing there with his fists clenched, and his jaw bulging.

"Careful, Captain. I'd resist her charms if I were you and get on that horse—unless, of course, you wish me to kill her on the spot."

Flaring his nostrils, Leopold took one look at Morgana and swallowed his ire before getting up on his horse. Lafreya observed the exchange with a grin. Satisfied that she had them under her control, she grabbed hold of Morgana's chin and looked her in the eyes.

"Aren't you a good little witch?" She leaned to whisper in her ear. "You should have listened to me and stayed put. Now you've forced my hand, and we need to put on a good show for these pitiful mortals."

With a smirk, the princess nudged her horse's side and rode forward, dragging her prisoner behind her. Perdetia was not a long way away, but the road was rough and uneven, making it difficult to walk, especially with Lafreya yanking on her chains. More than once, Morgana stumbled and fell, dragged behind the horse, and she fumbled to get back up as the soldiers roared in laughter. Her knees were skinned raw by the gravel, and her legs ached from the walk, but she pushed on, unwilling to give the impostor the satisfaction of watching her flounder.

Riding his horse beside her, all Leopold could do was look on and watch, helpless to save her from the torture. His stomach churned, and he kept his gaze down, gripping his reins until his fingers throbbed in protest. His head swam with everything he could have said or done to prevent this, and even the familiar stone towers of Perdetia and mottled red roofs coming through the slowly congealing mist did little to soothe the aching in his soul.

Feeling the chains tighten once more, Morgana watched the city she had called home for the past seventeen years draw closer, its iron gates raised to welcome its prisoner. As they crossed the sturdy wood bridge spanning the weed-choked mote, Morgana's eyes met those of the spectators. Townspeople gathered to look at her with unquenchable curiosity. Their transparent smiles did little to hide their contempt, and occasionally a small stone would fly from the crowd to sting her skin, but she did not flinch. She wouldn't let them see her break.

Stopping in the town square, Lafreya dispersed the mob and

summoned a soldier to her side. The man complied, and she handed him the chains, instructing him to put Morgana into the dungeon until the morning light. Grabbing hold of her arm, the soldier, whom Morgana knew well, yanked her forward and pushed her toward the prison as if their acquaintance meant nothing to him. Morgana didn't take it personally. She knew these men were trained to obey orders, and she complied with his demands by walking forward in silence. From her horse, Lafreya watched the witch disappear into a stone building, then turned to regard Leopold—who was shooting her a sharp stare—with a smirk.

"You did good today, Captain. I'm proud of you for being able to resist a witch's spell. It's not something many men can do." She licked her lips, and a chill ran down his spine. "Don't worry, I shall be sure to reward your loyalty to us. Perhaps another promotion is in order. For now, though, go get cleaned up. You reek of sewage. After that, go inform Baroness de Laurent of her daughter's impending execution."

Without replying, Leo jumped off his horse, grabbed hold of the reins, and rode to the stables, where his squire greeted him. The lad had a string of questions for him, but Leopold wasn't in the mood to answer any of them. The words seemed jumbled in his head. Waving his hand to silence the boy, he handed off his horse and then stumbled up the barracks stairs to his room, where he could be alone with his thoughts and away from prying eyes. He staggered down the narrow, torch-lit hallway, stepped into his chamber, and slammed the door shut, pressing his back to the cold, metal-studded wood.

Away from any witnesses, Leo felt the pain in his stomach

taking over him, and he collapsed on his knees with a guttural roar, which reverberated off the stone and rang in his ears. His heart hammered in his chest, and he fell on all fours, buried his face in his arms, and sobbed as his world collapsed around him. Morgana's name rose to his lips, and he wailed at what was going to happen to her and at his failure to protect her. He told—no, swore to her—that he would not allow anything to happen to her, and now she was going to burn because of him. He was helpless to save the woman he loved.

Crushed under the weight of his grief, he forced himself up to his feet. His stomach continued to slosh with fear. Lost in a stupor of melancholy, he walked over to the window, tears still shimmering in his eyes, and he looked out through the deep purple haze in the direction of Bragburg. He knew what he had to do, and he would need Leighton's help to make it happen. Fortunately for him, the demon king made the mistake of trusting him to deliver the news to the de Laurent estate. The baroness and Stephan would assist him in getting the word out to the duke, and he formulated a plan of how he would save her, until it was time to leave and put it into action.

CHAPTER 18

# The Wheel of Life

Sitting on the cool floor with her back pressed against the wall of damp stone, Morgana, dressed in a white execution gown, watched through the bars of her window as night took possession of the town beyond her prison cell. The hushed streets provided her with little comfort as she could see her execution site. The milky luminance of the moon vaguely illuminated her funeral pyre, which waited to claim her in a few scant hours. Staring at the veil of moonlight through the slats, she felt the cold arms of death around her, stealing away her hope. Reclining, she fought the tears threatening to come out, and her sinuses continued to sting.

Listening to her heart drumming in the hollow space of the dungeon, her ears perked at hearing deadened footsteps coming down the stone steps toward her cell. She listened closer, and her eyes stung to see through the deepening darkness. Soon the footsteps grew louder, and a familiar form eased from the shadows. His blond hair was a mess, and he wore no armor, but there was a strange glint in his eyes that made her heart jump into her throat, and she got up to greet him.

"What are you doing here, Leo?" She held on to the bars and frowned as she studied his face.

"I've come to break you out." He held up a brass skeleton key with a plain bow. "What does it look like?"

"What? Are you insane?" She stepped back and watched him open the cell door. "If they catch you, you will lose your position and your life."

"To hell with this position. And my life—well, it's not worth living without you."

Reaching into the cell, he grabbed hold of her hand, pulling her in until she was pressed up against him. Dense shadows of the dungeon embraced them, and nothing moved but time as her heart pounded in her ears. Her hands were still bound by the thalanium cuffs, but she pressed her palms on his chest and looked up as he continued to hold the small of her back, causing her gown to rustle in the stillness. The hand holding the key reached slowly for her cuffs when a clatter from the top of the stairs drew their attention.

A stern voice bounced off the stone walls. "The captain is breaking the witch out. Stop him!"

Darting her head up, Morgana saw a soldier charging straight at them, his blade raised over his head. Reeling around, Leopold grabbed hold of her arm, whirling her to safety before dropping the key and ripping the Heartseaker from his hilt to block the descending blade. The sharp steel slipped down the edge of the Heartseaker and grazed across Leo's bicep. A spurt of blood flew at the stone wall, and searing hot pain spread through his arm. Spinning around, he hit the soldier in the temple with the hilt of his sword and watched the lights go out in the man's eyes before more voices made him lift his head. Four more soldiers descended the stone steps, their sword drawn and ready to cut them down. They pointed their blades of burnished steel at his face, and he gripped the Heartseaker, coming back hard to meet their blades with a clang.

Standing back, Morgana watched with mounting frustration while Leo parried the strikes and twisted away from the blades. If only she had her magic, she could easily help him, but her hands were still bound with magic-restraining cuffs. She continued to survey the area when she spotted a mace hanging on a wall a short distance away, so she dashed and grabbed it by the wood handle, then carried it over to the battle. Seeing a soldier about to strike Leo, she strained her muscles to raise the weapon above her head and brought it down on his back. Spinning around in his spot, the soldier gave her a cross-eyed look before crumpling to the ground in a twisted heap.

Hearing the metal clang on the stone, Leopold looked behind him at the man sprawled out by his feet and Morgana holding the mace between her legs, shrugging. He shook his head and smirked, then kicked away another advancing soldier, who stumbled back and fell over a barrel. Pulling Morgana closer to him, he faced the last two men when a thunderous explosion shook the dungeon. Exchanging glances, the soldiers forgot about the prisoner and their captain and ran in the direction of the sound. Morgana looked suspiciously at Leo, who sheathed his sword and bent down to pick up the key.

"What was that, Leo?"

He shrugged. "A diversion, now give me your arms so I can remove the cuffs. Leighton is waiting for us at the gate used to cart out bodies."

"You got Leighton to help you?" She lifted her arms, allowing him to slip the cuffs off, letting them clatter to the ground, then rubbed the red marks on her wrists.

"You didn't expect me to save you alone, did you?" He laced his fingers through hers and began ascending the steps. "Not to mention, we have to get the real Lafreya back, and we want him for that as well."

After sneaking out through the dungeon doors, they stood in the town square and surveyed the chaotic scene unfolding before them. Townspeople and soldiers ran around with buckets of water as caustic smoke poured from the direction of the castle. In the distance, a small amber glow of a fire could be seen through the deepening gloom, and the gate they needed to use was only a short distance away. Leo tightened his grip on Morgana, then pulled her down the narrow alley lined with sleeping storefronts, away from the town center and closer to the freedom beyond the stone walls.

A cold voice stopped them in their tracks. "Traitor. How could you choose *her* over your own men? I'll kill you for this."

Morgana turned around and narrowed her eyes down the pitch-black alley and could barely make out the shadow of one of Leopold's lieutenants rushing toward them. He was the son of one of the minor noble houses, and she never liked him much, given the way he talked about Leo behind his back, but she hated him even more now that he threatened to kill him. Before Leopold grabbed the hilt of his sword, Morgana was already holding the guard up in the air with an invisible grip. The soldier thrashed and kicked around, even as she hung him up by his surcoat on the signpost above their heads.

"Let me down, you witch," he screamed, squirming. "Let me down, and I'll make your death swift."

Morgana shook her head. "Nah. I think you need some time to cool off and rethink your life choices. Especially the way you treat your captain."

The man continued to protest from the signpost, causing a loud commotion, which drew the attention of every soldier close by. Morgana could see them turning and running in their direction, and she turned to look at the half-open iron gate behind them. They did not have far to go, but they would never make it in time without a distraction to help them.

"Your dagger,"—she turned to Leo—"give it to me."

Leo pulled the knife out from his waistline and handed it to her. As she grabbed the silver blade, a vague smile formed on her lips, and she pressed the sharpened edge to her palm. Leo gasped, watching her dig the knife into her skin. Slowly, she moved her hand down and allowed the blood to pool to the surface. Handing the weapon back over to him, she turned to the pile of old rain-polished stone and flung the beads of crimson on their smooth surface. No sooner had the blood contacted the boulders did they move, one by one, rising and regrouping, forming some semblance of a body until two enormous creatures stood before them and stared out at the square. Stomping their feet, the bodies of stone made their way for the men, who were almost upon them.

"Rock golems." Leo smiled. "I knew there was a reason I love you."

Taking hold of her hand, he turned and ran for the closing gate. The golems were doing a decent job of distracting the royal guard, who were only dulling their blades against the stone. The diversion gave the two of them plenty of time to escape through the gate, which was left open enough for them to run through by ducking their heads. Beyond the castle wall, Leighton sat atop his black horse, holding on to the reigns of Leo's stallion.

"Finally." The duke heaved out a sigh. "I thought our plan failed and you two were dead."

"Not a chance." Leo jumped into his saddle and hauled Morgana up to sit before him. "Where to from here?"

"Quickest way to Mireworth is straight through Devilwood Forest."

"You're joking, right? Those woods are said to be haunted by blood-thirsty creatures from the Otherworld. No one who goes into the forest ever comes out alive."

"True, but my great-grandfather made it through there alive, and I bet we can too. What do you say, Captain, do you trust me?"

"All right." Leo drew in a sharp breath. "I trust you. Let's go. We'll take our chances in Devilwood."

Turning his horse around, Leo urged it to gallop toward the mysterious and obscure forest where wind often forgot to go. As they headed for the wind-stripped black trees, they could hear the guards regrouping somewhere in the distance, but it was still too dark for anyone to see them. The closer they got to the mist-wrapped trunks, the more the horses protested, but the men held tight to their reins, guiding them into the slit of the trees. The entire forest seemed to be shrouded in darkness blacker than night, and as they penetrated the shadows, they heard all sound from beyond the woods stop as if it were being swallowed by the pitch that surrounded and threatened to consume them.

CHAPTER 19

# The Nine of Staves

**B**reaching the deep purple haze of the foreboding tree line, Leo slowed his horse to a trot. After gingerly lowering Morgana to the soggy ground, he jumped from his saddle and glanced around at the fog clotting around them like mud. Morning was still an hour away. Above them, in the interlacing branches of charred trees sat a murder of crows, their purple and black feathers melting into the gloom. Occasionally they'd cackle and crow into the forest, but the darkness made no reply. Thinking how it's been a good hundred years since anyone dared to enter these woods, Leo glanced around at the deepening darkness, waiting for something to jump out at them. Shaking off the dread creeping up his spine, he glanced up at Leighton, who rode up beside him and was now also surveying the trail, which led deeper into the blackness.

Leighton's great-grandfather was the last person to make it through Devilwood and live to talk about it. Before that, only a handful of travelers had survived to spread the tales of creatures who lurked in the trees, waiting for unsuspecting victims—creatures unlike any found anywhere else in Dresbourn. Unlike Leo, Leighton knew the firsthand accounts of what lurked in the woods, not just the rumors. His great-grandfather escorted druids and witches through this forest to neutral territory beyond, and his journal from that period had some details of the things he encountered.

In one entry, he described a headless knight riding after them with a sword crafted from human bone. The knight rode on a pale horse, carrying his severed head on his side. The head grinned at the travelers as he chased them, and the horse dragged a cart of human bones. With his sword, the knight would behead human riders and toss their bodies into the cart. In another account, he wrote of a ten-foot-tall woman who lived in the trees, stalking anyone who stopped beneath her tree. If she got close enough to touch you, she'd infect you with the plague, and you would die in a few days' time. The verbal accounts of others were no less horrifying. The only reason the Bragburg party survived was that they were saved by the magic folk they were escorting. Staring at the undulating darkness in the path beyond, Leighton shook his head and looked down at Leo and Morgana.

"Why did we stop? We best get going if we wish to make it through here alive."

"I need to bandage up Morgana's hand." He reached into the

bag hanging off his horse, pulling out the dressing. "Just give me a moment, and we will get going again."

"Fair enough." Leighton glanced down at Leo, cleaning out the deep gouge in Morgana's hand. "Did you get hurt in the fighting?"

"No. I cut myself to create a diversion." She shot him a weary glance. "Why did you help us anyway? Why did you risk starting a war with Perdetia?"

"Aside from the captain here, you're one of my only friends. I couldn't allow them to kill you, and it's what Lafreya would have expected me to do. As for starting a war, I wouldn't worry too much about it. Bragburg has better weapons and several sorcerers. The demon king won't take the risk of attacking my province just yet, not until he can show my people my severed head. And now that he knows I'm coming for him, he will focus all his efforts on killing me."

"Does this mean you know where Lafreya is?"

"I have an idea, but we need to make it to Iatan to learn more. I already sent word to a friend of mine in Tel Hillar. He will be expecting us. He knows his country better than anyone, and he will be able to tell us where the demon king hides."

"In that case, we best get going. I don't wish to be in these woods longer than need be. As is, the energy they are putting out is making my skin crawl."

"I concur." Leo finished tightening her dressing. "I don't know what lives here, but I sure as hell don't want to find out."

As he turned to walk back to the horse, a dark crimson stain on his white sleeve caught Morgana's attention, causing her to let out a soft gasp. Beneath the faint light cracking through the trees, she could see a clean slash through the starchy fibers and blood seeping slowly from the wound.

"Leo"—she grabbed hold of his blood-sleeked arm, causing him to wince—"are you hurt?"

He gave her a short-lived glance. "It's nothing. I'll be fine."

"Shouldn't we get it cleaned and wrapped before we continue?"

"What's wrong?" He turned to look at her pouting face. "Are you worried about me?"

"Of course I am. I always worry about you."

"No need to worry, Morgie. I promise you." He gave her a boyish grin and cradled her cheek with his hand. "I'll be fine until we get to Mireworth. I've had worse during my campaigns, so this minor cut will not kill me. However, if we stay here longer than need be, the creatures rumored to live here might destroy us all. So let us just get out of here, and I promise to get treated as soon as we are safely in the village. All right?"

"All right." She bit her bottom lip. "But promise me it will be as soon as we get there. Not a minute longer."

"I give you my word as a knight." Leo mounted his horse and stretched his hand out to her. "Now come on, let us ride deeper into the forest. This place is already making me feel uneasy, and I don't wish to linger here."

Taking hold of his hand, she allowed him to pull her into the saddle, then wrapped her arms around his waist. Glancing into the undulating darkness ahead of them, Morgana felt the flesh chill on the back of her neck. She only heard stories from passing merchants of the creatures that were said to inhabit the forest. There was a black dog that would appear in your path, and if you saw it, you would drop dead on the spot. There was a winged monster who was part man, part horse, and the size of a bear, who lurked in the trees and swooped down to snatch unsuspecting travelers before ripping them apart. Few who faced the creatures in the forest survived. Wondering what horrors they would encounter deeper in the gloom, Morgana felt her spine go cold, and she tightened her grip around Leo, who guided his horse slowly down the trackless terrain.

As they rode deeper into the smothering silence, the overgrown passage narrowed, crowding them, forcing them to ride in a single file. Layered in shadows, they pressed on. Their breath sounded like a roar the further they rode into the trees, and the hooves on the ground resonated through the bleak space like thunder. The deeper they rode, the more the atmosphere changed, causing the hairs on the back of Morgana's neck to stand up. Even the horses seemed to sense the change. They froze, whined, reared, and refused to move forward. Still numb with cold fear, Morgana dismounted the stallion, and the men joined her, surveying the deep forest for hidden dangers.

The surrounding blackness was darker than night, and neither of them could see or hear a thing until a soft, distorted sound broke the silence. At first all they could hear was the sound of echoes overlaying echoes, but the closer the sound got, the more it sounded like the flapping of wings, and soon enough a large black mass flew over their heads, landing in the tree to their left. The creature made no other noise, but Morgana could feel its eyes upon them. The group huddled together, gripped by fear, and they inched for their horses. Suddenly a whooping howl came from their left side, cementing the three of them in their spots.

One howl was met with another, and the woods rang with

the cries of beasts talking to each other. The horses snorted and stomped their hooves, their eyes bulging in their heads. Branches creaked and snapped all around them. With this eerie forest song crept a low-lying fog, congealing by their feet as if summoned by a supernatural force. The air turned soapy, making them gasp for breath. Around them, the howls continued, drawing closer until a shrill, haunting cry shred the air, silencing everything around them. Their pulses throbbed painfully in their veins as they looked for what could have made the sound.

"What's going on here?" Leo's voice was sharp with panic. "Where is this coming from suddenly? And where did all the other sounds go?"

"I think . . ." Morgana shivered. "I think we're being hunted."

"By whom? Or should I say, *what*?"

"I don't know . . ."

Chilled to the bone, Morgana strained her ears to listen. Nothing came. Silence once again fell around them like a shadow, and the air went still. Sensing something move in the distance, she turned to where the road turned sharply and watched a crouching dark figure rise to all fours, distorted by the eddying fog. With no breath left to scream, she backed up and grabbed hold of Leo's shoulder. Growling, the creature leaped from the shadows, landing on the road a few feet before them.

A mélange of odors ranging from sweet to putrid filled the space, and Leopold spun on his heels to come face to face with a horrifying monster. Standing sixteen feet above them was a hodgepodge of parts—limbs made of bones and talons that pierced the earth. Melted flesh covered the emaciated torso, the twisted pieces of skin hanging off the blood-coated meat beneath. It was the color of clay, and it peered at them with its eyes like molten quicksilver, which bulged out from the flesh shriveled to its skull. As it peeled back its lips, saliva strung like taffy from its sharp fangs, and it let out an ear-piercing yell. Leo stumbled back, falling from the cry, hitting the soggy ground beneath.

"What is that?" He scrambled up to his feet, his voice trembling.

"A grave screamer, Captain." The duke drew his sword and pointed it at the beast creeping closer to them. "My great-grandfather encountered one too on his journey through here. It's a creature made from the parts of corpses it finds lying around. The more body parts it collects, the bigger it grows, and I'd say this one has been busy. Watch yourself with this thing. It likes to bite off the heads of travelers and drink their blood."

"Great"—Leo bore his blade which illuminated the darkness—"just what I was looking forward to today." He raised his sword in the air. "So how do we defeat this thing?"

"We need to sever its head." Leighton glanced behind him, his breath ragged. "They are also afraid of fire, so do you think you can help us, Morgana?"

"Certainly."

Lifting her hand up, she stole a glance at the maroon-stained gauze on her palm and took a deep breath before facing the creature. Collecting herself, she waved her hand, summoning a circle of fire to trap the grave screamer and keep it away. The flames crackled and sprang to life, causing the creature to shriek and spin around its flaming prison. Letting out a guttural snarl, it snapped its head to glare at Morgana. The creature shook the raining embers off its body and stretched its neck. As the head inched away from the body, blood spurted onto the ground. The skull detached from the torso, dragging a blood-slicked spine and a tangle of entrails behind it. Floating in the air, the head bobbed, dragging the slimy ropes of its guts on the ground, and unfurled its long, snake-like tongue to taste the air.

"Good Lord," Leo gasped. "That is disgusting. Far worse than the monsters of Synia or Vekureth."

"Sorry, I guess I forgot to mention its head can float and seek out victims remotely."

"Great." Leo tightened his grip on the hilt of his sword and brought it down on the head as it lunged for him. "I truly appreciate the warning, Your Grace."

Evading the attack, the head flew into the air, made a sharp turn, and flew for the knight again before he had the chance to respond. Morgana formed a green ball of lighting between her palms, threw it at the creature, and hit it square in the face, blistering its waxy skin and singeing its greasy black hair. Stopping in its tracks, the monster turned its head to glare at her, its lustrous eyes filled with cold hate. Its lips skinned back in a snarl, revealing its saliva-streaked fangs, and it lunged straight for the witch, dragging its bloody entails behind it. Immobilized by a primal fear, Morgana wanted to scream but couldn't even muster a whimper as the fanged mouth sped right for her. She fell back to the ground with her eyes growing wide and her skin turning to ice.

Spinning his blade in his hands, Leo gripped the hilt and lurched from his spot, running to intercept the head flying toward Morgana. He dropped to the ground and skidded along its slushy surface, positioning his blade above his head in time to block the beast just above her body. The mouth full of sharp teeth latched on the metal, and the blade severed the tongue, sending spurts of old blood flying into his face. Screeching, the head loomed over him, its mouth chomping on his sword, pushing him further into the sodden soil.

"Leighton." He turned to his side while trying to push up on his blade with both hands, struggling to keep the beast away. "Any day now."

"Right." The duke shook himself out of a stupor. "My bad."

Leighton swung his sword and brought it down, severing the vertebrae connected to the grave screamer's head. The mouth opened and let out one final shrill yell as a spring of blood flowed from the neck, raining down on Leopold and Morgana. Coughing, they looked up in time to see its molten eyes flicker out and go dark. The head dropped to the ground, and the body followed suit. Once more, silence crept up around them, swallowing them in the static-filled air. No other creature lingered in the darkness beyond the trail. Wiping the putrid blood from his face, Leo pushed himself up to his feet, sheathed his sword, and offered his hand to Morgana, pulling her off the moist soil.

"Are you all right, my lady?"

"I"—she glanced at her blood-speckled gown—"I think I'll recover."

"You didn't get hurt, did you?"

"No, and it's all thanks to you. I'm not sure what would have happened if you didn't block that thing with your blade."

"Glad I could help." He put his arms around her and rubbed her trembling shoulder. "I didn't save you from your dungeon only to lose you to some foul creature."

Leaning on his chest, Morgana heard faint rustling coming from somewhere in the trees and stiffened with the fear of another grave screamer coming after them. It wasn't until she heard a long, drawn-out moan that she knew something else had found them. Leopold seemed to know what it was because he tightened the grip on his sword and pushed her behind his back.

"Reavers," he gritted out. "I hate reavers."

Before Morgana had a chance to ask what they were, a herd of emaciated, flesh-colored creatures stumbled out from the shrubs. Their jawless mouths and exposed ribs made Morgana shudder, but it was the sight of their six blade-like arms that filled her with horror. Leo and Leighton charged in with their swords, blocking the appendages, working in unison as they dodged their attacks. At her side, a reaver crept closer to Morgana, and she summoned a vine to restrain the monster, but the blades of its arms simply cut through as it headed straight for her. The pointed tip of an arm swung for her throat just as something swooped out of the tree and grabbed hold of her, lifting her into the air.

Morgana let out a shrill yell as the creature took her deeper into the woods and Leo's horror-stricken face vanished from sight. Squirming in its grip, she could see the ground beneath her and feel the attacker's muscular arms holding her tight. Not daring to move any further, she waited until they landed in a nearby tree before she began her struggle anew against her kidnapper, who was almost two feet taller than her.

"Let go of me!" she screamed, thrashing against the creature's hold. "Let go, or else—"

"Stop squirming unless you wish to fall out of this tree," the cool, husky voice commanded. "And stop screaming. You'll draw the reavers straight to us."

"You . . ." Morgana looked up wide-eyed at the white-haired

man with amber eyes holding her to his chest. "What are you doing with me, you bastard?"

"Saving you, little one. What does it look like?" The demon king smirked, and she could see his fangs glisten in the light of dawn breaking through the foliage. "Unlike your knight, you can't fight those things."

"Saving me?" she hissed. "You were planning to kill me."

"Was I really, though?" The demon king cupped her face in his large hand, stroked her cheek with his clawed finger, and tilted her head up to look at him. "Think about it, baby girl. If I wanted you dead, I'd have killed you a long, long time ago. I would have never allowed your precious captain out of my sight. Truth is, I *wanted* him to save you."

"Why—"

"I have my reasons."

The demon king peered into her eyes, and despite her burning hatred for him, she felt safe in his grip. There was something in his wicked smile that put her at ease and a quality to his icy touch that soothed her. She wanted to ask him more questions, but the snapping of branches behind them made him turn around and click his tongue.

"These woods really are infested," he snarled. "Your knight really ought to do something about this. But I guess I have no choice but to leave you." He turned to look at her and she shuddered. "Stay here, and don't move until your boy gets to you. And, darling"—he leaned down to kiss her forehead—"heed my warning: stay away from the cursed duke. Remain in Mireworth, keep your knight, but whatever you do, do not follow me. I only want the Charmant, not you, and I would hate to hurt you if you continue to insist on coming after me."

Without giving her a chance to reply, the demon king took off toward the sound of snapping branches, and the only thing Morgana heard was howling, followed by silence. Sitting in the tree, she dared not move until she heard nothing coming from the gloom below. Shifting her weight, she attempted to get her legs over the branch but slipped and fell to the ground with a thud. Sharp pain shot up her shoulder and down her arm, and she had to bite her lip to keep herself from crying out in pain. Too scared to move, she pressed herself closer to the soil and waited in the stillness, blanketing herself in the shadows.

She finally heard Leo's voice in the distance after an unknown amount of time. "Morgie! Morgie, where are you?"

"Over here!" she yelled, sitting up and wincing from the stabbing pain in her shoulder. "I'm here!"

Straining her eyes, she spotted Leo emerge from the trees in his blood-soaked shirt, the Heartseaker sheathed at his side. Seeing her on the ground, he ran to scoop her in his arms, and she almost cried when the pain in her shoulder burned harder than before. A moment later, Leighton came out of the same tree, holding on to the reigns of the horses.

"Are you all right?" Leo held her shoulders and peered at her face. "What the hell took you?"

"I—" She paused, wondering if she should tell them it was the demon king himself who saved her. The connection she felt with the Devoth prince frightened her, and she didn't wish to explain to them something she didn't yet understand. "I don't know. I didn't get a good look before it dropped me."

"Did you get hurt?"

"Only my right shoulder."

"Let me see." Gently pulling away the gauzy fabric of her dress to the side, Leo frowned at the small lump at the top of her shoulder. "Damn it. Looks like you dislocated it. I can fix it, but I'm afraid it's going to hurt."

"It's all right." She nodded. "I can take it."

Drawing in a sharp breath, Leo placed one hand on her collar bone and grabbed her wrist with another. After giving her arm a quick pull, the bone snapped back into its socket with a loud pop, and Morgana yelped from the pain. Letting her go, Leo looked at her with his brows drawn.

"I'm sorry. I didn't mean to be so rough."

"It's fine." She winced and gripped her throbbing shoulder. "It still hurts, though."

"I think I have something that may help." Leighton reached into his pouch and placed a small white ball between her lips, which melted into a bitter ooze on her togue. "It's a painkiller my apothecary concocted a while back. It will help ease the pain. Let us get out of here now. The captain and I spotted the exit not far from here, and I don't know about you, but I don't wish to encounter any more monsters. As is, the reavers almost got the best of us."

Nodding his head in agreement, Leopold placed Morgana in the saddle before jumping in behind her. Her trembling arms wrapped around him, and he held her tight, growing hot at his core as they made their way into the murky tunnel of trees. They caught sight of the distant luminous clouds of fog and ashen light breaking through the saggy branches of their trail, and their hearts pounded with excitement. They survived their journey through Devilwood Forest. They were closer to saving the princess and restoring order to Perdetia—and even if they failed, at least they were safe.

CHAPTER 20

# Judgment

**T**rotting out of the blackened forest, they rode up the singular muddy street running through the tiny village nestled among the trees. Beyond the town, foam-laced waves crashed rhythmically against the windswept shore. Only a dark sage sea, flecked with white sails, lay beyond the main strip. Glancing about at the oxcarts laden with grain rumbling by them, the three were met with icy stares. The women sweeping their stoops ushered the children inside and closed their shutters while men with pitchforks spit on the ground by their feet, watching the new arrivals, sizing them up.

"Friendly lot here," Leo said, glancing down the soggy track. "Love the warm greetings."

Morgana fidgeted in the saddle. "I can't say I blame them for being leery of us. After all, we did just ride out of Devilwood Forest looking like we've been through hell. I'm sure to them we look like trouble, and no one really wants trouble, especially no one in a humble little fishing village."

"I must agree with the lady on this one," said Leighton, dismounting from his horse. "I'm sure these folks are just protecting their best interest, and we sure don't look like the people someone would want to put up for the night. I'm sure they will warm up once they know we mean them no harm. In the meantime, I suggest we split up, get more things done, and get out of these people's way. I'll go board the horses at the stables and get us tickets on the next boat out. Leo, you can go get us some rooms at the Glacial Forge Inn. It's the only one in town, so it's hard to miss. As for you, Morgana, you need to go buy yourself some new clothes." He tossed a small pouch of gold nuggets at her. "You need something that doesn't scream that you just escaped near death twice—and preferably something not streaked in blood."

"All right." She gripped the pouch and leaped off the saddle. "In that case, I shall see you soon."

Waving to her companions, Morgana set off down the dirt track, searching for a clothing shop open at this hour of the day. The clouds clotted up the sky, and the afternoon light dwindled with the sun dipping below the horizon, darkening the gray-green sea. After inquiring a passerby for a store that may sell what she needed, she was pointed toward a small shack a few feet away. Ambling toward her destination, she observed the dusty window with sparsely filled shelves and stepped over the ruts in the road standing between her and the door.

Oil lamps flanked the weather-beaten oak door, which had a crude dress painted on its surface. She pulled the rusted handle and stepped tentatively into the shop. Inside the musty interior, a stout middle-aged woman greeted her with a scowl. Forcing a smile, Morgana didn't say a word as she headed for the racks cramped with hangers of clothing and began to look around. The shopkeeper watched the young woman in the dirty white dress, narrowing her beady eyes as she took a hanger off the rack and looked over the floor-length green dress.

"So," the shop keeper barked, "what crime do you stand accused of?"

"Witchcraft," Morgana said unblinkingly, "and treason."

"The charges true?"

"The witchcraft"—she paused—"yes. But I'm afraid I'd never betray the crown, not with my best friend wearing it."

"Yet it was your friend who accused you or took the accusation seriously."

"Not her. An impostor standing in her place."

"I see." The woman frowned, carving deep grooves into her brow. "And that handsome young knight you rode in with, did he save you?"

"He did." Morgana grabbed a nightdress off the rack. "He always does."

"Good man," the woman said, bobbing her head. "We need witches, you know. Things were so much better when they were in abundance. The Devilwood Forest was actually a viable path back in the days before the demon king. Now, well, as you have seen, *now* the place is crawling with monsters he brought with him, making a passage through the cursed woods impossible, and only the brave and the foolish try. No, since that damned man was summoned and the number of sorceresses dwindled, life has become a lot harder for us simple folk." The woman hacked and spit by her feet. "Say, what *is* a witch doing living in Perdetia, of all places? That is where you are from, isn't it?"

"I am, and . . ." Morgana placed her clothing on the counter. "I guess I had no choice. I was orphaned at a young age, and the woman who took me in lived within Perdetia's border, even if her estate didn't fall within the king's jurisdiction."

The shopkeeper began calculating the cost. "Yeah, but what kept you there? Surely when you turned of age, you could have married a passing merchant or traveled to some other place, living your life out peacefully with a farmer, or a count."

"That's true." Morgana deposited the gold nuggets on the counter and smiled at a time-sweetened memory. "But I had fallen in love long before I became eligible to wed, and he was not able to leave. I stayed so I could be near him, no matter what happened to me as a result."

"You talking about that dashing knight of yours?"

"I am."

"I see." The woman smiled. "In that case, here." She slid a small glass jar across the tabletop. "Some healing salve for you, on the house. You and your companions look a bit banged up, and this will help heal you in a day's time."

"Thank you." Morgana took the salve with a smile and turned to walk away.

"I hope you thank that boy well tonight for all he's done for you—if you know what I mean," the shopkeeper called after her, making Morgana's cheeks redden. "Just remember, all you got in this cold, cruel world is each other. Never forget that."

Thanking the woman again, Morgana opened the door, stepping

into the cold, damp air and placid village streets. In the time it took her to purchase new clothes, night had taken possession of the town, and shadows hung over the buildings like a wet rag. She walked uphill a short way, then stopped when she spotted a wind-battered building. Mists of light pooled beneath the windows, and an age-eaten wood sign dangled on rusty hinges, declaring it to be the Glacial Forge Inn.

She pushed through the silver-studded oak door and surveyed the murky interior. Cobweb-laced candle chandeliers swung above, vaguely illuminating the dusty space. Trailing her eyes past the innkeeper and dust-filmed wood tables, she landed on her companions sitting in the corner by the fire, drinking from porcelain cups, with a plate of food set out for her. She shuffled over and placed her bundle on the bench, sat down beside it, and dug in ravenously into the pheasant breast before her.

"This place looks deserted." She wiped her hands on the napkin. "I take it we are the only guests."

"I'm thinking you aren't far off in your assumption. Don't seem like too many people pass through here." Leo placed his glass down. "I got us three rooms, although I'm afraid a bath is out of the question. However, the innkeeper said there is a bucket of water in all the rooms, so I guess that will have to do."

"I think we'll manage." Leighton pocketed his key. "And we really should retire to our chambers and get some rest. I was told a passenger ship for the shores of Iatan is docking in the morning and that I can buy tickets then. So as soon as the sun comes up, I'll go book us a passage. For now, let us put this day behind us."

Washing her meal down with the warm ale in her cup, Morgana plucked her key off the table, took her clothes, and bid the men a good night before heading up the stairs to her chamber. Inside the monotony of the inn room, she placed her clothing on the chair and stripped off the bloodied white dress, allowing it to crumple by her feet before kicking it away and heading for the washbasin. The water inside the chipped porcelain tub was ice cold as she dipped a rag in and wiped the grime off her skin.

Staring at her shattered reflection in the mirror, she listened to the wind howl savagely in the background. The semblance of an approaching storm grew closer. Somewhere from the hallway, the creaking of the door across from her echoed down the hall. Leo had gone into his room. She knew because she had caught a glimpse of his key number while she was eating, then made note of the door numbers before she went into her room. Heaving out a sigh, she pushed the thoughts of him aside and slipped on a fresh gown before sitting on the bed.

Laying her head down on the burlap pillow stuffed with straw, she glanced up at the ceiling and stared at the wood showing through the pocked plaster. Outside, the wind picked up, slamming violently against the inn, vibrating the sole window in the room. The howling reminded her of her brush with death, and instantly thoughts of Leo trickled into the back of her skull. Listening to the gale toss the trees of the nearby Devilwood Forest, she recalled the promise she had made in her prison cell and sat up on the edge of the bed, gripping the sheets in her hands. The visions of blood continued to haunt her, but she could no longer fight what she was feeling, and she held her breath while her mind continued to race.

*What's wrong, Morgana? Can you not sleep, or is the young captain on your mind again?*

"And what if he is?"

*Then perhaps you should finally bed him . . . if he will have you, that is.*

"Maybe I just will."

Narrowing her eyes, she sat on the lip of the mattress and watched the shadows leaping on the wall before getting up to head for the door.

*What would your father say if he knew you were going to lie in a bed of a simple soldier?*

"I don't know"—Morgana shrugged and reached for the door handle—"I don't remember my father that well. But from what I do remember, I'd assume he'd want me to be happy even if he did not approve."

*You keep telling yourself that.*

Watching the shadow evaporate into the gloom, Morgana shook her head at the strange exchange and flung open her door. The narrow hall was awash in the dim light of the candles hanging on the wall. Closing off her room behind her, she took a step forward and stared up at the door of Leopold's room. She raised her hand and then paused, her heart pounding in her throat, her breath ragged. She wondered if she could enter his room on the fragile pretext of wanting to talk to him, but as she heard him mumbling inside, she pulled herself together and rapped on the door.

CHAPTER 21

# The Lovers

**W**alking into his room, Leo let out a sigh and stripped down to his leather pants. Leaning the Heartseaker against the wall, he stole a fleeting glance at the trees swaying outside his window. Recalling the events of the day, he strolled over to the brass-framed mirror across from him and looked at his blood-streaked face in the mottled glass. Leaning on the wood tabletop, he grabbed the washcloth and dipped it in the icy water, washing away the stains from his face before turning his focus to his right arm. The bicep still stung from where the sword hit him, and gummy blood continued to ooze from the deep wound when he flexed.

Sucking in the stagnant air of the room, he reached to pick up the healing salve Morgana handed him at the table and smiled to himself. He was filled with desire to go see her, his heart slammed painfully, and he wondered how her shoulder was doing. He wanted to go ask, but he figured she was probably asleep after the day she had and left her be. Instead he placed the glass jar down on the counter and walked over to the bag resting by the bed, then dug out the dressing he kept on hand. He was about to return to the washstand when a gentle rapping on his door drew his attention. Once more, the discreet knock broke the silence, more determined this time, and he got back to his feet. He padded over to the door, pried it open, and nearly fell over in surprise.

"Morgana?" he gasped.

Leopold's eyes drifted over the woman standing outside his door, puzzled. A peach nightgown fell above her knees, clinging to the elegant lines of her female body, and he could not peel his eyes away from her. She traced her eyes along the muscles of his abdomen, and her cheeks tinted while she chewed her bottom lip. The sight of her blushing made him smirk. He loved seeing how the sight of him shirtless still drew such a response. She blushed like that since she was eight and it always made him feel hot inside. As she continued studying him, her gaze met his, and she tilted her head to the side. Staring into the deep pink sapphires that were her eyes, he felt his body temperature rise, and he gripped the door jamb while he continued to admire the frightening beauty.

"Is everything all right, Morgie? Did something happen? Is your shoulder still bothering you?"

"Everything is fine, and my shoulder still aches, but it's not why I'm here," she said in her sensual, breathy voice. "I just couldn't sleep and wanted to check in on you. Can . . . can I come in?"

"Of course."

Stepping aside, he motioned for her to come in, and she glided inside, standing at the center of the room as he shut the door, taking in her surroundings. Turning to him, she held him in her gaze, and he was unable to move, seduced by her stare. Strolling closer to him, she reached out and slid her slender fingers up his arm and over his blood-sleeked skin, stopping to study the pulsing cut on his bicep. He tried his best not to move, but her touch on his bare skin made his spine tingle, and he flinched, causing some blood to ooze from his cut. Gently wrapping her fingers around his arm, she let out a soft, barely audible whimper, and her eyes flew up to his face, the darks of her pupils almost covering her irises.

"You got seriously hurt today," her voice quivered, "because of me, didn't you?"

"It's nothing." He peered down at her as she continued to study the gash. "I told you, I've had worse in battle. There is no need to worry about me."

"How can I not?" Her silky voice dripped with pain while her eyes glided over his body. "Would you like me to clean and bandage it for you?"

"Sure, if you'd like." He whispered, pulling his heart out of his throat. "The salve and bandages are on the dresser, next to the cleaning rag."

Curling her lips, she pressed on his collarbone and pushed him into the velvet, moth-eaten cushion of a nearby chair. Trying to still his galloping heart and the rushing of blood to his head, he watched with bated breath as she ambled over to the basin and grabbed the supplies before coming over to him with the wet rag. She focused her attention on him, and Leo feared his pulse might burst through his wrist if he stayed with her any longer. Ignoring his reddening face, Morgana brought the rag up to the cut, washing it gingerly, making him wince as the water stung the wound.

"What's wrong?" She pierced him with her soft stare. "Am I hurting you?"

"Just a bit," he mumbled, "but don't worry. I can take it."

"You know," she dipped her finger into the balm and tenderly massaged it over the broken skin. "I never did get to thank you for saving me back there."

"It was nothing," he breathed out. "I'd do it again if I had to."

"I know, but . . ." She smiled at him, winding the gauze around the hard muscle. "What you did meant a lot. Thank you."

"You know," he quavered, "you better be careful. I can get used to you taking care of me like this."

"Can you, now?"

Fixing her gaze on him, she reached out her hand and hesitantly ran the tips of her fingers through his hair, causing a shiver to run down his spine. Wrapping his arm around her, he placed the hand on the small of her back, pulling her in until she fell in his lap, almost straddling him, and his throat tightened. He looked up, swallowing hard while looking at the hard nipples of her round breasts poking out through the lightweight fabric of her gown. The silken aubergine strands of her hair cascaded around her shoulders, and the faint scent of vanilla hung in the air. Somewhere in the distance, the hollow sound of rain slashed through the trees, but Leo did not hear it. All he could focus on was her proximity to him and the growing tightness in his pants.

"Why are you really here, Morgie?" he finally asked her through a raspy breath. "Can you really not sleep, or—"

He dared not finish the sentence, even as hope bubbled up to the surface and his erection dug painfully into the buttons of his pants.

The tension lacing the air almost crackled, and his heart rammed into his sternum as waves of scolding heat crashed through his body. She leaned toward him, tracing the tips of her fingers up his rippled abdominal muscles, then rested her palm on his chest. As she caught him in her gaze, her eyes twinkled and bottom lip wavered. Inhaling a tight huff of breath, she craned her neck down to whisper in his ears, and her hot breath on his skin made him groan.

"Sleep with me, Leo."

"W-what?" He pulled her back, his eyes wide. The pulse throbbed in his temples; he had a hard time believing what he heard. "Why . . . why are you asking me this suddenly? I . . . I thought you wanted to wait until everything was settled?"

"I know, but . . ." she glanced at the floor, glass-eyed, her voice dropping. "I have already cost you everything. You gave it all up . . . for me." Her eyes found his again, their gaze more determined. "I love you, Leo. Ever since we met, I've always loved you. Until now, I've held myself back, waiting for the right time. But after coming so close to death twice, I realized what really matters in life. I wish to *live* for once, and there is no other person I'd rather do so with than you. It's always been you. Not to mention, we may not return from this alive. Then I will end up regretting never allowing things to progress between us. So what do you say? Will you still have me?"

"I thought I'd never hear you say that."

Pulling her into him, Leo stood up, and his lips covered hers. She eagerly welcomed him, wrapping her arms around his neck, bringing him closer. His tongue parted her lips and moved inside her mouth without hesitation. Tracing the roof of her mouth, he pressed her against the wall, framing her with his legs. The erection in his pants pressed against her, and she let out a soft gasp as he broke away from her, her sweetness still lingering on his lips. Hungry to taste her again, he leaned in and traced the fine line of her collar bone with his lips, trailing his faint kisses up her neck while her nails dug into his back, her body quivering. He worked his way up, sucked on her earlobe, then tugged on it with his teeth, making her grow stiff in his embrace.

"Leo"—she pressed her arms on his shoulders, pushing him away breathlessly—"wait."

"What's wrong, Morgie?" He hung his head in defeat, pressing his hand against the wall. "Change your mind already?"

"No." Her eyes flashed wildly, her face taking on another shade. "It's just . . . well, you're really turning me on. That's all."

"Is that so?"

A devilish grin crossed his lips. He looked at her flushed face in the ethereal candlelight. His hand followed the curves of her body downward until it found the opening in her gown. Tucking his fingertips beneath the hem, he skimmed across it until he landed on the bare skin of her thigh. Trailing his fingers up the silky softness of her leg, he stopped when he reached her slit and her wet heat covered him, soaking his hand. Seeing her panting at his touch made his pulse quicken, and he had to restrain the urge to take her on the spot while he played with the coarse hair of her sex.

"I guess I am. You're drenched." He stroked his fingers against her, and her body shuddered with a hoarse moan. "Don't worry,"—he leaned in to give her a deep kiss— "I'll take care of that in a minute. Right now, I wish to savor you for a while longer."

Leaning in, he pressed his lips against hers, getting more aroused by the heat coming off her body as she melted into him. Her tongue took hold if his, and she let out a soft groan into his mouth, her hands working their way down his back. This was not how he pictured their first time, but then again, he never imagined her to be a witch nor being alone with her in a ramshackle inn of a coastal town—not to mention everything that happened in between—but none of that mattered because he finally had her. She pulled his hips closer and tucked her fingers into the waistline of his pants, undoing the button and allowing them to pool by his ankles. Leo pulled himself away and found the buttons of her nightdress, then expertly undid them while he kept his eyes locked on her. The fabric slipped away from her body with a soft whisper, dropping to the floor like a billowy cloud.

Leaning against the wall, he studied the gentle curvature of her body as she stood before him, naked, her luscious breasts swollen and waiting to be touched. He traced the lines of her seductive curves with his fingertips until his hands found the swell of her breast and cupped it. She purred with his touch, arching closer. No longer able to resist her, his hands molded her bottom, lifting her up. Her legs wrapped around him, holding him tight, and he carried her to the bed, laying her down on the scratchy covers.

He climbed on top of her, and she spread her legs to accommodate him, squeezing him with her thighs. Rubbing his shaft against her, he felt her scorching warmth lubricate him, and he pressed the head of his hard penis against her, making her squirm beneath him while her eyes begged him to take her. Thrusting his hips forward, he plunged inside her. Her moist walls clammed around him, and she let out a passionate yell, grabbing onto his back to pull him down into her. Pushing up off the mattress, he peered into her eyes, panting, trying to calm his mind.

"Careful, now." He grinned. "You wouldn't want anyone to hear us."

"I don't care who hears us," she moaned softly. "I want to enjoy you. So please, don't hold back."

"I wasn't planning on it."

Suppressing a smile, he rolled his hips back and pushed forward again, causing the headboard to crack against the wall while Morgana purred and wrapped her legs around him, pushing him in further. With every thrust, the bed creaked, and her walls grew tighter around him while her screams got louder, until her body shuddered beneath him, covering him in hot juices as she arched her back with a raw moan, small muscles fluttering around him. Looking down on her, he watched the sweat drip off his chin and pool in the valley between her breasts, and he felt his own muscles tighten as she continued to clamp around him. This would have been the time he would normally pull out and finish himself off into the covers, but he couldn't tear himself away from her. He needed to feel himself spill inside her. Reaching the point of no return, he groaned, pushed down deeper into her, and the sweet release of ecstasy flowed into her. Collapsing into her waiting arms, he tried to catch his breath while she stroked his hair, cradling him against her.

"Stay with me, Morgie." He tangled his fingers in the delicate waves of her hair and peered into her eyes, which sparkled in the darkness. "Spend the night."

Glancing up at him, she smiled, resting her head on his chest. Nestled into the nook of his arm, she draped her leg over him while her fingers ran along the muscles of his abdomen and up to his pecs. Her deep purple hair flowed around him, and he wrapped his arm over her shoulder, pressing her closer. Holding him tight, she let out a soft sigh and drifted off to sleep, leaving him to lie in bed, stroking her arm with his fingers. Then Leo lay awake, scolding himself under his breath for being happy at their circumstances. Lafreya was his friend, too, and his princess. He knew they had to get her back, or else shabby inn rooms were the only place he'd ever be with Morgana again.

CHAPTER 22

# The Ace of Chalices

At the break of dawn, the cawing of a lone rooster rousted Morgana from her dreams, and she fluttered open her lids. Shaking off sleep, she glanced up at the man lying beside her. A warm ray of light slipped through the crack in the curtain and landed on his face, making his eyes sparkle. His sweat-darkened blond hair stuck to his brow as he looked over at her with a smile, caressing her bare skin with his hand, which was still draped over her. Seeing her wake, Leo creased his brow, and she saw the silent questions flicker in his eyes, clouding their brilliant blue color.

"What's wrong, Leo?"

"Nothing . . ." he said, exhaling sharply. "It's just . . ." He flipped over to his side and reached over to brush a loose strand of hair behind her ear. "Please tell me this wasn't a onetime thing."

"No." She smiled and stole a kiss from his lips. "I don't think it was. Not unless you want it to be."

"Never." He tightened his grip on her as if she would slip away if he didn't. "All I ever wanted was to be with you . . . always."

"And I wish to be with you. In every way possible."

"Good. That's exactly what I needed to hear."

Grinning, he slipped his arm over her back, pulling her in for a kiss, his warm lips enveloping hers. He still smelled of last night's sex, but she didn't mind. The musky sent brought up those memories, making her tingle with his touch, sending jolts of electricity down her spine. She pushed her body up against him and felt him grow hard against her inner thigh, making her shudder. His tongue continued exploring her mouth as he rolled over on top of her, pulling her legs apart and rubbing himself against her in leisurely strokes. Morgana arched her back, and heat washed over her in waves. She felt herself grow moist, her hands grasping his wrists. Pulling away from her, he tugged her bottom lip between his teeth, and she peered into his face while her cheeks continued to burn.

"Leo," she purred. "What are you doing?"

"I was going to make love to you again." His lips curled into a smile and gave a her a quick kiss. "What does it look like?"

"But . . . isn't Leighton waiting for us downstairs? Shouldn't we get going?"

"I've waited seven years to be with you." He pressed his mouth on hers, tracing her bottom lip with his tongue. "I think Leighton can wait another thirty minutes or so."

"But we have to go. We must find Lafreya."

"Morgie." He peered at her. "The ship won't leave till at least noon. I won't take that long. I promise."

Leaning over, his tongue massaged her neck, making her moan, and she clung to his sculpted back. Usually she didn't allow the man to be on top, not since the professor forced himself on her. She loathed the position since that day, and from then on she enjoyed being in control of the situation, but there was something different with Leo, something that broke down the barriers. Feeling his weight on top of her made her body grow hot, and a tingle crept along her spine. She pressed herself up, rocking her hips into him, asking him to take her again. Taking his cue, he slipped inside her with a throaty groan, and she felt her walls swell around him as he filled her out.

The night before, he treated her as if she were oxygen and he were running out of breath, but he was less eager this time around. The rocking of his hips was gentle and slow, allowing her to feel his full length inside her, and warmth fizzled at her core. She could still taste his salty sweat on her lips as he continued to kiss her, hungrily grabbing hold of her lips. Her pulse quickened, and her breasts hardened as he continued to swell inside her, rubbing up against her walls as she moaned his name breathlessly. The more he thrust himself inside, the more she felt a familiar sensation as she climbed to her peak. Her toes curled and her body spasmed, and she let out another passionate scream, clinging to his back.

Looking down on her, his expression changed, and he brought his lips on hers, his movements getting faster. Still shaking from her orgasm, she held on tight and moved her hips to meet his every time he plunged inside her. She felt his muscles harden. Tilting his head back, Leo closed his eyes and released inside her with a guttural groan before collapsing on top of her. Still shaking, she gasped as he slipped out of her and lay beside her, running his hand over the dip of her hips. Stealing one last kiss, she combed her finger through his hair and got up from the tangled sheets, finding her nightgown on the floor, slipping it over her sweat-glazed frame.

"Leaving me already?"

She glanced over at him on the bed. The stained sheet draped leisurely over his hips while he propped up on his elbow, fanning her with his eyes, and she felt herself getting aroused again. She could hardly believe she had denied herself his phenomenal pleasure for the past seven years, and she craved to have it again. If circumstances were permitting, she would have spent all day in bed with him, loving him with her body, but she knew they had to get going. She walked over and sat down on the bed beside him, and his fingers worked their way up her arm, sending sparks throughout her core.

*Stay here with him, Morgana. Heed the demon king's warning and remain here with your knight. Forget the princess and leave the cursed duke to his fate. You don't owe those people anything.*

"Leo." She traced his bottom lip with the tip of her thumb, ignoring the shadow. "I would love nothing more than to make love to you all day, but we really ought to get going. We have some place we need to be. Without Lafreya, I'm afraid dingy rooms of coastal inns are all I foresee in our future."

"I know. But I still don't want to let you go," he moaned, falling back into the covers. "At least promise me that we will spend a day together in bed as soon as we return home to Perdetia."

"Mmm. I got one better for you." She leaned in to give him a fleeting kiss. "We can spend all week together if you'd like."

"All right, fine." He stroked her cheek with the back of his finger. "Go on, then. Get dressed. I'll meet you outside your room, and I'll hold you to your promise once we return."

"You better."

She winked at him, got up from the bed, walked out the door, and entered her room, where her clothing waited for her. After slipping into the simple green peasant dress, she braided her hair into a single loose braid and took one last look in the mirror. There was something different about her reflection; she allowed herself to smile as Leo's touch continued to loiter, warming her from the inside, making her tingle.

Leaving the shabby room behind, she walked into the narrow, dusty hall where Leo was already waiting for her, leaning against the wall. Standing up on her toes, she kissed him and laced her fingers through his, tightening her grip on him. He held her close and turned to walk down the stairs, never once letting go of her hand. Waiting for them at the table, Leighton was tapping his fingers on the wood, and he stopped when he spotted them come down. Seeing them together, holding hands, he raised his brow, and his eyes darted between them, his lips curling into a teasing grin.

"Well, well, Captain." He brought up a gloved hand to cover the smile on his face. "I thought I heard you entertaining company last night. I just didn't picture it being Lady Morgana, of all people. But I suppose I should have guessed that you wouldn't have anyone else, and with the way you were looking at one another last night . . . well, it was only a matter of time until she fell into your bed."

Morgana's face flushed at his words, and she glanced over at Leopold, who was turning a bright shade of red that spread to his ears. This caused Leighton to chuckle and slap his knee. Rolling his eyes, he motioned for them to join him for breakfast as the barmaid placed three plates on the table. Letting go of Leo's hand, Morgana sat down between the men and picked away at the eggs on her plate while the duke continued to study her face. Beside her, Leo placed a hand on her knee and gave it a squeeze. Looking up, she met with his gaze, his face still pink, and Leighton snickered, causing them both to turn and glare at him.

"Relax," he said, shaking his head. "I'm not judging you, if that's what you're afraid of. I'm just glad you finally got together. Now"—he pushed away his empty plate—"what do you guys say we go get on that ship and get my real fiancé back?"

"I'd say, what are we waiting for?" Leo placed his fork down and looked at the woman beside him. "After all, I have Morgana's good name to clear and my position to restore here. You have my sword for as long as you need it."

"All right, let us go, then. I already got tickets this morning while you two were preoccupied. As for our horses, I paid the stable master handsomely. They will be fine here until we return. Well," Leighton said, getting up from the table, "what are you waiting for, an invitation? Lafreya is waiting for us."

Still blushing, Leo got up from his seat and offered Morgana a hand, smiling. Averting the duke's gaze, she stood up and snaked her arm through his, drawing their bodies together. She never wished to let him go again, and he held her tight, assuring her he would always keep her close as they walked out of the inn and headed down the groove road for the harbor. Turning her head away from him, she spotted a mass of white sails on the horizon and gasped. She'd never been far outside Perdetia before, and she had never seen a ship up close, let alone been on one. Morgana wondered what it would be like on board. Her feet hesitated to move, and Leopold rubbed her arm to reassure her everything would be fine as they got in a long queue to wait to board the vessel.

CHAPTER 23

# The Ace of Coins

By the time they boarded the ship, the mild afternoon sun warmed the wind-scarred deck, and Morgana stood basking beside a railing, admiring the ship. The main deck was the size of the courtyard in Perdetia. Three masts rose into the air, draped in white sails with the crest of a red eagle in their centers, and a staircase led up to the top deck on either side. People shuffled past her, heading up the steps or down into the ship's bowels while she spun around with her mouth open, taking in everything one bit at a time. She couldn't wait to tell Lafreya all about her journey on the sea vessel, but recalling her friend made her heart sting, and she turned to watch the mist slowly swallow the town.

Morgana stood on the upper deck and watched the men scurry

about below, pulling the heavy hemp ropes off the pylons beside the hull. With the last cord tossed up to the ship, they hoisted the sails, and the vessel picked up wind, jerking from its spot, making her stomach lurch. She continued to scan the deck, and for the first time since they boarded, she noticed something wrong with the ship. Faint silhouettes mingled among the bodies of the passengers, and distant sounds rang in her ears. Memories she tried so hard to forget crept back up, making her mouth go dry, and she leaped back with a yelp right into Leo's waiting arms.

"Everything all right, love?" He rubbed her shoulder. "You look like you've just seen a ghost."

"No, not a ghost." She tilted her head back to look at him. "It's this ship. It's not safe."

"What are you talking about? You've seen it, it's as solid as they get."

"Not like that, Leo. It's filled with echoes."

"Echoes?"

"Yes. When something traumatic happens in a place, the negative energy gets absorbed into the surrounding materials, like an imprint. Those of us who use magic can see those echoes. First time I've ever seen one was at the potions lab at the academy. I saw palm prints on the desk and heard screams of girls. I didn't know what it was until he—" Her throat clenched up. "Until—"

"It's okay, Morgie." Leo squeezed her shoulder. "You don't need to repeat what that bastard did to you."

"Thank you." She sighed. "Anyway. This boat is infested with echoes. It's filled to the brim with bad energy."

"What kind of echoes? Can you tell what they are from?"

"No. They are so faint and numerous I can't make much out. I heard screaming and crying and water splashing, and I see the faint silhouettes, but that's about it."

"All right. We will keep an eye on things and take extra caution. Whatever evil is here, I promise to keep it away from you."

She smiled at him. "I have no doubt you will. So, Leighton"— she turned to the grand duke— "how long are we on this thing for?"

"Not long. Iatan is only three days away across the Sea of Suldant."

"Fair enough." She looked at the people ambling about. "So . . . what now?"

"I'll show you our room first and then the rest of the ship. We'll be staying on deck two. You and Leopold can share the bed, and I will sleep in the hammock across from you."

"Are you sure about this, Leighton?"

"I'm not sharing the bed with either of you, if that is what you're asking." Leighton sniggered. "I'll be fine. I was going to suggest the captain and I take shifts in the hammock, but it's no longer a problem. Not to mention, I am used to less-than-ideal accommodations, so a hammock shouldn't pose a problem. Come"—he turned to walk toward one of the staircases—"shall we go check out our cabin? Then we can explore before going down to the mess hall for dinner."

Taking hold of Morgana's hand, Leopold set off after the duke, who vanished into the opening between the stairs on the stern side. Following Leighton down several flights of rickety, winding stairs, they found themselves in a narrow hallway, where they took a left turn and studied the doors with pitted brass numbers on them. Humming as he went along, the duke stopped before a door and pulled out a rusty key from his pocket, which allowed him entrance into their accommodations. The couple squeezed in behind him.

The unassuming room—filled with lingering mildew—reminded Morgana of her dungeon cell, and she shuddered at the memory still fresh in her mind. Across from her a tiny, square porthole window looked out at the sprawling expanse of the ocean. To the left and right of the window sat a tattered velvet armchair and a shabby cot barely big enough for two people. Beside the cot stood a pine washstand with a cream porcelain basin and a pitcher on top. Above the stand hung a gold-leaf mirror—flaking and crusting over with age—and across from that, a rope hammock.

Leaving the few things they had on hand in their room, they left to look around the rest of the ship. Morgana noted the echoes were mostly confined to the upper deck and the rear of the ship, where, according to Leighton, the supplies were kept. Frowning, she pondered where they all came from. Perhaps the ship used to be a war vessel, and she was witnessing the last moments of the sailors' lives. Whatever the echoes were, though, they made her uneasy, and she wished that their trip across the sea was over before it even started.

Finishing their tour, the three strolled into the mess hall—where there was an unusual concentration of echoes—and grabbed the evening meal provided for the passengers. Sitting at the table next to Leo, Morgana glimpsed at the congealing slop on her plate and crinkled her nose. She picked up the unidentifiable gruel with her spoon and was about to put it in her mouth when her flesh prickled at the sensation of eyes burning a hole in her back. Hearing the echoes get louder, she dropped her utensil and looked for whoever was staring at her.

To her shock, three men in sailor uniforms glared at her from across the room, the silhouettes crawling across them like ink stains on parchment. One was a lanky, pockmarked man with a large scar running down his milky eye, licking his lips. On his left stood a portly, bulbous-nosed man, flipping a silvery blade in the air. And on his right was a potbellied giant with a face covered in horrid purple grooves, smirking lecherously. The scarred man shifted his weight from one leg to the other and gave her a nod that rocked her to her core. Whoever they were, the echoes focused around them, and that made her uneasy. She sensed they were trouble, even without the blackness crawling around their feet—just by the way they undressed her with their eyes.

"What's wrong, darling?" Leo rubbed her back, and she turned to look at him. "You look as white as a sheet. Are you seeing more of those echoes?"

"I . . ." she glanced over her shoulder, but the men were no longer there. "I thought I found their source, but maybe my mind is playing tricks on me, because they are gone now."

"In that case, did you want to return to the room? We can relax there for the rest of the night, where you know you're safe."

"Yes." She jumped up, still shaken by the sailors. "I think a little sleep would do me some good. And I'd like to be away from the general area and the negative energy it holds."

Excusing them from the table, Leo took Morgana to the room and curled up on the bed beside her, draping his arm over her, pulling her close. Lying in his embrace, she stared at the damp corner of the room and the glow from the red eyes in the shadows. Her companion didn't move, not until Leighton returned to the room and collapsed in the hammock. Slinking closer, the shadow regarded Morgana with a hard stare as she lay still, listening to the wind keening outside the porthole window, lobbing waves against the hull, which filled the room with tapering echoes.

*What are you doing, fool? The demon king gave you a chance to live, and you threw it out. Why are you following that cursed man? What's in it for you?*

"He is my friend," she hissed under her breath. "I promised to help him, and that is exactly what I plan to do, even if it kills me."

*And what would your lover say to that? Think he wants you to die?*

"Leo"—she stole a glance behind her—"he'll protect me. He always does. We will all get through this."

*And yet you don't believe the words you speak. I know you can feel it: death . . . it's closer to you than ever. Someone close to you will have to die, and you will be the cause of it.*

"No," she snarled, sitting up in bed. "I won't lose anyone I care about again. I won't allow it to happen."

*You think you can save them? You couldn't even stop your daddy from walking out on you.*

"You know as well as I do that my father never left." She got up to her feet and glared at her shadow. "The demon king took him from me, just like my mother. It's about time that Devoth bastard pays for what he did to me."

The shadow only laughed. Huffing out a stale breath, Morgana walked to the door and flung it open. Ignoring the echoes following her, she strolled for the top deck, where she hoped to think without anyone interrupting her. But the phantoms were not the only thing following her, and if she only paused for a moment, she'd have noticed the company trailing behind her, watching her every move.

CHAPTER 24

# The Six of Swords

**S**trolling onto the deck flooded by moonlight, Morgana tightened her arms around herself and shivered from the brisk ocean gale tousling her hair. It was late, and the ship fell silent because most of the passengers had gone to sleep, and she only heard the din of drunken sailors from the decks below and the whispers of the echoes. Inhaling a lungful of the crisp, salty air, she closed her eyes and breathed out all the ire she had been harboring since the conversation with her shadow. Then she walked over to the port side and leaned over the railing.

Below her, dark, foam-crested waves lashed the side of the boat, murmuring in hushed tones, which filled the empty space around her. Morgana recalled what the demon said to her back at the cabin, and a crystal tear glistened in the corner of her eye as faint memories of her father came back to her. Pushing it back, Morgana closed her eyes, wishing to at least recall his face, but it was a blur, no matter how hard she tried to focus on it. Her father's face was erased by time, but the warmth he left behind remained, and she focused on that as she wished to have him close. Lost in her thoughts, Morgana didn't notice the soft footsteps swallowed in shadows behind her, not until a rough voice grated the silence and she reeled around to look at the three sailors from earlier, strolling closer, their lecherous gaze fixed on her, the echoes wailing behind them.

"Well, well," said the lanky man, licking his lips, his one eye undressing her. "What have we got ourselves here, boys?"

"Looks like fresh pussy to me," sneered the robust man. "Same one we were admiring in the mess hall earlier. And she looks ready to get a good pounding."

"Mmhm." The scarred man grabbed hold of his crotch, yanking it upward. "I think you're right, Pasco. She looks like an exotic little vixen, too. What do you think, Rowan, think the curtains match the drapes?"

"No clue, Hayrig." Curling up his lips into a sneer, the pockmarked man took a step closer. "We could always ask the man she was with, but . . . I think I prefer to find out for myself by ripping that dress off her and pounding her juicy cunt against the barrels in the storeroom."

"Stay away from me." Morgana pressed herself against the rails. Her heart slammed in her chest, and the blood drained from her face at the memories of the last man to force himself on her. "Don't come any closer."

"Or what?" The sailor named Rowan lurched, grabbed hold

of her arm, and pulled her in close. Morgana could smell the rum on his breath. "What are you gonna do, girly? You gonna scream? It's too late in the night. No one will hear you, or they will blame it on the siren calls. Not even your man will come running, as he is probably out cold at this hour. And by the time morning rolls around, you'll have long gone overboard in a tragic accident."

"Tragic," nodded Hayrig. "It happens all the time. Someone always gets drunk and falls into the water, never to be seen again. And you can only hold your head above the water for so long in that dress of yours."

"I'm warning you." She kneed Rowan in the balls, and he toppled over, letting go of her arm. Morgana stepped back and glared at the men flanking her, her heart racing. "I said stay back, or you will regret it."

"So, you're gonna put up a fight, are you, girly?" The pockmarked man stood up, still clutching his crotch. "That's fine by me. I like a little fight in a bitch before I take her. It makes having my way with her that much sweeter."

The three men closed her in, surrounding her. Fear gripped her at the thought of what they planned to do with her, and her mouth grew dry as she recalled the professor. Morgana readied herself to throw them overboard with a spell when a figure, cloaked by shadows, slipped past her and stood before the men. It was Leighton, with his steel sword drawn, its blade glistening with the moonlight.

"Didn't the lady tell you to leave her be?" Leighton blocked her with his body and sneered at the sailors. "Or are the three of you as dumb as you look?"

"Shit," muttered Pasco and turned on his heels, "seems we have company, boys. Let's get out of here. We can find some other pussy to bang."

The sailors left them be, scattering in every direction of the ship. Leighton sheathed his sword, turning to look at the woman behind him. She glanced up at him, and his scowl softened as he placed a warm hand on her trembling shoulder.

"You all right, my lady?"

"I'll be fine." Morgana glanced up and rubbed her arm. "As for them"—she watched where the men had gone—"well . . . they will wake up with a nasty case of crotch lice tomorrow morning."

"You are devious at times." Leighton raised his brow. "You know that?"

"So I've been told on several occasions by your fiancé." She smirked and gave him a wink. "And, um, thank you for saving me."

"Oh, something tells me you didn't really need saving. But I'm glad I came when I did, for their sake." Strolling over to the railing, Leighton turned his back to her, leaned on the wood, and stared at the inky darkness beyond. "So, you going to tell me what you are doing here all alone this late at night? I know you didn't come here to get assaulted by sailors, and the captain might wake up and lose his head if he finds you missing."

"Just came to clear my head"—she joined him at his side and observed the moon bobbing in the surf—"that's all."

"From what? Or should I say, whom?"

"What are you talking about?"

"No need to lie to me, Morgana." Leighton turned his head to regard her with a soul-piercing stare. "I heard you arguing with something in the cabin before you left. Something I couldn't see or hear. Now why not tell me what it was? What's really going on with you that has you running around a ship late at night, meeting the company of drunken rapists?"

"Promise you won't tell Leo?"

"You have my word."

She sighed. "All right. I have this demon that follows me around."

"Like, an actual demon?"

"I don't know, maybe, but that's what I call it. It's a shadowy figure that lurks around me, and I'm the only one able to see and hear it."

"I see." Leighton nodded his head and wrinkled his brow. "How long has this been going on?"

"Ever since my mother died. I'm not sure how or why it happened, just that it happened after her death."

"And *this* is what you don't want Leopold to know about? Surely this is not something he would care about."

"I know he wouldn't care. That's not what worries me." Morgana pursed her lips. "I just feel like it's connected to the demon king somehow, and that he uses it to spy on me and possibly even control me. Even now, I feel his eyes upon me. Watching me and plotting his next move."

"But Morgana, that's impossible." Leighton shook his head. "Not even a Devoth can see something they are not there to witness."

"I know," Morgana said, gripping the railing. "And yet I can't help feeling the way I do. I can't shake this fear that he's here with us and that he knows what we are up to. Like he always knew. Because"—she bit her lip and took in a deep breath—"it was him who swooped me up back in Devilwood Forest."

"What? Why wouldn't you tell us?"

"He said he was saving me from the reavers, and, well,"—she looked at Leighton—"I didn't want Leo thinking the same thing I was. That the demon king was among one of the men I slept with, because I really can't come up with any other reason he'd want to save me. And, believe me, I tried while I lay there waiting for you, but not a single thing came to mind."

"I see." Leighton gritted his teeth and nodded his head. "Did he tell you anything else?"

"He warned me to stay away from you. He said I should stay in Mireworth and leave you to your fate."

"Ah, guess he underestimated your loyalty to Lafreya. My Lafreya . . ." He ran his hands through his hair, clutching the strands at the end. "Oh, Lord. I miss her."

"We'll get her back." Morgana reached out to touch his shoulder. "This is why I came with you despite his warning. You need to stop worrying. It's not good for you. Strong negative emotions might just accelerate that curse of yours."

"Who said I was worried?"

"Oh, Leighton, Leighton. You don't have to pretend with me. I've known you for as long as you've been with Lafreya. I can tell that beneath that cool, composed exterior, you are in a world of panic and agony. How could you not? She was the first woman you've been with. The first person you have given your heart to."

He side-glanced her. "You know, sometimes I hate how you can read me. But you're right. Deep down, my heart is breaking, and I fear losing her. What if she's already dead? He knows we're coming. So what's the point of him keeping her alive?"

"Don't think like that. You won't lose her. He'll keep her alive—he has to. I can't imagine him killing the person he needs to control Perdetia. His little stand-in is only good for a month or two. He needs the real thing."

"True." Leighton bobbed his head, continuing to glance at the murky horizon. "Say, do you remember what you told me when I asked you if Lafreya would marry me?"

"Which part? That she would marry you regardless of the card you hold because your curse insured that you were not long for this world?" She peered at his scowling face and smirked. "Or the part where I told you that we could cure you if you held the Hanged Man card?"

"Yes, the last part. I recall you said there was no way I could hold the World card because of my sunny disposition."

"Yes, I remember. What brings this on now?"

"Do you still believe that?" He tilted his head toward her. "You still believe in the power of our fate cards? Do you think I can end this, save Lafreya, and give her what she wants? Or will I leave her broken-hearted when I succumb to my curse in a few more years?"

"I'll never stop believing in the cards. I told you before, if you can bring down the demon king, you can end this curse, which is bound to his power. Once we find him and destroy him, you can give Lafreya all the children her heart desires, without the fear of passing your condition on to them. And we will find her because the Golden Empress is destined to live a long life, and I refuse to believe the cards lie. Cards never lie . . . at least that's what I choose to believe until they prove me wrong."

"I hope what you say is true." Leighton turned around and leaned his back against the railing, bending his head to the murky sky. "But then, why is the demon king luring me toward him? Why would he risk me putting an end to him?"

"He's arrogant, and he doesn't think he can lose, not when it's just you. I think that's why he attempted to make me a deal, to keep me and Leo away from you. I think he fears the three of us together. He believes he can kill you if you are alone. After all, your fate card isn't exactly promising. You are teetering between life and death—your future is uncertain. And my card is not much better."

"That's true. One wrong move, and I can go into the direction I don't want to. But what of Leopold and Lafreya?" He looked at her. "What of their fate cards?"

"Our soul cards? The people destined to be with us because our cards are bound together?" She drew a sharp breath. "What of them? If we die, they will move on. Lafreya still has another card, which she can be bound to, and maybe he's out there. As for Leo . . . well, I'm his only soul card, but his destiny is one of glory, even if it is in death."

"I see. So even if I die, my Lafreya will live. I guess I can take some small comfort in that notion. Question is, do you really want to go down with me?"

"Yes. Because I want to see him pay for what he did to my mother and possibly my father."

"Very well. I will accept that answer for now and give you another chance to leave when we reach Iatan. But for tonight"—he took her wrist—"let's not think about it. Instead, what say you we return to the cabin? It's getting late, and you need some rest. Not to mention, we don't want to run into any more company who are looking to play with you."

Thinking of Leo alone in the bed and the sailors, Morgana

agreed to leave the deck and its echoes behind and return to the relative safety of the cabin. Holding on tightly to her wrist with one hand and gripping the hilt of his sword with another, Leighton walked briskly down the steps, avoiding drunken sailors stumbling around the decks as they headed for their room. Once they made it down to the lower hall leading to their cabin, he let her go, and she shuffled behind him as he headed for the door, gasping as she saw Leo sitting on the edge of the bed, darting his eyes between them.

CHAPTER 25

# The Five of Swords

Sitting in the darkness of the dingy cabin, Leo glanced between Leighton and Morgana. Neither of them had to say a word. He could tell something happened up on the deck, but he couldn't begin to even think of what it was. Tightening his grip on the edge of the mattress, he gritted his teeth. She ran off on him and took Leighton with her—after all the talk of echoes and the ship being unsafe. If only she'd asked Leo to go with her, he would have followed and kept her safe, but that duty fell to the duke. Part of him was jealous of the man, but more than anything, he was upset with her. Ever since they were little, she'd run off without saying a word, and it was always up to him to go find her, yet she still refused to ask him for help. Finding her gaze once more, he heaved out a sigh and shook his head.

"Leo," she whispered, stepping around the duke, "what's

wrong?"

"Where were you, Morgie? Where did you run off to this late at night?"

"I went out to clear my head for a bit. I couldn't sleep in here."

"And you." He turned to Leighton. "What were you doing with her?"

"I was awake and followed her when she left to keep her out of trouble. I didn't want her to be alone when she was talking about echoes."

"I see. Well, I guess at least one of us was with her."

Getting up from the bed, Leo headed for the door. He needed some time alone to think. Not wishing to take his frustration out on Morgana or his friend, he reached for the door handle when a small hand grabbed a hold of his wrist and pulled him back. Turning around, he looked down at Morgana, glancing up at him, her eyes wide and filled with tears. He was still angry with her, but a part of him softened at seeing the remorse in her eyes.

"What do you want?"

"Where are you going, Leo?"

"I need to get some fresh air and get away from you for a bit and figure out why you can't trust me. Go back to bed, Morgie."

Without another word, he turned and went out the door, shutting it behind him. Morgana's jaw dropped, and no matter how much she tried to speak, her throat refused to allow any sound to come out. Catching her breath, she darted after him, but Leighton grabbed hold of her wrist, pulling her back into the room. Holding her in his tight grip, he looked down at her, shaking his head, frowning.

"Don't." His voice was hoarse but gentle. "Give the man some time to think. He has a point, you know. You really don't trust anyone. Tell me, are you trying to get him to give up on you?"

"No." Her voice came out as barely a whimper.

"Then allow me to give you a word of advice, as your friend." He let go of her wrist and lifted her chin up to look at him. "Start lowering the walls you have built around yourself. I know people have hurt and let you down in the past, but not everyone is out to get you, especially not those of us who care about you. You need to start letting your friends in, and especially Leo, if you wish to keep him."

*What would he know about trust? It's not something one gives away so easily, not when they know that everyone is out to hurt them. That is our destiny.*

"I try, Leighton, I do. But I find it so damn difficult sometimes, even when I *know* I should trust those closest to me."

"You think I don't know how hard it can be?" Leighton gave her shoulder a squeeze. "Did you forget who you were talking to? Did you think it was easy for me to tell Lafreya about my curse and show her what my hand looks like?"

"No," she sighed. "I can't imagine it was."

"But I still did it because I care about her. I never wanted to mislead her, and as much as I wished to hide that part of me from her, I knew it wouldn't be fair to her. And right now, you are hiding a lot from the captain, and it needs to stop. You need to start being honest with him if you want him to stick around. I know he's stubborn when it comes to you—I've seen it firsthand. But even he might give up eventually, and I'm guessing that is not what you want."

"Not at all." Morgana shook her head and met Leighton's stony gaze. "And you're right, I need to be more open with him. But the best I can do is try, because right now I don't even trust myself."

"All right." Leighton wrapped an arm around her and pulled her in for a tight hug. "Start one small piece at a time, and you'll get there. But for now, why don't you go back to bed? You need to sleep, and I'm sure Leo will be back shortly."

"Actually"—Morgana looked at the door—"why don't you go to bed? I want to go sit by the window and think a little more."

*What are we going to think about? How to push everyone away from us? You seem to be remarkably good at it already.*

"Fine." Leighton gave her a soft smile and wiped a stray tear away. "Just don't stay up too long."

"I won't."

Walking away from him, Morgana curled up in the chair by the window and pressed her knees to her chest while Leighton returned to his hammock. Looking at the shadow sitting beside her, she rolled her eyes at the grin on its face. She had always found interpersonal relationships difficult, but Leighton was right: she couldn't keep people at arm's length all the time, especially not Leo. Not wishing to think about it any further, she turned away and glanced at the swell of waves rise and fall outside the window. Thinking of what she could do to remedy the situation, her eyes flooded with tears, and her eyelids grew heavy. Before she knew it, she was drifting off into a deep sleep with the rhythmic lull of the ocean outside the window.

Barreling out onto the deck bathed in moonlight, Leopold slammed his fist into the wood planks of the wall with a roar, pressing his head beside it. Smoldering with resentment at his last words to her, he pondered why she couldn't fully trust him. After everything they've been through since they first met, he had been the one person to know her the best, but there were still parts of her he couldn't reach, no matter how hard he tried. Every time he made it over one wall, he simply found another one he'd have to climb. But then he recalled what the old witch told him back at her hut, and he sighed. Morgana was almost impossible to be with, but he refused to give up on her, not after he made it this far.

Tilting his head up toward the sky, he pondered how he should approach her next. The direct approach has usually worked in the past, but back then he at least knew what the truth was—here he was lost. No, he figured a gentle approach would be best this time around, and that given enough time, she may just let him into that turbulent, dark world of hers. Turning on his heels, he walked back down the stairs, hoping to apologize to her for their last conversation and assure her that he'd wait for her to open up.

When he reached the cabin, the latch to the door seemed to have conspired against him and refused to budge. He rattled it for a few minutes until it finally gave, allowing him inside. The room beyond was dark, barely lit by the ghostly spray of light fanning in through the porthole window. To his left, Leighton lay sleeping in his hammock, and in the chair across sat Morgana, slumped against the wall, deep in slumber. He wondered if she fell asleep waiting for him to return, and regret filled him at taking so long up on deck. He kneeled beside the chair and peered at her face, brushing the strands of hair draping her cheeks with his fingers.

She shifted slightly with his touch, but she did not wake, and on her skin he could make out the dried splotches of tears.

His heart twisted—he hated making her cry. He scooped her ragged body into his arms, lay her down on the bed, curled up beside her, and draped his arm, pulling her close. From a sleepy haze, she murmured his name in a pained voice, her lips flinching slightly. His heart continued to thump wildly in his chest, and he buried his face in her silky aubergine hair. In that moment, he decided that whatever she was hiding didn't matter much, so long as she was with him. Tightening his grip around her, he pondered what the morning would bring and if they could survive the journey together—or if the prophecy from years earlier would come to pass.

CHAPTER 26

# The Two of Chalices

Stirring to the gentle rocking of the ship, Morgana shot up once she realized she was lying on the covers of the bed. She recalled drifting off to sleep the previous night and wondered how she wound up sleeping in bed. Figuring Leo must have put her there when he returned, she placed her face on his pillow, deeply inhaling the subtle woody scent still clinging to the fabric. A tingle of warmth ran down her neck, and then she recalled the previous night, and wretched, ugly feelings rose to the surface. Her mouth felt like clay at the memory of what Leighton told her. Thinking she needed to clear things up between her and Leo, she frowned, got up, and glanced about the room. In the corner, the hammock swung empty, and by the chair she fell asleep in sat the Heartseaker, resting against the wall, sending a kaleidoscope of light across the teakwood floor.

Figuring Leo was still avoiding her, she left the cabin and began her search for him. Starting with the mess hall, which she found completely empty aside from the echoes, she thought about what to say to him when she found him. She was terrified at the thought of telling him the truth, but she kept looking for him, making her way outside. She walked up the stairs, where the echoes lingered and reached out to her, then strolled onto the deck, which was awash in the warm sun. Standing at the center, she listened to the thrum of the waves and the squawking of gulls fusing with the chattering of passengers, hoping to catch Leo's voice among them. Shielding the sun from her eyes with her hand, she surveyed the mingling crowds for her companions, then spotted Leighton leaning on the railing, viewing the specks of land in the distance. She heaved out a sharp breath and strolled over to him.

"Morning." She tapped him on the shoulder. "Have you seen Leo?"

"Yeah." Leighton tilted his head to look at her, thumbing over to his left. "Saw him over on the quarterdeck not that long ago. I didn't see him come down, so he must still be there."

"Thanks." Morgana turned to walk away. "I'll go find him then."

"Hey." Leighton grabbed hold of her wrist, spinning her around to look at him. "Remember what we talked about last night. You don't have to let him in all at once, but you have to start somewhere."

"All right." She gave him a smile. "I'll try to keep that in mind."

Morgana turned and strolled up the steps. The quarterdeck was almost empty except for the man sitting on the floor, leaning up against the mast. He looked pitiful, with his shoulders sagging, his head dangling between his knees. Taking care to not make a sound, she moseyed over to him, gathered up her skirt, and sat down beside him. Leo turned to look at her and his eyes shot up, then he quickly darted his head back down without saying a word. She knew she'd have to open up to him, as Leighton said, and she placed her hand over his, giving it a gentle squeeze.

"I take it you were the one who placed me in the bed last night." She glanced over at him, but he simply nodded his head in reply. His lack of response made her throat tighten and go dry. "I see . . . are we no longer on speaking terms?"

"It's not that," he mumbled. "It's just . . . I don't know what to say to you."

"Well," she sighed, "you can start by telling me what's bothering you."

"You really want to know?" He looked at her, and she nodded. "Fine. It's your need to always run away from me."

"I don't run from you, Leo. I only run from myself."

"That makes things even worse. If you only told me what's eating away at you, I could help you, but you don't trust me enough to do so."

"It's not that I don't trust you." She swallowed the lump in her throat. "I just don't want to burden you with my problems."

"Is that what you think? That you are a burden?" He frowned at her, and she nodded once. "If only you knew how wrong you were. If you were such a burden, I wouldn't have spent all my free time with you. And, if you only let me into your world once in a while, you'd know that. It's like that time when you ran away from home, when you thought that everyone hated you. If only you trusted me or Lafreya back then, you'd have known how much we all love you."

"I know"—she cast her gaze to the ground—"and for you, I'm willing to try."

"That's all I ask."

Smiling, Leo cupped the back of her head, pulling her in for a soft kiss. He always made her feel safe, but the looming threat of death still scared her, as well as her connection to the demon king. Parting his lips from hers, he pressed their foreheads together. He held her close, and she wanted to tell him everything—when a firm hand grabbed hold of her arm, yanking her away from him. Falling back onto the planks, Leo looked up in time to see Morgana whirl around and come face to face with the lanky, pockmarked man with a scar across his eye. Her face paled at the sight of him, and she struggled in his grip as echoes surrounded her.

"What do we have here?" the man snarled at her. She gagged at his rotten breath. "If it isn't the nasty little witch who gave us all a burning crotch itch last night." He yanked her arm, causing her to cry out from the painful grip. "I think my boys and I have a few things to discuss with you, harlot."

"Leave her alone, ruffian."

Leaping to his feet, Leopold rushed for the man holding Morgana when a colossal fist slammed into his gut and stopped him in his tracks. His diaphragm spasmed as the air was forced out of his lungs. Clutching his midsection, wheezing, he collapsed on one knee. Gasping for breath, he looked up to see the giant with the molten head cracking his knuckles. The enormous fist came down again, striking him in the face, sending him crumpling to the ground. The echoes of the murdered women gathered around him, crying out in pain.

"Stay out of this, pretty boy," the scarred man sneered. "Your whore has some unfinished business with us."

"Say, Rowan," the stout man kicked Leo in the ribs and pulled a switch blade from his pocket. "Want me to carve up that face of his?"

"Please do, Pasco." The pockmarked man curled his lips to reveal his green teeth. "Let's see if this slag still fancies him when he looks like us."

"You bastards," growled Morgana. "How dare you hurt him."

Watching Leo writhe behind her, a fiery glint flashed in her eyes, turning them a blazing shade of rubellite. Grinding her teeth, she let out a growl and stomped on her captor's foot. Yowling, he released his grip on her, bouncing on one leg while holding his foot with both hands. She then turned to the other men flanking her, and the air surrounding her grew oppressive. Dark tendrils of mist swirled under her feet, and she peeled her lip back into a sneer.

Focusing on the stocky man with the knife, she flicked her wrist. With a crunch and a howl, the man dropped his blade to the ground with a clang. A splinter of his radius and ulna peeked through the flesh, and blood squirted out of the wound, splattering on the planks by his feet. Ignoring the burning ache in her fingers, she twirled her hand, and with a harsh pop, the assailant collapsed to the ground, shrieking, his right foot pointing in the wrong direction.

A sharp pain shot up from her arm to her shoulder, but she paid no attention to it; instead, she turned to the purple-faced man backing away from her. Turning her hand around, she clenched her fingers, and the scarred man bellowed as an invisible hand took possession of his balls. Jerking her arm down, she severed the testicles from the body. Hayrig fell to the ground with a bloodcurdling wail, grabbing onto his crotch. Smirking at her handiwork, Morgana drew her hand close to her chest and pushed out, flinging the sailor away. The man ruptured through the railing and hit the deck below with an echoing thud. Gasps and whispers from other passengers drifted up to her ears.

Morgana licked her lips as she whirled around to face the pockmarked man, whose sweat glistened on his face. A dangerous glimmer flashed in her eyes. Lifting her arm, her dark violet hair flew behind her, and she clenched her fingers, grasping his throat in her phantom grip. The man put his hands up, desperately trying to free himself, but his struggle was useless. Raising her arm above her head, she dragged him into the air as he thrashed against her attack, and the familiar shadow creeped out from behind her, nodding in approval.

*That's right. That's my girl. Show him what you are. Let him taste your power. Make that degenerate regret ever messing with you.*

"Morgana," Leo coughed. Clutching his midsection, he staggered to one knee, looking at the man dangling in the air. "Please," he begged, "stop. You'll kill him."

"That's the intent," she hissed through clenched teeth. "Scum like him deserve to die."

*They do, Morgana, they do. Men like him don't deserve the oxygen they waste. Think of all the women you are saving by disposing of this piece of human garbage. Think of all the women he raped and killed. Break his neck and be done with this scoundrel.*

"Please . . . this isn't you."

*Oh, but this is you, Morgana, the real you. He knows nothing of who you are. He doesn't know what you are capable of. Go on, kill that disease-riddled bastard. Show the captain what you can do.*

Hearing the demon's words caused the pulse to throb in her temples. Her body grew hot with a cold sweat. She watched the man in her grasp kicking at the air. His eyes bugged out of his blue face; his swollen tongue convulsed between his lips. Then she turned back and looked at Leo, who was kneeling on the ground, the bruise blooming on his face as he gasped for air. She thought of all the things the vile man threatened to do—and everyone he had hurt before her. The demon had a point. The world was better off without this man in it, but after another glance at the pleading look in Leopold's eyes, she found herself unable to kill him. Leo was always her anchor. He kept her darkness at bay and calmed the rage inside her, even if he didn't know it yet.

"No," she whispered to the shade. "You're wrong."

*What did you say? You're not actually thinking of sparing this criminal, are you? You can't be this weak, Morgana. I know you. I know what you've done in the past.*

"No, you know nothing. Leo's right." She unclenched her hand, and Rowan dropped to the ground, flailing, and gasping for breath. "This isn't me. I'm not a killer. I'm better than this."

*That so? Well, you just wait. You'll regret this in a minute. Your love for Leopold will destroy you one day.*

"You filthy wench." Rowan caught his breath and leaped to his feet, lunging for her. "I'll kill you, you dirty witch whore."

"No,"—the tip of Leighton's sword pointed at his jugular notch—"you won't."

"You again," Rowan barked. "Why are you protecting that witch? Her kind should be burned. We all know this."

"And where, may I ask, do you think we are?" The duke chuckled, pressing the sword into his skin, causing a bead of blood to trickle down the man's chest. "Do you think this is Perdetia or something? Witch-burning has been outlawed everywhere else for the good part of fifty years now. And even if it wasn't, we are in neutral waters. It's up to your captain to decide what he wants to do, and I think he wants you to join your buddies in the brig for the duration of the voyage." Leighton waved his hand, and a set of sailors rushed up the deck to collect the men. "Seems to me like you and your buddies were never popular with the crew. They can't wait to hand you over to the authorities in Iatan."

Rowan thrashed in the grips of the sailors dragging him down behind his blubbering friends. Watching them vanish from sight, Leighton sheathed his sword and turned to look at Morgana. She was helping Leopold off the ground, and he went over to assist them, taking hold of one of his elbows.

"Getting yourself in trouble again, I see?" He steadied Leo on his feet and smirked at Morgana. "Can't leave you alone for a minute, can I?"

"What can I say?" She trembled from the pain burning her body. "I have a knack for finding trouble."

"That you do. And as for you, Captain, why don't you have your sword on you? I thought you never take it off."

"Hey, now." Leo straightened out with a wince. "My mind was a bit preoccupied this morning. Not to mention, I didn't expect to be fighting thugs on a passenger ship, of all places."

"Ships are the most dangerous places, my friend. And, may I

add, those sailors sure worked you over. It's a good thing we have the healing salve Morgana got us. How about I help you back to the cabin where she can treat your wounds . . . in private?"

"I think that's a fine idea." Leopold grimaced, clutching his ribs. "I think I've had enough excitement for one trip."

Flanking Leo on both sides, Leighton and Morgana steadied him as they walked him down the steps. Even before his feet hit the bottom landing, his stomach cramped, and his breakfast crept up his throat. His world spun and he broke away, rushing for the railing. Leaning over the side, he spewed the contents of his stomach into the ocean before collapsing on the deck, clutching his side. Then he glanced up at Morgana's horror-stricken face through blurred vision while his head swam, making his stomach churn again.

"Leo." She kneeled beside him, brushing his hair out of his face. "Are you all right?"

"No," he groaned, "I feel like I need to throw up again."

"Damn it." Leighton clicked his tongue, crouching beside them. "I think that punch to the face did a lot more damage than we expected." Digging in his pouch, he pulled out a small white ball of painkiller and placed it between Leo's lips. "Here. Take this. It will make you feel better and make the pain go away."

Leaning his head back against the wood, moaning, Leopold closed his eyes and took in shallow, ragged breaths while the medicine worked. Tremors continued to rattle down his spine. He felt drunk until the sensation slowly faded away and the twisting in his stomach stopped. He pried open his eyes and met Morgana's gaze, smiling at her. The crease in her brow made his heart stutter, and his cheeks flushed at the thought of her worrying over him. Still clutching his throbbing ribs, he grabbed hold of the railing to pull himself up, and Morgana and Leighton rushed to his side to grab hold of him, worried he might fall over again.

"I'm all right," he croaked. "Whatever Leighton gave me is working. I think I'll be fine now."

Exchanging worried glances, his two companions took hold of each side, in case another bout of sickness hit, and gently guided him to the stairs leading below the decks. A din of whispers reverberated around them as they walked to their cabin—mostly talks of what transpired on the quarter deck and what would have happened if Morgana wasn't a witch. The trio ignored all of them, even the occasional stares sizing them up as they passed. Reaching their room, Leighton opened the door and helped Leo onto the bed, strolling over to hand Morgana the jar of healing salve.

"Here you go." Leighton placed the balm in her hands. "I swear, you two will be the death of me. Is this your idea of revenge? Are you still upset at me for asking you to teach me how to please Lafreya in bed that one time?"

"Oh, I'm not mad at you." She grinned. "But perhaps it's a cosmic joke for involving me in your relationship with my friend."

Leighton smiled. "Well, don't get used to it. Go take care of the captain, will you? It looks like your sailor friends really worked him over. I'll give the two of you some privacy for now."

"Why? What are you going to do?"

"I have to go talk to the ship's captain. Make sure those rapists and killers get what they have coming to them once we dock. After that, I just want to breathe in some fresh air and figure out our next move. Plus, you and Leo could use some alone time." He gave her a playful wink. "You have until dinner to sort out things between you."

Walking out of the room, Leighton left Morgana and Leopold alone with a lot of spare time on their hands. Inspecting the bottle in her hands, she turned on her heels and faced Leo, who was reclining in bed, sweeping her with his gaze. She sat beside him and took hold of his chin, tilting his head to the side, frowning at the bright red bruise that screamed at her from the side of his face. He gave her his sheepish grin, and she shook her head, opening the salve, taking a hefty dose into her fingers. She rubbed it on his face, and he flinched with her touch.

"Am I hurting you?"

"No," he said, wincing, "it just stings a bit."

"All right. In that case, I'm going to need to take your shirt off next."

He grinned at her. "Why, Morgie, I've been waiting to hear you say that. You can strip my clothes off any time you wish."

Rolling her eyes, Morgana drew in a deep breath, thinking that this was how he always was. Leo always made jokes to ease the tension and always played down his injuries so she wouldn't fuss over him. Shaking her head, she reached for the shirt tucked into his pants. She worked her fingers under the cotton fabric and yanked it out from the waistline, then slowly dragged it over his head, assessing the angry red splotch on his ribs. She tossed the shirt to the floor by the bed, then reached up to touch the hot skin, and he recoiled. His ribs were bruised and would take a while to heal, even with the salve. Grumbling, she scooped up the balm, gently working it into the injured area until his breath relaxed and he stopped shaking.

Closing the jar, she stood up and started to walk away when he grabbed hold of her wrist and pulled her back down. Landing in his lap, she looked up as his arms wound around her waist, drawing their bodies closer. The heat from his body cut through the fabric of her dress, making her tingle with desire, and she pushed to get away. He responded by tightening his grip, bringing her even closer. She felt the stiff flesh in his pants poke her in the thigh. Her eyes locked on his, and her breath hitched. Their faces were inches apart, and his sweet breath fanned her collarbone.

"So, Morgie." He leaned down to kiss her neck. "Are you going to tell me what's bothering you? After all, you let me touch you like this." He slipped his hand under her skirt, caressing her thigh. "I feel you tremble with delight. You don't recoil for me like you do for everyone else. And"—he rolled her over onto the mattress, pressing his body against hers—"you allow me to strip your clothes off. So, what will it take to get you to bare your soul to me?"

"Time." She wrapped her arms around him. "Only time can undo all the damage done."

"Fine." He teased her mouth open, taking hold of her tongue, pulling it into his mouth. "You can have all the time you need. But you need to give me something. At the very least, you need to tell me why I see such turmoil in your eyes. What are you afraid of?"

Running her fingers through his hair, Morgana searched his face, which remained unchanged. Around her, the room hung in weighty silence. The echoes had vanished, but a darkness still lingered. She could almost see the hand of death reaching out for them, threatening to take him from her, and her heart slammed in her chest. The demon king had already stolen her birth parents, her best friend, and now she could almost see him plotting to take Leo as well. She didn't want to admit to him how much she feared for him, but recalling Leighton's words, she closed her eyes and took in a deep breath.

"Losing you," she finally said, then fluttered open her eyes. "I don't want the demon king to steal you from me like he has everything else."

"I won't allow it to happen." He rolled off, wrapping her in his arms. "I'll do everything in my power to stay alive."

"I sure hope so."

Swallowing her doubts, Morgana put her head on his shoulder and wrapped her arms around his waist. He held her tighter and pressed a kiss to the top of her head. Tears welled up in her eyes. Her fate card was an ominous one, which threatened destruction and upheaval, but his card was there to rebuild her—that much she knew. But what if she was wrong? She never once asked him what his card was. She only assumed she knew because of the connection she felt between them. Not daring to ask him, she pressed herself closer and cried silently while he comforted her until Leighton returned to the cabin. She pushed her fears aside for the duration of the trip.

The healing salve helped, and the bruises vanished after a day, even if the ribs took longer to heal, and the rest of the trip proved to be uneventful. Word of what Morgana did to the sailors spread like flames on tinder. Passengers of the ship were either eager to thank her for bringing down the vile sailors—or they steered clear of her, fearful of what she could do in a moment of anger. In any case, after another night, their ocean voyage drew to a close, and they abandoned their cabin at the break of dawn to watch the shores of Iatan come into view on the horizon.

CHAPTER 27

# The Four of Staves

Leaning on the railing, Morgana watched with sparkling eyes as the city came into view on the molted skyline over the foaming surf. A tan tower of brick, trimmed in turquoise tile, rose to the gauzy clouds above. Pink terracotta houses sprawled around its base, broken apart only by palm trees. The ship drew closer to the dock, and Morgana's lips parted when she spotted the vast square of colorful stalls, baskets, and people in robes going about their day, the scent of spice wafting up to meet her. She had only read about distant lands back at the academy, but no books did Iatan's coastal city of Al Suljaf justice. She held her breath as the ship docked and passengers began to dismount.

Blending in with the hoard of people stampeding off the ship into the bustling marketplace, Leighton herded them to the side, glancing about for their guide who was promised to meet them. A tall, dark-skinned woman with a shaved head adorned in a gold headband of coils turned to look at them, tapped her spear on the ground, and approached. Endowed on the top and bottom, she sashayed her hips as she walked, her golden chain dress clicking against her solid glistening thighs. Stopping to tower before him, she grinned at Leighton with porcelain white teeth, studying him with her umber eyes.

"Grand Duke Leighton Charmant of Bragburg, I presume?" Her commanding voice boomed through the docks.

"You assume correctly." He bowed. "And you must be Dengele of X'aris, Sultan Rasil's new bride."

"Indeed. We both hope to foster a happy relationship between our nations with this union. And the people in your company"—she glanced behind him— "are these your friends?"

"Indeed. These are—"

"Don't tell me," she belted, putting a hand up to his face. "The young woman with the purple hair, pink eyes, and the skin the color of cotton must be none other than Princess Lafreya's advisor, Lady Morgana de Laurent."

"Yes . . ." Morgana twitched in surprise. "How did you know who I was? We never met."

"My older brother is Kasaru, of X'aris." Dengele grinned. "I have heard a lot about you."

Upon hearing the name of the young man she met two years ago, Morgana's eyes grew wider. The handsome advisor from X'aris was a decent negotiator, and she enjoyed the intimate time the two of them spent together, but she had Leo now and didn't want him to know about all her exploits. Feeling her cheeks grow hot at the memory of her time with Dengele's brother, she avoided the woman's face and cast her eyes toward the ground.

"Oh, I see. I didn't know the advisor of your tribe had siblings."

"He does, indeed. There are twelve of us in all, and Kasaru always spoke highly of you. He tells us that Princess Lafreya's right-hand woman looks as delicate and fragile as the petal of the druite flower, but underneath the façade lies a cunning soul and an expert negotiator. He also mentions you are skilled in other areas as well. It is a high compliment coming from a man in our tribe. I'm sure if he thought your princess would allow it, he'd make you his fourth wife." She beamed at the reddening Morgana, who was avoiding her gaze. Chuckling at the reaction, Dengele stole a glance at Leo and frowned. "And the light-haired man with eyes the color of water standing beside you? Who is he?"

"Captain Leopold Ellingham of the Perdetia Royal Guard." Leo bowed. "And I am the man who is to marry Morgana."

Dengele raised her brow. "Interesting. From what I heard, I did not expect Lady de Laurent to be the settling down type. But perhaps a small man like you is a desirable choice for a lady like her, and that is why she picked you."

"Small?" Leo exclaimed, turning to look at Morgana. "How big was this guy that you slept with?"

"About twice your size," she said, wincing, averting his gaze, "without armor."

"Twice my size?" Leo yelped and fell back in shock. "Well, dang, I suddenly feel inadequate being by your side."

Leighton clapped him on the back. "Don't be. Morgana chose well with you. I can't think of a better match for her."

"What the duke says is true." Dengele nodded her head. "Our mating rituals would break such a delicate woman. A man from her own country is more suitable to her, and you are the best specimen I've seen from Perdetia thus far."

"Thank you . . . I think."

"Come, let us not talk of the past any longer. My husband has a lot to discuss with you, and Tel Hillar is a two-hour elephant ride away." She turned, waving her ebony hand. "Follow me, my friends. We have prepared a feast for you that you will not want to miss."

Morgana took hold of Leo's hand and squeezed it to reassure him that Kasaru meant nothing to her. The two followed Leighton, who trailed behind their host as she led them to a set of wooden stairs propped up against a massive gray beast. She had never seen a sight as strange as this wrinkled creature, with ears the size of sails and a tube for a nose, which it raised in the air, letting out a trumpet-like sound. Stunned, she timidly stepped back, but Leopold tightened his grip, calming her nerves, and she saw the red-and-gold blanket on the beast's back, upon which sat a tent-like structure.

Dengele climbed the stair, then sat inside the platform, waving them on. Morgana watched Leighton scale the steps to sit on the monstrous animal and reluctantly climbed up behind him. Sitting by a small railing, she glanced down, and a bead of sweat trickled down the back of her neck. The ground below almost seemed to pull away from her. High places made her blood run cold, and she squirmed in her spot until Leo placed an arm around her shoulder, pulling her close until she could finally breathe. She reminded herself that somewhere in the desolate sandscape of Iatan, Lafreya was waiting for them—and for her best friend, she was willing to face all her fears.

Placing two fingers in her mouth, Dengele let out a sharp, oscillating whistle, and the platform swayed as the elephant took a step forward, making Morgana's throat grow dry. Beside her, Leo rubbed her arm, and she melted into his embrace. They watched the terracotta houses, inlaid with colorful tiles, fade from sight and be replaced by a vast desert landscape. The iridescent air shimmered delicately among the humps of red sand, which stretched as far as the eye could see. Occasionally a patch of palms and low-lying shrubs broke apart the swelling in the dunes, but beyond that, the monotony of the landscape stretched well beyond the horizon. Studying the undulating dunes, Morgana wondered where Lafreya could be and hoped that, at the very least, the demon king gave her some shelter.

Waving her hand over her face, Morgana heaved from the scorching dry air, sucking the moisture out of her lungs. She was about to inquire how much longer they had to go when Dengele pointed her hand up and told them to look. Turning in her seat, she peered over her shoulder at the wall of white standing against the painted sky. Beyond the wall, in what she could only surmise was the center of the city, a huge white building rose from the ground. The late afternoon sun beamed and bounced off the gold dome at the center. At each corner of the behemoth, white towers rose to the horizon, which was as pale as the palace.

As they approached the walled fortress, the wooden entrance gates swung open, allowing them inside, where a large crowd of people greeted them. The elephant ambled over to a set of steps draped in red carpet and stopped, allowing them to get off. Walking down to the bottom, Morgana glanced at the felt runner, which stretched into the palace, and spotted a man in a starch-white robe and turban waiting for them at the end. Seeing Leighton, the man grinned, rushed over to him, and wrapped the duke in his single-arm embrace.

"It's good to see you again, my friend." The man with the golden-brown skin parted from Leighton, clasping his hand around his arm. "How long has it been?"

"Five years, Rasil. We haven't got together since I helped you with your crusade to unite Iatan."

"Has it really been that long?" The sultan chuckled. "Alas, it has. And how is that curse of yours progressing? You still have use of all your limbs?"

"I'm happy to report that the spread has been slow, and my left arm is still somewhat useful. But, as you can imagine, I can't be a gambling man. I must find a way to end this. Which brings me to why I'm here. I need to know if you know where the demon king is. I'm afraid that bastard took my fiancé, and I must find her."

"I see, my friend, that is grave news indeed." Rasil placed an arm over Leighton. "I think I can help you. Come. Follow me into the banquet hall, where we have a feast prepared for you, and I will tell you everything I know."

Morgana watched the sultan guide Leighton away, and at the urging of Dengele, she took hold of Leo's arm and followed them through the multifoil arch into the palace. Dust drifted lazily around the stone hallway lit by gold chandeliers, which cast haunting shadows on the walls of tiled mosaic. The whispering of their footsteps echoed off the walls as they walked to another set of foiled arches, which were decorated with intricate carvings in the stone. Beyond the archways lay a set of wood doors adorned with floral-cut panels.

Guards on either side swung open the doors, and they were led into a hall with long, low-sitting tables running along the perimeter. The sultan and his wife guided them to the table at the far end, sitting them down on the colorful velvet pillows trimmed with gold thread. A spread of food lay before them, gold plates of fruit and meats as far as the eye could see. Leighton offered Morgana a date while she listened to the murmuring waters in the azure fountain behind her. Eating the sickly-sweet fruit, she watched Leighton lean back on his cushion and regard the sultan with his piercing gaze. Their host sighed, nodded his head with a weak smile, and took a sip from his jewel-encrusted gold goblet.

"I take it you are eager to learn what I know, my friend."

"Pardon my rudeness, Rasil, but yes. I'm afraid that the wellbeing of my fiancé, my duchy, and the safety of my friends here, depends on it."

"No need to apologize, Leighton. I too would be impatient if my beloved was kidnapped and the future of my people hung on the line. So listen closely." The sultan leaned in closer to the duke, and Morgana strained her ears to hear them. "As you know, there is a tower that sits at the far edge of Iatan. My people know it as Burh Almat, or the 'Pillar of Death,' as it marks the beginning of the Black Sand Barrens. This is where the demon king is rumored to have been summoned, and some say a door to the Otherworld is still there. It is there you will have to go if you wish to confront the Devoth prince."

"I see." Leighton cradled his chin. "Tell me, how do we get to the Black Sand Barrens?"

"It's a few days journey through the desert. You exit through the western gate and ride toward the edge of civilization. After that, the road ends and you are on your own. Go in the direction of the setting sun, and you will spot the black tower on the horizon, nestled in sand dunes as black as night. It's a route fraught with dangers, and my people need me here, so I'm afraid the best I can do is loan you my best camels and some equipment for the trip. After that, it's up to you to make the journey. I'm sorry, my friend. I wish I could help more after all you did for me all those years ago."

"No need to explain, Rasil. I couldn't possibly ask you to accompany me, even if you insisted. What you are doing is more than enough, and I can't thank you enough for the information you've given me."

"Will you be able to fight your way through if you need to? You know as well as I that the desert is filled with animals that can kill you, and monsters lurking in the caverns. And that's not even mentioning what the Black Sand Barrens may hold."

"No need to worry. I have a witch and the captain of the royal guard with me. They have proven to be more than capable of taking on menacing foes. The three of us will be all right."

"I sure hope you're right, my friend. But I can't allow you to leave now that the sun has fallen. Stay here the night, as my guests. Delight in my bath house and rest up from your trip. You can leave first thing in the morning."

"I think my friends will be happy to take you up on your offer."

"In that case"—the sultan waved his hands—"my servants will guide you to your rooms, and I shall provide some garments for the lady, which will be more suitable for a trip through the desert."

At his command, two women in colorful headscarves and matching robe-like dresses came over, bowing to Morgana, then helped her to her feet. Leaving the banquet hall, they guided her down the hall to another set of carved doors, this time engraved with patterns of swirls, and ushered her into a dimly lit stone grotto. Pressing a hand to her chest, Morgana looked in awe at the cream walls glowing with the designs of light cast from the bulbous brass lanterns hanging above. Before her, steam rose from the aquamarine waters of the glistening pool, stretching the length of the room as roses bobbed on the surface. The ladies in her attendance stripped off her dress and bowed as she walked into the scolding waters of the bath, sinking below the surface to wash clean the stains of the past few days.

CHAPTER 28

# The Ten of Chalices

Nestled in the fragrant water laced with oils of jasmine and orchid, Morgana imagined herself sinking beneath the surface and never coming back up. The aches in her body melted away, and the memory of Lafreya's kidnapping felt like nothing more than a bad dream. Feeling refreshed, she emerged from the pool with a splash of water, summoning the ladies waiting for her. The servants dried her with a plush towel before dressing her in a silk black gown with silver trim, which landed just below her thighs. After slipping on a matching robe of shimmering organza that hit her ankles, she followed the ladies into her room, strolled onto the stone balcony, and waited for Leopold to join her.

Resting her elbows on the railing of white stone, she slipped a knee between two pillars and glanced down at the night-shrouded kingdom below. She watched the sand migrate across the vacant street, stopping to loiter among the stalls. Not finding anything of interest in the town, she lifted her head up to gaze at the deserted expanse of moonlit sand beyond the wall, wondering where her friend was in the vast emptiness, or if she was even still alive. Thinking of Lafreya somewhere out there in the void, she felt as if they were all specks of sand, drowning in the dunes. Suddenly a deep emptiness gripped her, and her heart lurched at the thought of it all. She could feel death more intimately than ever. Its hand was close enough to rake her spine, and she shuddered at the thought of it.

That was how Leo found her when he entered the room: standing beyond the archways framed with silk curtains, staring out into the boundless desert beyond. Watching her lean against the stone, faintly illuminated by the blooms of moonlight, he felt his pulse quicken. Ethereal moonlight bathed her in its glow, but there was a darkness around her that he could finally see for the first time. Undeterred by the storm clouds gathering around her, he snuck up behind her and wrapped her in his arms. With a breath of sentiment, she fell back into his chest, allowing him to bury his face in her luxurious locks. The scent wafting off the strands was far from her signature perfume of musky vanilla, but the exotic notes made his crotch tingle, and he let out a soft moan.

"What are you doing out here?" he mumbled into her hair. "I thought you'd be waiting in bed for me."

"I was just admiring my surroundings. I've never been outside Dresbourn before, so this entire landscape is foreign to me, but at the same time, I feel so at peace here, despite the reasons that brought us here in the first place."

"I have to admit"—he watched the sand floating beyond the palace walls—"you're right. There is something oddly serene in this desert wasteland, even if our circumstances aren't."

She smiled in reply, chasing away the shadows lurking behind her eyes, and he leaned in to kiss the top of her head before spinning her around to look at what she was wearing. Her supple breasts puckered through the silken fabric of the gown, and with the hemline as short as it was, he could not help but stand at attention for her. Running his fingers along the sparkling, sheer fabric tied with a lace ribbon below her chest, he let out a sigh, then lifted her chin with his index finger.

Leo smiled. "That outfit looks lovely on you. Is that one of the garments the sultan gifted to you?"

"It is." She trailed her fingers along the ripples in his abdomen and placed a palm on his chest. "But I'm afraid you only have tonight to enjoy it. I'll have to leave it here tomorrow morning, at least until we are ready to go home."

"Does this mean"—he pressed his lips to her forehead—"that you intend to wear it for me when we get back to your estate?"

"Maybe . . ." She winked, working her long fingers through his hair. "I guess you will just have to wait and find out."

"Ahhh, so you're just going to tease me, is that it?" He wrapped his hand around her back, bringing her in for a deep kiss as she sighed in his mouth. "Tell me something." Then he pulled away, regarding her with a pained look. "Do you think we have a chance of returning home?"

"I don't know." She cast a gaze at the desert behind her. "But I sure hope so."

"In that case"—he pulled her against him—"allow me to spend the night with you, as this might be the last chance we will ever get."

"I have a better idea." Backing him up to the bed nested in an arch carved out of stone, she pushed him down onto the white satin sheets and climbed up to sit on top of him. If they were going to die, she didn't want to think about it. "How about tonight I show you exactly where my reputation comes from?"

"And here I thought I already knew."

"Not even close." She leaned over for a kiss. "The last few times, I allowed you to have control. I haven't allowed a man to do that since, well . . ."—she chewed the inside of her lip—"you know. Since that day, I don't like feeling vulnerable. You are the first man to get that pleasure, as I trust you. But tonight, allow me to show you what happens when I get the top."

Morgana straddled him, her thighs gripped his hips. She felt the bulge in his pants rubbing up against her, making her moist. Bending down, she placed her lips over his and slid her tongue into his mouth as he fiddled around with the lace bow of her robe until he managed to slip it off her. She sucked on his lower lip, then pulled away. His hands gripped her thighs, sliding up to pucker the fabric of the silk gown that fell between his fingers. Her breath caught when his hands continued trailing up her curves, tickling her skin as he pulled the gown off and tossed it to the ground.

She placed her hand on his pecs, and her fingers slid down until they caught in the waistline of his leather pants. Slinking her body down, she ripped them off, reaching up to grasp his erection. Her expert hands worked him over in slow, steady strokes, making him grow harder. Groaning, Leo gathered the satin sheets at his sides into knots, and he looked up to watch her as she continued to work, the glisten of sweat shimmering on his forehead.

"Morgie," he moaned, "you're going to make me come before you get to show me anything."

"Don't worry"—she leaned closer to him—"I'm in full control here. Just trust me and relax."

Bringing him into her mouth, she flicked him with her tongue, and he fell back onto the mattress with a guttural groan. Working his shaft with her lips and tongue, she savored the moment as he flinched on the bed, gripping the sheets, arching his back. She released him from her grasp, then slid the curves of her soft, luscious breasts up along his sweat-slicked body until her legs draped over him and he gazed up at her, panting. Scraping his defined abdominal muscles with the light touch of her fingers, she squeezed her thighs around him, licking her lips while watching his eyes light up and his mouth open as he exhaled, his erection pressing against her.

The feel of his hot, damp skin pressing to her made a shiver run down her spine. She rocked onto him, arching her back with a soft purr. He filled her up instantly, stretching her, and she closed her eyes, swaying her hips, feeling him rub against her walls, making her even wetter than she was. Pressing her hands down on his collar bone, she undulated her hips and allowed the heat to bloom inside her. His hands shot up, his fingers dug into the flesh of her thighs as she slowly moved up and down, timing her thrusts so as not to allow him the sweet release of an orgasm.

Her breasts bounced steadily as she continued to ride him, and he pushed himself up, wrapping her in his arms as she rocked her hips. Grasping a breast in his hand, he brought it up to his mouth, wrapping his lips around it. She arched her back and moaned in response. He stroked her with his tongue, then pulled away and grasped her nipple between his teeth, giving it a gentle tug. Letting out a breathy sigh, she felt the warmth grow inside her. She gained steady tempo before throwing her head back with a shattering moan, crying out his name, allowing her scorching heat to flow out of her and pool in the soft hairs of his crotch.

Deep shadows of a sleeping city swallowed her screams, and Leo's hands wrapped around her bottom as he thrust himself deeper inside her. Pressing her hand into his collar bone, she regained control and leaned over as her hips continued to pick up speed. Clenching his jaw, he gripped her waist, meeting her with his thrusts until he could no longer control the tingling inside him. Falling into the mattress, he exploded inside her with a roar, arching his neck into the pillow while his body convulsed.

Giving him one last kiss, Morgana swung her leg over him and lay on the bed beside him, her hand still caressing his skin. Their hot sweat cooled and dried with the light breeze coming off the balcony, and he stroked her arms with his fingers while he attempted to catch his breath. Turning his head, he placed a kiss on top of her head and turned back to stare at the ceiling as she wrapped herself around him, making him shiver.

"Damn," he heaved. "I never imagined it could be like this. Do I dare ask where you learned all that?"

"From mother . . . who else?" She glanced up at him with a smirk. "She had me read the *Ways of Desire* after she learned what happened at the academy. She told me there would be more men like *him* out there, waiting to take advantage of me, so I had to learn how to gain the upper hand. And that's what I did. Wait"— her hand trailed up his side to rest on his pec— "did you think some other man taught me?"

"It may have crossed my mind." Leo turned his head away from her. "Is that so bad?"

"No," she giggled. Then she turned him back to face her with her long pointer finger. "I just think you're adorable when you get jealous, that's all."

"Is that so?" He rolled over, pinning her down, giving her a deep kiss. "Well, you better not make me jealous from here on out. My heart can't take it."

"I won't." She stroked his cheek. "I have no reason to."

"Good." He kissed her forehead before rolling off to hold her. "Now get some rest. We still have a long journey ahead of us if we are to get married. Unless, of course, you want to stay here."

"No, afraid not," she cooed. "As much as I like this place, I'd rather reclaim my best friend and return home, where we belong."

"That's what I thought."

Leaning down to kiss her forehead, Leo draped the sheets over their naked bodies and wrapped his arm around her while her head rested on his chest. The sweet aroma of jasmine and orchid floating off her hair and the hissing of insect wings outside the window made his lids grow heavy, and he plunged into a deep sleep. Watching his chest rise and fall in a flood of the moonlight, Morgana closed her eyes, draping her arm around his waist. Once again, sleep refused to take her. Dark thoughts wormed into her mind—thoughts of death and destruction. Worry over what was to come stole away her peace, and she stared into the gloom until she thought Leo wouldn't wake up.

CHAPTER 29

# The Hanged Man

The darkness of the room pulsated with the buzzing of the insects outside the window as Morgana sat on the edge of the bed and opened the nightstand. Before she took her bath, she had requested the servants leave her a potion in her room, and they came through. Picking up the bulbous vial, she brought it into the shaft of moonlight falling in her lap to study the viscous black fluid inside. The sludge was thick enough to stick to the glass but not thick enough to be chewed. Swirling the potion, she placed the bottle back into her lap, pondering what she should do next. If Lafreya were there, she would have asked her advice, but that night she did not have such luxury.

Indecisiveness crept up from her belly and settled in her throat as she stared at the muck inside and pulled open the cork. Mixing with the sweetness of the hibiscus in the garden below, the pungent scent of sulfurous mushroom burned in her nose, causing her to heave. The smell always got her, but that was not why she was afraid of taking the tincture. It wasn't even the taste of black licorice, nor the spasms of cramping pain it would cause her. None of that ever stopped her. She knew it was best to get it over with so she could sleep through the worst of it, but her hand refused to move. She was held back by something she didn't understand, and she continued to clutch the bottle in her shaking hands.

*What are you waiting for?* The shadow hissed from the corner of the room. *Hurry up and drink it. If you get pregnant, he will drop you faster than a hot chunk of coal. If you wish to stay with him, you must drink it. Go on. One gulp is all it takes.*

Glancing at the shade, she chewed her bottom lip, unsure why she hesitated. It was something she had done countless times without a moment of doubt. Confused, she returned her gaze to the vial in her hands, heaving out her stale breath. *One big swig,* she thought to herself. *One swig and I can return to sleep. The pain will be gone in the morning. There is nothing to worry about.* Halting her fragmented breath, her trembling hand went up, slowly drawing the slender neck of black ooze closer to her lips, and she closed her eyes tight.

"Wait." Leo's hand grabbed hold of her wrist, pushing it back into her lap. "You don't have to drink that if you don't want to."

"Leo?" She turned her head to look at him. He was propped up on his elbow, holding on to her hand. "But"—she glanced back at the potion—"if I don't drink this, then—"

"I know what the risks are." His thumb rubbed her wrist, and his brow creased. "I'm telling you, I don't care as long as it's with you."

*Don't listen to him. He only says that because he thinks your womb is as barren as the desert outside.* The shadow lurched from its spot, coming closer. *How many vials have you taken over your lifetime? Dozens probably. Maybe even hundreds. Certainly more than a normal woman. He probably thinks you can't bear children after drinking that much poison, but he won't stick around if he's proven wrong.* Grabbing hold of her hand, the shadow attempted to push it up, but Leo's hand pressed back down, overpowering it. *Drink it. Drink the potion. Don't let him stop you.*

"Do . . ." Morgana's voice broke. Her eyes filled with tears. "Do you even know what you're saying? What you're asking me to do?"

"Of course, I do." He reached up to caress her cheek, flicking the lone tear away. "And I understand if you don't feel the same. But for me, you're it, darling. There will never be anyone else after you, there never has been. If I didn't want this, then I'd have pulled out like I have with every other woman. Not to mention, I still intend to marry you as soon as we rescue the princess and restore order to Perdetia. Don't you understand? All I ever wanted was a life with *you*. That includes a home with children. And, if one happens before the other, then that's fine by me. So please, don't poison yourself on my account."

*He lies . . .* The demon cowered in the corner. *All men lie. You know this. He'll turn out just like your father. He'll abandon you too. They all do.*

Looking at the sincere flicker in his eyes, Morgana's heart pounced in her throat. Her face grew hot; the vial in her hand shook violently. Soon her entire body quaked, and the tears freely fell into her lap. Sitting up, Leo wrapped her in his strong arms, pulled her close, holding her tightly, and rubbed her back until she calmed herself down. Pushing off his chest, she gazed at his face, silently questioning him with her eyes, trying to figure out if he meant what he said.

"I want this with you, Morgana." He cradled her face in his hands. "Put the potion away. We don't need it."

"Are you sure about this? Can you promise me you won't leave? That you'll always stay with me, no matter what, and that there will never be anyone else for you?"

"I'm not your father, Morgie." His blue eyes were piercing, his voice determined. "I won't walk out on you. Nor would I allow the demon king to get between us. Now, close that damn bottle before I take it and throw it out the window."

"All right." She closed the vial and slipped it back into the drawer. "I'll believe you. I won't drink the potion."

"Good." He pulled her down and lay on the bed, cradling her against his chest. "Let's go to sleep. What are you doing up at this hour of the night, anyway?"

"Thoughts of the future kept me awake."

"You need to not worry about what our future holds." He kissed her forehead. "All you need to know is that it will be a bright one, filled with children and happiness."

"And how long have you been plotting this future for us?"

He turned and smiled at her. "For the past seven years. It was one of the only things that kept me going while I was away. Haven't you ever thought of it?"

"No, can't say I have. But now that you mention it, I sure hope that if we have children, they'll look more like you and not me."

"What?" Leo knitted his brow. "And what's wrong with you?"

"Everything," she murmured, looking away. "I'm different, just like the rest of my kind, and not in a good way. I stand out in a crowd, and I hate it."

"And yet I love everything about you. The fact that you stand out is what attracts people to you. And I was sure hoping to have children that are a mix of us both." Planting a kiss on her head, he shifted his body to lie on his side so he could look at her better. "Although, that was *before* I knew you were a witch." His fingers rubbed her cheek while he peered at her through the hair falling around his face. "Do you know what our chances are of having a child be a witch, like you?"

"About half. Why? Is that a problem? Because the potion is right there."

"No problem at all. I was just hoping they were higher."

"Are you being serious right now?"

"Of course I am. There are so few witches left that I feel like it is our duty to make sure there are more. And I am more than happy to loan you my body to ensure that happens."

"You're ridiculous, you know that?"

"What can I say?" He leaned in and stole a quick kiss. "It's part of my charm."

"Hmm." She pressed her forehead against his. "I suppose it is."

Curling up in the nook of his arm among the chaos of the sheets, she tilted her head up, grazing his abdominal muscles with her fingers. Her hair fell around him like a waterfall, and the tips of his fingers stroked the warm skin of her arm. The scent of desert flowers encircled their naked bodies. She draped her leg over his and shimmied closer, gliding her hand past the bruise on his ribs to the small charm hanging off his neck. She wanted to believe him, but with death so close she could almost taste it, she needed to get something off her chest.

"I need to ask you something." She looked up at him. "I need you to tell me what your fate card is."

He smirked. "Don't you know? I thought you would have it figured out by now. It's your soul card, after all."

"So, you're the Chariot of Fire after all."

"I am." He kissed her head. "Now, will you stop worrying about every little thing and get some rest?"

"I can certainly try."

In the tranquil stillness of the night filled with the hissing and buzzing of insects, Morgana closed her eyes. A serene calmness washed over her with the knowledge that Leo was her soul card. Even if death was near, she hoped it wouldn't touch him, and she drifted off into a peaceful sleep. In her dreams, the demon king visited her once again, but a blinding darkness obscured him, and the only thing she heard was his voice, pleading with her not to follow him. The end was drawing near. Like a fortuneteller flipping her fate cards, Morgana sensed this spread was about finished and she prepared to come face to face with her destiny.

CHAPTER 30

# The Page of Swords

Before the sun split the horizon with an amber-yellow glow, the sultan's servants spirited Morgana away, leaving Leo alone in the room. Stealing a glance at the murk of dawn outside the balcony, he pulled on his pants right as Leighton walked into the room, dressed in the traditional robe of the Iatan people. He offered him a similar garment to stay comfortable in the desert, but Leopold refused, feeling more comfortable in his own clothing.

Taking a cotton head covering from the duke, he followed the man outside to the stables, where three horrible, smelly beasts were waiting for them. One such creature—the lighter brown of the bunch—side-glanced at him, snorted, and hocked a giant globule of spit by his feet. Curling his lip in disgust, Leopold looked at Leighton, who simply chuckled and pointed him to a different camel, which would serve as his ride through the desert. Leo cautiously approached the gray animal from the side and placed some equipment on its back, trying to not let the creature sense his fear. He much preferred horses to camels, and he couldn't wait to ride on the back of his stallion once more.

Before he finished strapping on the rolled-up tent, Morgana walked up behind him and ran her fingers down his back, making his spine shudder. Turning to look at her, he felt a rush of blood to his head as she peered at him from her turquoise, gold-trimmed head covering. A matching ankle-length tunic clung to her curves—not accentuating them like the bodices found in Perdetia, but making them subtle enough to let the imagination run wild. His mouth dried, and he rubbed the back of his neck, speechless as she walked over to the evil beast that spit at him earlier, which allowed her to rub its misshapen snout.

"Hey," he said, finally. "You sure you'll be okay riding by yourself? I think I might feel better if you ride with me. These things don't seem like the friendliest lot."

"I've ridden horses plenty of times. You taught me to do so, remember? And this little guy doesn't seem like he is hostile at all." She rubbed the animal's rough, straw-like hair, and it let out a strange rumbling growl before nuzzling her. "Plus, we will cover more ground if I ride my own camel and not overburden yours. As is, yours and Leighton's are carrying all the tents and sleeping pads."

"Very well." He studied her with the camel, noting how animals always seemed to love her. "Have it your way. But if you need us to slow down, say something. I don't want you to fall behind by accident."

"As if, Captain." She snorted and effortlessly swung her leg over the saddle. "The two of you best try to keep up with me."

Reluctantly Leopold did the same and nudged his beast, nearly falling off as it lurched up on its back legs. Gritting his teeth, he wished he could have his horse for the trip, but he knew even if they took the steeds with them, the nasty creature he found himself sitting on was far more suited for the environment. Spinning his camel toward the western gate, he spotted the sultan strolling out of the palace to intercept them.

"What are you doing up so early, Rasil?" Leighton said, smirking. "You wouldn't want your subjects to catch wind of this. They may think their sultan likes to work or something."

"Very funny, my friend. I've come to see you off and tell you to return safely, for I shall have a feast prepared for you in celebration."

"And what a celebration it will be, for we shall not only be celebrating our triumphant return, but the death of the demon king himself."

"In that case, safe travels, my friend. *Al qudab as'amma wadukishi.*"

"*A'n atama aktari 'baki.*"

The sultan smiled and gave them a nod before Leighton took off, heading for the gate at a light, cumbersome trot, with Morgana close behind. Squeezing the camel with his calves, Leo held on tight as the animal trotted along to catch up, swaying side to side, while the streets slowly filled up with people. Coming up to flank the duke's right side, he slowed the beast down and looked over at his friend.

"What did he say to you?"

"He said, 'Let the sun guide you and keep you.'"

"And how did you respond?"

"'May the wind bring you news of my tidings.' It's a standard Iatan exchange when one goes off on a dangerous journey from which they may not return."

"Well, hopefully these foul, evil beasts we have been given will be the most dangerous part of the journey."

Leo's camel responded with a rumble and a shake of his head, and Leighton grinned. The western gates were open and waiting for them, and they rode through them. Leaving the safety of Tel Hillar behind, they headed deeper into the unforgiving sprawl of the desert beyond. At first they passed by small settlements of tan houses built into the hills, their people walking by, carrying baskets on their head, guiding oxen along lugging buckets of water. But as the rivers dried up and sand took over, any semblance of civilization vanished and was replaced with crumbling ruins and tumbleweeds.

The sand told a sad tale, swallowing up the remains of crumbling buildings and wilting palms. The underground springs that once proliferated their civilization had run dry, sopped up by the demon king, who forced this desert's inhabitants to retreat to other sources of water. Control through resources was his specialty, and he enjoyed making people leave their homes and their lives behind to migrate into cities where he had the most control of the people. Riding past them caused Leo to clench his jaw and twist his reins in his hands. This was exactly what the demon king had planned for the rest of the world if he wasn't stopped.

By the time they left the ruins behind them, the sun was at the highest point in the sky, scorching the ground. Shimmering waves of heat rose from the sand, blasting them with stifling air, drying everything it encountered. Wrapping his head covering over his nose, Leopold squinted as the road ahead ended abruptly. Swells of scorching sand rose ahead, blocking the view of anything that lay ahead of them. Slowing their camels down, the trio rode into the tangle of dunes and pushed toward the horizon until the sand shifted, obscuring their guidance point. The beasts stopped, snorted, and protested by stomping their padded feet on the ground, refusing to go further.

"Damn." Leo put his hand up to his forehead, glancing about the ever-changing landscape. "Where to now? I can't make heads or tails of things."

"Rasil told us to go west, which would be in the direction of the setting sun, but it's high noon and the dunes are disorienting, even to me."

Leo glanced up at the sky. "So, do we just sit here and cook until we see what direction it begins to set in?"

"Men," Morgana sighed. "What would you two do without me?"

She reached behind her neck and unclasped a chain holding a small charm. Before she left to get to the camels, Dengele stopped her and gifted her the metallic gray stone. She wondered the reason behind the obelisk of onitite—a magnetic stone of the desert lands where compasses were not widely used—but now she understood the gesture. Placing her other hand over it, she focused her energy into the gem. Her skin blistered as it rose in the air and began to spin wildly. It continued to twirl above her palm until it stopped, then darted from left to right before settling slightly to the right of her hand, indicating north. Giving her camel a nudge, she pointed him slightly to her left, placing the necklace back on her neck.

"There you go. The stone points north, much like a compass from our land. So we go that way."

Exchanging glances with the duke, Leopold tapped the sides of his camels with his heels, and the foul brute ambled after her, snorting at its rider. They continued to ride, covering considerable ground with the stone continuing to point their way. By the time the sun moved halfway down the sky, they had made substantial progress and were moving deep into the heart of the arid desert. Glancing about the vast expanse of tan, Leo heaved out a dry breath. The stiff air caused his throat to grow dry. Even the camels slowed down and stumbled over the dunes, which stretched on as far as the eyes could see.

Once the sun dipped below the sand line, the desert took on surreal hues of pink and yellow, and the air cooled. The three pressed forward, kicking up plumes of dust as they went, looking for a spot to settle down for the night. They made it a few hours before a surreal gale came from out of nowhere. Sand rose like a wall, obscuring their vision and battering their faces as it swirled around them, steering their camels from the path they were on. Straining to see, Leo attempted to guide his camel back, but the churning sand made it impossible to move forward, and his face stung from it scraping against his skin. Coughing, he tightened his head covering around him and turned his camel so he could face Leighton.

"Where is this coming from all of a sudden?"

"I don't know." Leighton spun his camel around. "Sandstorms are unpredictable, but this one came out of nowhere."

"We need to find shelter, or we will be buried in this sand."

"Over there." Leighton pointed his finger, and Leo's eyes traced it to a cave glowing a short distance away. "I think we can get there."

Something about the faint yellow-green glow coming from its gaping maw, which resembled a mouth of an animal, made Leo uneasy. He didn't like the idea of spending a night in there, but it was better than taking their chances in the storm. Nodding his head, he nudged his camel forward and tried to keep up with Leighton, who was already halfway to the shelter. Pushing forward, he kept his eyes on Morgana while the sand-filled wind whipped his back. By the time they reached the pillar rising out of the sand, with its sole opening glowing in the gloom, he could barely make out her silhouette beside him.

Leaping off his smelly mount, he took hold of the reins and led the creature up the slope. Something about the cave—how it was so conveniently nearby when the storm hit—didn't sit right with him, but they had little choice but to take shelter where they found it. The inside was shallow, only about two furlongs deep, but it kept the sand out, and he immediately saw what caused the haunting glow. Above their heads, the ceiling was dotted with pulsating bioluminescent slime. Having encountered the creatures before, he knew they were harmless, and he heaved a breath of relief knowing it wasn't anything sinister. Letting the camels loose to wander deeper into the cavern, Leo set about making fire from the little kindling they had on hand, and the three of them settled down for the night while the wind continued to howl outside.

CHAPTER 31

# The Monk

Flames leaped and swayed, casting shadows onto the cavern walls, which almost seemed to take on a life of their own. Staring off into the wind-blown abyss beyond the opening by which their camels gathered, Morgana noted that the heavy surrounding air smelled faintly of bitter almonds. The entire atmosphere of their makeshift camp seemed oppressive, and she didn't like being there one bit. Huddling close to Leopold, Morgana continued to glare at the opening from which the camels had moved, retreating toward the fire, rumbling loudly in protest. The wailing from the sand-torn landscape grew louder, and a shadow figure, barely lit by the moon, peeked over the drop in the cavern before it vanished.

"Did you see that?" She jolted in her spot.

"See what, love?"

"The shadow that entered the cave."

"I didn't see a thing." Leo frowned, looking at the narrow slit in the stone. "Are you sure the light wasn't playing tricks on your eyes?"

"I don't think so. I feel it in here with us."

"She's right." Leighton jumped to his feet, drawing his sword. "My cursed arm is tingling. Something is here with us, and it reeks of the demon king." Tightening his grip on the hilt, he walked closer to stand beside his companions. "Stop hiding and show yourself."

"Clever." A hollow voice chortled. Then the shadows on the wall twisted, churned, and melted together, morphing into a being resembling a human, but with no identifying features. "At least you know who sent me, Duke Charmant, but it's not you I've come to see. I am here with a message for your witch."

"For me?"

"Yes, for you." The creature hissed and slid across the floor to tower over her. "My master says that he warned you back in Devilwood to stay out of Iatan, but he is giving you one last chance. Take your knight, find a small village here, and settle down, live whatever life you envisioned with him. Stay out of his way, and he will not harm either of you. His fight is with the duke of Bragburg, not you."

"And what if we refuse?" Leo unsheathed his sword. "What then?"

"I'm glad you asked, knight. I was told I could eat everyone but the witch, starting with you." The shadow lurched for Leo, who brought his blade down on it, cutting it in half. The form vanished and rematerialized behind him, grabbing hold of his neck. "Foolish man. You can't kill me—you can't even hurt me, for I am immortal."

"Rubbish." Leighton brought his sword up, releasing Leo from the shadow's grip. "Voidnots are difficult to deal with, but you are not immortal." Then he turned to the woman. "Morgana, this is a corrupted soul, bound to the land by greed. If you find the object it's attached to, you can destroy it and the voidnot. They can't wander far from their possession, so it must be in the cave somewhere."

"All right. I'll look for it. You and Leo keep this thing occupied."

She went to go searching when the voidnot lunged and grabbed hold of her leg. It pulled her to the ground and dragged her across the floor before Leo's sword cut through its hand, releasing her. Scrambling to her feet, she watched the creature fling Leo across the cave by his leg and saw his body hit the wall and crumble to the floor. Leighton was quick on his feet, and he leaped in to swing his sword up at the shadow before it had the chance to suck him dry. Thinking the men could handle the monster, she turned her head to peer over her shoulder at the footpath leading deeper into the cave behind her.

Not stopping to think, she ran down the path deeper into the cave, guided only by the haunting green glow of the slime creatures above her head. Halfway down, the stifling air became so oppressive that even the bioluminescent creatures vanished, and Morgana had to form a ball of light between her palms to get enough light to find her way. The further she went, the more oppressive the energy became, and she found it difficult to breathe. By the time she reached the end and found a yellowed skeleton in rotted-out rags leaning against the wall, she felt as if a boulder sat on her chest.

From somewhere above, the sounds of the fight became more prominent. The shadow's snarls melted with metal clanking against the stone, followed by Leo's scream. Realizing her companions were in trouble, Morgana began her search for the object that held the negative energy of the voidnot. Pushing the skeleton aside, she traced her hands along the moistened stone of the wall and found a small crack. Slipping a finger into the opening, she could feel something smooth and solid, but it was too deep for her to get a hold of. The commotion from above grew silent and her heart sped up at the thought of the voidnot winning.

She tried again to pull the object closer to her, but without luck. Blowing a stray strand of hair out of her face, she placed her palms against the crack. The pulse lines beneath her were almost dry, but they would have to do. Tightening her jaw, she focused a blast of energy into the opening to break the trinket free. Sharp pain cracked her hands and spine as the stone wall flew apart, sending small chips of rocks and moss hurling past her in every direction. Using her orb of light, she crawled around on all fours, searching for the hidden object and spotted the luster of stone and metal an arm's length away.

Pulsating before her was a broach of a cabochon and sea-green aqualite encased in a gold-leaf wreath, stained with reddish-brown spots. Morgana went to take it when something grabbed hold of her leg and yanked her back. Screaming, she spun around on the ground and observed the skeletal hand of the voidnot's original body tightening around her ankle. Kicking at the brittle bone, she broke herself free and crawled across the floor to grab the broach.

Her fingers reached for the metal, but the darkness grabbed her again, pulling her back. Digging her nails into the soil, she resisted long enough to reach the object the creature was trying to protect.

Gripping the jewel in her hand, she brought down her palm and slammed it against the stone floor, cracking it. The shadow's grip loosened, and she brought the broach down again, shattering the stone. A hollow scream filled the cavern, and the bitter air rushed out past her as the skeleton disintegrated into dust, leaving only darkness behind it. Scrambling to her feet, she ran up the path, hoping to find her friends alive.

"Leo!" she screamed, "Leighton!"

Ignoring the pain in her body, she rounded a boulder and skidded to a stop in the main portion of the cave. She spotted Leighton first, crouching by the wall behind the fire, and then her heart dropped. He was tending to Leo, who was laid out on the floor, clutching his side with a grimace. His chest rose and fell in shallow strokes, and she ran to kneel beside him.

"Is he going to be all right?"

"I think he'll live." Leighton opened Leo's shirt to reveal a dark red splotch on his skin. "I think he broke a few ribs hitting the wall. They'll heal in time, and I will give him some more medicine, but he will need to take it easy."

Getting up from his spot, Leighton went to find the camels, who had wandered outside, and fetch his pouch. Left alone with Leo in the cave, Morgana felt her heart slam against her rib cage, and she reached out to take hold of his hand. Squeezing it in his, he turned and regarded her with a pained look.

"Why," he said, "why didn't you tell me it was the demon king who grabbed you in those woods?"

"I . . ." She looked away. "I didn't want you to think that—"

"That you slept with him?"

"Yes."

"It doesn't matter." His voice was pained. "Your past doesn't matter to me."

"I know." She stroked his hair. "I'm sorry I lied to you. I just didn't want you to worry."

"I always worry about you. Even when you don't want me to."

Leighton snuck up behind them. "And you can continue to worry about her when we patch you up." He dropped the supply bag on the floor, then crouched beside them and rummaged through it. "You should take the demon king up on his offer and settle down in a village nearby. You two have done enough for me as is, and I can't ask you to continue risking your lives for me."

"Never," Leo groaned. "I promised you my sword until you get Lafreya back."

"And what good are you to me now? You can barely move, and even after I wrap you up, your mobility will be limited. You are better off hiding out with Morgana until this is over. After all, that Devoth has some vested interest in her."

"More of a reason we come with you." Morgana placed her hand on his shoulder. "We are in this together until the end."

"I'm thankful to hear you say that." Leighton looked up at her as he continued to work the healing salve into Leo's skin. "But what of Leo? I don't want him to get hurt anymore because of me."

"I'll be fine," Leo groaned, sitting up. "You forget that I am used to fighting with injuries. I'll get through the pain, don't you worry. Friends stick together."

Leighton smiled. "I'm glad to call both of you friends. Now, let's get some rest. Tomorrow is another long day, and you need to heal up, Captain."

Settling down on the clay heated by the embers, Morgana cuddled up against Leo, laying her head on his shoulder and draping her arm around him. Laying in silence, she peered into the flames, catching her reflection, occasionally shuddering to think of what the demon king wanted with her. There had to be a reason why he kept trying to keep her away from him, but she couldn't think of one. She figured he had plans to kill Lafreya and Leighton, and she could not allow it to happen. He already took everything from her once, and she would not allow him to steal her friends as well. Vowing revenge against the Devoth prince, she continued to stare at the darkness beyond the cave, unable to sleep.

CHAPTER 32

# The Star

**R**esuming their journey through the landscape that never seemed to change, Morgana guided the group with the use of the onitite necklace. The dull repetitiveness of the desert made her sigh from boredom, and she longed to see the rolling hills and green forests of Perdetia once more. When she was five, she ran away from home, wishing to be anywhere else. Now, as the dust stung her cheeks, she realized everything she had ever wished for was always there. Gripping the pommel of her saddle, she hid her face from the sand and pressed on as the scorching sun burned above them.

Once the glowing orb settled behind the dunes, the bitter cold snapped at their joints, and visibility diminished, signaling it was time for them to stop. Upon finding a relatively flat patch of sand between a dense tangle of shrubs and fallen trunks of palm trees, they dismounted the camels, tying them up nearby. Morgana helped Leighton take the tents and sleeping pads off the beasts while Leo hacked away at the thorny bushes, gathering kindling for their fire. Above, waves of clouds drifted over the crescent moon, covering them with shadows as they worked.

"Do you think we are getting close?" Leopold struck the flint with his dagger, sparking a fire. "I feel like we have been in this desert forever."

"We must be very close. I can't move the fingers on my left hand anymore."

Morgana looked at Leighton. "Is . . . is your curse progressing?"

Shrugging, Leighton removed the black glove from his hand, and she yelped at the sight of it. The once gray hand was completely white and unmoving. Specks of crystal twinkled in the firelight Morgana reached out her fingers to touch the icy flesh. It was as hard and smooth as polished marble. The fingers didn't flinch, not even when she pressed on the joints. Leighton's hand had completely turned to stone, and the graying area of skin spread past his wrist, up to his elbow.

"Yeah . . . it's not pretty." The duke sighed. "I guess the curse is speeding up because we are close to the Black Sand Barrens. At this rate, my entire arm will be useless by the time we get there."

"Perhaps you and Leo should wait here. I can get Lafreya on my own."

"No way." He shook his head and put his glove back on. "She is my fiancé, and I am getting her back myself. Plus," he added, smirking, "I'm going to kill that demon bastard and break this curse once and for all. And if you go alone, he will have exactly who he seems to want—you. I won't let him take, my friend."

"Are you sure about this? You may not even make it that far with how fast this is spreading."

"I only have seven years left as is. If I don't end this, I won't be able to give my woman the child she desires, not if it means passing this sickness on. I have no choice but to try."

"He's right, Morgie, he must end this. And don't you worry. I'll be there to aid him. As for you"—he placed a hand on her shoulder—"I think it would be best if you take Lafreya with you and leave the barrens. The demon king seems awfully attached to you, and I don't want to risk putting you in danger."

"Are . . . are you really asking me to stay behind while you go fight him on your own?"

"I'm sorry, Morgie, but I don't want you near him, not when we don't know what he wants with you. I think it would be better if you allow me to handle this with Leighton."

"Know what?" She stood, huffing. "I refuse to argue with you over this. I'm coming with you whether you like it or not."

She didn't say another word as she stormed away from him, chin up, kicking sand in her wake. She wasn't angry at him for asking her to stay behind; she simply didn't wish to allow him to die without her. It was true the demon king wanted something with her, and she wanted to find out what it was before she ended him. Figuring Leo would eventually come find her, she strolled up the hill where the sand met the horizon and glanced up at the stars, which were falling from the sky.

"Morgana!" Leo called after her as she vanished from sight. He flung his arms in the air, then turned to Leighton, who was laying out a tent on the ground. "Tell me honestly. Am I being unreasonable here?"

"I don't know." Leighton looked up from the wood stake he was driving into the ground. "With Morgana, it's hard to tell sometimes."

"Fine." Leo came over to him and grabbed hold of an extra mallet. "Then tell me what you would do if this was you and Lafreya?"

"Me?" Leighton snorted and drove another spike into the ground. "I'd tie her up and leave her at that outpost we're heading for. But"—he looked at Leo with a smile—"I'm not you, and Morgana isn't Lafreya, now is she?"

"No, she's not. And she's helped keep us alive thus far. But you know, there is still a reason I don't want her to come. I fear for her safety."

"Then why not tell her that? You should go find her and tell her how you feel and why. Then you need to listen to what she needs to tell you."

"You know as well as I do what she needs to tell me."

"Yes, that she's coming with us." Leighton chuckled as he put up the center pole. "But you still need to listen to her. And who knows, maybe some miracle will happen and Morgana will come to a compromise with you."

"As if." Leo smiled. "I love her because she's impossible. But you think she's willing to talk to me?"

"I don't know. Why not go check?" Leighton smiled at Leopold, who stood up and went to walk away. "Oh, and Captain." Leo turned to him, frowning. "Can the two of you make up quietly tonight? As much as I enjoyed hearing your conquests back in

Mireworth, I'd like to get some sleep tonight."

Shaking his head with a smirk, Leo turned away and flipped the duke a finger before searching for Morgana. Her trail wasn't hard to follow; the desert lay calm, and her footprints remained in the sand where she left them. It didn't take him long before he stopped at the top of a jagged cliff overlooking the valley. At the edge, Morgana stood with her back to him, arms crossed over her chest, watching the stars streak by in the sky, leaving behind long, glowing tails. Standing behind her, Leo wrapped her in his arms and rested his chin on her head.

"You want to tell me what all this is really about, Morgie, or will you have me guessing for the rest of the night?"

"You first."

"What do you mean?"

"Don't play stupid with me, Leo. I know you. You wouldn't ask me to stay behind unless something was eating away at you. I can almost smell the fear on you, so why not tell me what it is? You always want me to be open with you, so why not be open with me?"

"All right," he sighed. "You got me. So I'll tell you. When I left for my second campaign, our party camped in the Notch of Bones. There I had an encounter with a shadelych. He showed me a dream where I had to choose between you and my career, and then he showed me your dead body. I didn't think much of it then, but when I found out you were a witch . . . well, let's just say that brought the memories of the dream back, and now I fear that if you go with us, you will end up dead, or worse, you'll leave me for the demon king. And Morgie, I can't stand the thought of spending my life without you."

"I see." She turned around and peered into his eyes. "But you must know that I would never leave you for him. He killed my mother and possibly took my father from me. I want to see him dead as much as you and Leighton do. Not to mention"—she ran her hand up his chest—"I know you'll keep me safe."

"You know I'll always be there to catch you when you fall." He wrapped his hands around her waist and pulled her closer. "But now you need to be honest with me. You need to tell me why you want to meet him, and don't say revenge, because I know that's not it."

"You're right. This isn't about him—it's about you."

"Me?"

"Yes, you." She looked him in the eyes. "I've watched the king drag you off on two campaigns which I knew were a death trap, and there was nothing I could do to help you. Every day you were gone, I held my breath and waited for any news from the field. When reports of the dead came in, my heart ached with the thought your name might be on that list. I feared the day I may see only your body return, and I prayed every night that it would never come to that. But I'm here with you now, in the most dangerous battle of your life, and for once there is something I can do about it. This time, I can stand by your side and aid you, or at least I can die with you. You say you can't spend your life without me—well, I can't spend mine without you. So please, don't put me through the hell of wondering what happened to you again. Allow me to come with you and see this to the end."

"Very well." He leaned in to kiss her. "I won't make you wonder. Tomorrow, come what may, we'll face it together."

Wrapping her arms around him, Morgana held him in the desert's stillness as the stars continued to come down around them. Death was close now; she saw its outline standing beside her, waiting to claim whoever it came for. Bracing herself for the inevitable of what the next day would bring, she took Leo back to the tent for one final night before they had to face the demon king. Falling asleep in his arms, she met the Devoth prince once more, and once more he bargained with her. This time, he promised to return Lafreya to them and allow them to return to Perdetia. Sensing he was desperate, she once again refused and prepared herself for the fall that was to come.

CHAPTER 33

# The Enchantress

**S**nuggled up to Morgana, Leopold forgot he was in the desert—and the reason they were there to begin with. Instead he dreamed of having her in his bed back at the barracks of Perdetia, where they were both safe and Lafreya was queen. It wasn't until Leighton's voice drew him from his slumber that he remembered where he was—and that the princess was far from safe. Grumbling at the realization, he stole a glance at the woman next to him and smiled as the specks of sand glimmered in the deep purple strands of her hair. Even if he was to die in a few hours, he'd have his memories of her, and that was enough to keep him going. Nuzzling her neck, he kissed her clavicle, and she stirred. Her eyelids fluttered open, and she pulled him in, pressing her soft lips against his. He could have remained there with her for the next few days, but duty called, and they dressed and left the tent to see the duke loading up his camel.

"Glad to see you two made up." Leighton strolled over to help take down their tent. "How did you sleep?"

"Well enough, I guess." Leo gathered the tent parts into a pile. "I have sand places it doesn't belong, but aside from that, it wasn't bad."

"You know, Leopold. It helps if you sleep with your clothes on." Leighton winked at his friend. "Now come on. We have a trap to walk into, and afterward you can be with your lady in places where sand won't bother you."

"Your Grace"—Leo smiled—"you must be stressing out about the last leg of our journey if you are giving me a hard time."

"You've finally caught on to me, Captain." Leighton loaded up his camel. "But you are right. I am afraid. Something about this whole thing doesn't sit right, and I worry one of us won't make it out alive."

Leo patted him on the back. "We'll all make it through alive. We have to. We didn't come this far only to fall here."

Watching the men load the camels, Morgana swallowed down the bitter fear building inside her. Death lingered at her side, and she knew it would claim someone in a few scant hours, and she feared who it could be. She couldn't see the fate line on her hand, but she felt it getting tighter. This was where the fate of her card played out. One way or another, her world would crumble around her, and she would simply have to face it. Biting her lip, she mounted her camel and set off in the direction the necklace pointed to, drawing closer to the demon king and his hostage. Leighton said there would be a small outpost about a mile outside the Black Sand Barrens, and they made haste to reach it before the sun was at its highest point in the sky, which would make foot travel difficult.

Traversing the barren dunes, their camels stopped before a low-lying valley with a crater and refused to proceed any further. Puzzled, the trio jumped from their saddles and glanced around, but aside from a lone tumbleweed rolling along the flat pass of the shelf, they could see nothing that would spook the beasts. Leaving the animals behind, they made their way into the crater, sliding along the sand. Stopping in the center, Leopold placed his hands on his hips and muttered curses under his breath. He was about to drag his way back up the dune and force the foul creatures down—when suddenly the ground beneath his feet quaked.

Morgana yelped and looked at him wide-eyed. Beside her, Leighton frowned and unsheathed his sword. The sand beneath their feet funneled downward into a deeper crater, dragging them down with it. Gripping the sides of the collapsing wall, Leopold pulled himself out and grabbed Morgana's hand, dragging her onto the flat surface despite the pain from his ribs. In the depression below, sand blew up like a fountain while the ground shook and something huge burst from the hole. Sand and stone showered them as the creature collapsed beside them, rocking the earth. Leopold's face drained of blood at the sight of the thing that came from the crater.

Part of the giant, slimy, segmented body was still buried in the sand, but the parts that were exposed were enough to make him gag from the foul stench they produced. Even partially covered in sand, the monster stood as tall as a Perdetia battle tower. Small, bristly hair covered every cylindrical portion of the monster's tubal

*Cards of Fate* ✤ 283

body, helping propel it along the ground. Twisting around to face them, the creature let out a guttural squawk, which shook the valley, making the camels flee. Opening its wide, circular maw, it revealed rows of needle-like teeth spiraling their way down the gullet. Leo pushed Morgana behind him and retreated to regroup with Leighton, never once taking his eyes off the monster wiggling in the ground.

"What is that thing?" He drew his blade, spinning it in the air.

"That, my friend, is the legendary death worm of Iatan. Rasil and I faced one years ago when I was helping him to unite the land under his rule. Don't let your guard down around it. These guys are slow but powerful. We'll need to work together to take it down."

The men flanked the worm, taking caution to not fall into the funnel of sand from which it emerged. Seeing this, the beast thrashed from side to side, and they barely had time to avoid its blows. Leo was struggling to wield his sword, clutching his injured ribs with one arm as he swung his blade to strike the worm's sides. Standing a safe distance away, Morgana raised her hands in the air, forcing a rope of sand to rise from the ground and wrap itself around the beast, keeping it down. Grabbing the opportunity, Leopold turned and slashed the worm with his sword. The creature screeched as rust-colored blood squirted to the ground, filling the air with the caustic scent of ripe carrion.

Gagging on the bile coming up her throat, Morgana tried to keep her hold on the worm, but a rush of air to her head blurred her vision and caused her ears to ring. Her body swayed as the light narrowed before her eyes, forcing her to drop her hands. Pressing her fingers to her throbbing temples, she glanced up in time to see the monster, still bleeding, open its jaw and lunge down for Leo, who was bent over from the pain. Jumping from her spot, she ran to him, pushing him out of the way right before the tooth-filled trap clamped around her, swallowing her whole.

"Morgana!" Leopold howled.

Grabbing the hilt of his sword with both hands, he gritted his teeth past the pain in his side and rushed the beast. He dragged the tip of the blade against its side, covering himself in its rancid blood in an attempt to cut it open. The monster reeled with a low groan, spun around, and tilted its serpentine body back. Leo stood below it, his lungs stinging, and he raised the blade above his head, waiting for the worm to fall on top of him. The tip of the sword almost touched the glistering red flesh when Leighton grabbed his shoulder and yanked him back, sending him falling to the ground just as the worm slammed down, sending out a shock wave and causing his broken ribs to throb with blinding pain.

"Are you insane?" Leighton growled. "Or are you trying to get yourself killed?"

"I'm trying to get her out!" he screamed. "That thing ate Morgana."

"And you think becoming a stain on the sand will get her out? That thing weighs as much as a building. It will crush you. Only way to cut open a death worm is from the top."

Staggering to his feet, Leopold clutched his side and glanced up at the worm. The pain in his ribs was barely tolerable, but he took in a deep breath and nodded up at the duke, who understood the plan. Leighton then began jabbing the beast in its side, and the worm spun around to face him, oblivious to the knight. Running along the side, Leo jumped on its back and made a dash for the head.

At the apex of the crown, four beady black eyes rolled up to look at him, and he drove his blade into the cavity between the head and the neck. The monster responded with a resounding roar and thrashed around, trying to shake him off. Hanging on to his hilt, he tried to regain his footing, but as the pain in his ribs spread through his body, he knew he needed to let go. Yanking the blade out, he slid down the segmented back and fell into the crater as the beast suddenly stopped moving.

Scrambling out of the pit, he stole a glance behind him as the worm made peculiar thrashing motions while continuing to growl. Its body expanded at the center, swelling to abnormal proportions until it burst open, sending putrid blood and meaty, blood-buttered chucks of flesh falling around them. Wiping the blood, sweat, and sand from his face, he ran over to where the body lay and spotted Morgana on her hands and knees, coughing in a puddle of murky green and rust-colored goo. Sheathing his blade, he slid down to her, grabbed her out of the slime, and brought her into his arms, squeezing the air out of her with his hug.

"You're alive," he sobbed. "I can't believe you survived that."

"I put a shield spell up right before it grabbed me." She pulled back, flicking the tear off his face. "I knew it wouldn't hold long, and it started to fade after a few minutes, so I figured I would try expanding it, hoping it would irritate him enough to regurgitate me, but I guess it exploded him instead. And boy, am I glad it did."

"You have no idea how relieved I am to see you. I thought I'd lost you."

Leighton strolled down to join them. "Yeah, he was a mess. I'm glad you're out, even if we all smell like death now."

"I don't suppose there is a shower at that outpost?" She looked at her stained clothes, remembering her vision of Leo's blood-sleeked face, which she had just now witnessed. "I can only imagine this will get worse with the sun."

"Afraid not. But if we hurry, maybe we can make it to the tower before we begin to smell like a grave of a thousand corpses."

"Sounds like a plan." Leo spit out sand. "And where is this outpost, may I ask?"

"I don't know. I was told it was a mile from where the sands begin to change."

Morgana gathered the camels, which had returned. "Gentlemen, I think I can help. Look there."

She pointed her finger behind them at the black roof poking up just above the dunes opposite of him. Dark clouds swirled above its peak, flashing with ominous sparks of blue. The Tower of Death was visible from where they stood, the same tower Morgana saw in her nightmares for years. The demon king had been teasing her all along, showing her the extent of his power. The group mounted their camels and carried on, using the pillar for guidance until they found a washed-out road leading to where the tan grains of the desert melted with dunes that were black as coal.

After a short distance, they came down the hill where a small shack stood. A colorful, tattered cloth spanned from its side, providing shade for the three guards gathered around a well. Glancing up, the sun-worn soldiers greeted them, and Leighton dismounted his camel to stroll over to them with Morgana and Leopold not far behind.

"Gentlemen." Leighton nodded his head. "Rasil said you would hold our camels for us and provide us with information needed to face whatever is in the Black Sand Barrens."

"Your Grace." One of the men approached him with a bow. "You still insist on going in?"

"I have no choice. My fiancé is there."

"As you wish. In that case, here." He handed Leighton a small pouch. "This is ash powder to put on your blades. Inside you will face skin hunters and bonetooth terrors. Ash powder is the only thing effective against skin hunters. Well, unless you happen to know their name, in which case you can get them to revert to their human form. They are also said to fear fire, and your witch can help you there. As for the bonetooth terrors, I'm afraid the only way to kill one is to stab it through the heart. Take caution with them. Not only do they have long, razor-sharp claws, but their saliva is venomous. I'm afraid that is all I can tell you, for no one has ever been beyond the gate."

"Thank you." Leighton nodded. "I think with your information, my friends and I stand a fair chance of survival."

"Good luck, your Grace." The man took hold of the camels. "You and your friends will need it."

Stealing one last glance at the outpost, the three friends took the crumbling track toward the ominous wasteland within their sight, preparing themselves for a fight that still lay ahead. As Morgana watched the all-too-familiar tower draw closer, her blood iced over at the thoughts of what would happen beyond the gate. She recalled the dream in which the demon king killed Leo in the very tower they were now trying to breach, and a whimper escaped her lips. Her visions of the day were sparse and blurry at best, but she knew death was on the horizon; she could almost taste it in the air. Through a thick veil of fog churning behind her eyes, she could see their fate lines converging in the moment. But their path afterward was unclear, and their future was not set in stone.

CHAPTER 34

# Strength

The air changed as the sand gradually began to turn black, replacing the stifling desert heat with an arctic chill, which stung the flesh. Dark storm clouds swirled above their heads, occasionally split by ribbons of cobalt as the wind howled in the distance. The closer they drew to the border, the more their skin prickled and their hairs stood on end. Wrapping her arms around herself, shivering, Morgana stopped as if she had walked into a brick wall. The path before her was clear, but the air stood still, thick with an ominous, weighty energy that made her want to run.

Turning to look back at her, Leopold stretched out his hand to her, and she took hold, lacing her frozen fingers through his. Giving it a squeeze, he pulled her close, and they pushed on, walking behind Leighton until they reached a wall of dark-gray sandstone rising twelve feet above them. The sloping tower of black brick stood just beyond the border, along which they walked until they stopped at an intricate iron gate. Panels, which were decorated in carvings of serpents and skulls, held a large, iridescent black stone at the center with a scintillating green line running across its surface. Leighton ran over to the doors and pressed on them, but they refused to budge.

"Damn it." He rattled the cages. "This thing is sealed shut. How are we supposed to get in?"

"This is strange." Morgana approached the gates, frowning. "This stone at the center looks almost like a lock. A Devoth device, perhaps?"

"Think you can use your magic to break it?" Leighton kicked the door. "Or should we look for another way in? Perhaps we can climb over."

"I don't know . . . let me see what I can do."

Reaching her hand out to touch the stone at the center, Morgana gasped and reeled back as it reacted to her presence with a luster of sea-green skidding across the surface. Raising an eyebrow, she stole a glance at the men gathering behind her, who were putting the ash powder on their blades. For some reason, her touch was enough to cause the stone to react, and she believed she could open it that way.

"This is strange," she muttered. "The stone seems to be responding to me touching it."

"What . . ." Leo said, scowling, "what does it mean? Does it react to those who possess magic?"

"I don't know." Morgana swallowed her fear, knowing all too

well the answer couldn't be that simple. It never was when the demon king was involved. "But I think I can open it. Are the two of you ready to go?"

"Ready when you are, darling."

The men gathered behind her, their weapons positioned before them, and they listened to the keening coming from the other side. Morgana wished to swallow the fear again—visions of death fresh on her mind—but her parched throat wouldn't allow it, and she reached her hand to touch the stone. Instantly it reacted with a turquoise glow, morphing from the iridescent solid into a polished shamrock stone with a resinous luster. She pressed against its smooth surface, and it shifted and moved inward beneath her palm. The gates groaned, and the wall rumbled as the metal separated and retreated into the wall, granting them access to the other side.

Stepping through the threshold, she turned to survey the black sand spanning the flat, static ocean of open expanse. Nothing moved. Even the churning clouds above the tower seemed to have frozen in time. Her eyes darted around frantically, and the skin on the back of her neck crawled with goosebumps as she sensed something near them. Trembling, she readied her hands to fight, and from the corner of her eye she spotted something creeping along the wall. Whirling around, she finally saw it: a milky creature with pointed ears and skin the color of the plaster, sliding across the wall to catch Leo off guard.

Its hollow eyes flashed at being spotted, and it let out a bone-shattering hiss before lunging forward, aiming its rake-like claws at them. Quick to react, she sent a wave of concentrated air into its belly, slamming it back against the wall. Turning to look behind him, Leopold flipped his sword and thrust it into the monster, piercing it through the heart. The bonetooth dropped to the ground, gurgling in a puddle of ink that spread from its body. All around them, howls and chirps rang out. Huddling against the men, Morgana encircled them in flames and waited for the monsters to come, puzzled about why she felt fine.

"That's odd," she mumbled, looking at her hands.

"What's wrong?" Leo shot her a worried glance. "Are you feeling ill from the psipher?"

"No . . . that's the thing. I feel nothing. It's almost like I'm not using magic at all."

"That's probably because"—Leighton backed up against them—"the barrens are a sacred site, much like the Sunhill Grove and the Black Forest. There are more pulse lines crossing here than anywhere else, making magic more potent. And since you draw your power from your surroundings, the energy concentration here is minimizing what you need to siphon from your own body to compensate."

Morgana grinned. "Makes sense. In that case, I think we may have the advantage. Get ready, they are almost here."

Right as the words left her lips, a deformed creature covered in brown fur leaped over the flames, landing in front of them. It rose from a crouch to stand on its long, human-like legs, dragging its arms, which turned into paws on the ground. Lifting its head, its human features faded as its nose and lips morphed into a muzzle partially covered in fur. Its glistening caramel eyes shone with hunger. Peeling its lips back to reveal its jagged canines, it let out a throaty growl and lunged at them. Spinning around, Leopold held his sword close to his side, blade up, grazing it across the monster's neck as they moved past one another. Stopping where it stood, the skin hunter's body twitched, and its head slid off its frame and crumpled to the ground by its feet.

Flicking the blood from his sword, Leo winced, stood, and readied himself as more skin hunters leaped into the battle. Swinging his blade and sidestepping from side to side, he fought off the attackers that clawed at him, tearing into his skin even as his breathing became labored from the pain in his ribs. He gritted his teeth, the blood dripping from his arm, and swung his sword downward, splitting a beast in half. To his left, Leighton was struggling against a bonetooth, pushing against the claws looming above his head while another horror snuck up behind him, the rakes on its hands ready to cut him down. Dropping to one knee, Leo turned halfway around, swung his blade up, and thrust it deep into the waxen chest cavity. Seizing the opportunity, Leighton kicked away his opponent, spearing it on the tip of his sword. Yanking the blade from the corpse, he turned to the captain and gave him a nod of appreciation.

Pressing their backs against each other, they walked in a circle as more skin hunters and bonetooth terrors surrounded them. Behind them, Morgana cracked a whip of fire, wrapping up the furry beasts in the flames and scorching them alive. The arena filled with howls of pain and the scent of burned fur as she continued to engulf the throngs of skin hunters in her blaze. Drawing his dagger from his belt, Leopold watched an ashen, hairless creature dart for him. Using his sword to parry the razor-sharp claws aiming for his throat, he lunged forward and thrust the dagger up into the heart. Foaming at the mouth, the emaciated figure hissed and dropped to lie in the pile of bodies gathering around them.

Morgana gripped two skin hunters in her invisible grip and lifted them in the air, igniting their blood from within and tossing them aside. Exhaustion took hold of her, and her legs turned to rubber as she panted, sweeping another line of brown-furred humanoids with her flames. Their numbers didn't seem to dwindle; more beasts leaped over the flames, rushing toward her. Clenching her jaw, she growled and released a stream of fire before they attacked. Her back ached, and she found it hard to lift her arms. The heat of the fire caused her to sweat, and her hair matted itself to her forehead.

Using her sleeve to wipe the moisture off her brow, she glanced behind the men to see a bonetooth galloping straight for them. Wincing, she forced her arms up. Lifting a stony spike from the ground, she pushed her palms out, sending it hurling through the sternum of the terror, stopping him in his tracks. No longer able to stand, she collapsed to the ground, gasping for breath. Digging her fingers into the blackened soil, she flinched when she heard a low growl next to her ear and something dark leaned in close to her face. Tilting her head, she glanced up to see a crooked face staring at her, dripping saliva from its partially formed jowls. She fell back, but before the skin hunter attacked, a steel blade whistled above her head, cutting the face of the beast in half. Looking up, she found Leo standing over her in his blood-soaked shirt, offering her a hand up.

"Are you all right, love?" He yanked her to her feet. "You're not hurt, are you?"

"No," she heaved, "just worn out. There are just too many of them. Even with the pulse lines, I am exhausting my mana supply."

"Don't give up now, you two." Leighton backed up to them while cutting down another skin hunter. "Look over there. I think we're winning."

Licking her parched lips, Morgana glanced over past the mountain of corpses at the few remaining skin hunters leaping away, retreating deeper into the barrens. Tracing her hand before her, she recalled the flames and looked past the blood-stained battleground at the black tower looming in the distance. Only a handful of bonetooth terrors lay between them and the demon king. Her throat tingled from the dust, and her limbs felt heavy from exhaustion, but she steadied her hand, giving Leighton a side glance.

"What are we waiting for? Let's go get your girl."

"That's the spirit. Let's take down these last few bastards while we're at it."

Catching her breath, Morgana smiled, reached out, and grabbed the first monster in midair with her magic grip as it made a leap for them. Stepping in, Leo jabbed his sword up, skewering the creature through the heart, and she allowed it to drop to the ground. Working together, they slashed their way through the rest of the beasts. The crumbling tower grew closer with every step, and the wind picked up the closer they got. When they reached the building, they could see the dried-up vines on the black brick and how the dilapidated spire pierced the swirling vortex in the clouds. Leighton rushed for the studded black door and pulled on the handle, but it sat firmly planted in the frame, denying them entrance.

"Damn it." The duke growled and pounded on the surface with his stony hand. "This one is locked as well."

"Stand back." Morgana shoved him out of the way. "I'll find us a way in."

As she studied the latch and hinges pitted with years of rust, a hint of a smile crept across her face—before dread pierced her heart once more. Recalling the dream of the tower, her hands shook at the thought of what would happen up there. She wondered if the demon king was giving her a preview of what he would do to them—to Leo—and Morgana faltered for a moment. She glanced at Leighton, and he nodded to give her enough strength to swallow her fear.

Placing her trembling hands on the opposite ends of the door, she concentrated all the energy she had left into her palms. The air surrounding her vibrated. She sucked the energy of the pulse lines into her body and released it through her palms in a rapid burst that sent splinters of wood flying past her. Morgana swayed from the spell, and Leopold grabbed hold of her elbow to keep her from falling over. The three gathered in the empty archway, staring up at the slanted stone steps spiraling into the gloom. Exchanging glances, they shrugged and set off up the stairs, skipping steps as they made their way toward the top at a sprint, neither knowing what they would be up against once they got to the end.

CHAPTER 35

# Ten of Coins

The trio bounded up the steps of the tower, which seemed to go on endlessly, but after a few minutes they reached a time-worn landing and a plain oak door framed in human skeletons. Leaning on their knees, they huffed, trying to catch their breath before turning to face the entrance, on which the skulls' vacant eye sockets peered back at them from between the femurs. They heard nothing coming from the other side, only the suffocating air between them. Nodding her head toward the door, Morgana glanced up at Leighton, urging him to open it. His hand reached for the brass handle, hesitating. Pushing him aside, she grabbed the latch and moved it with ease, flinging the door open with a crack against the wall.

Leighton moved past Morgana into the chamber and looked

around before collapsing on his knees with his head hung to the floor. Stepping through the doorway herself, Morgana glanced at the chamber and her heart sank to her feet. It was devoid of life, much as it was in her dream. A lone curtain fluttered in the window to the left, and dust drifted lazily across the floor while a single staircase spiraled up to a wooden platform above. Leopold rushed past the two of them and began scouring the chamber while silence fell around them. Only the sound of Leo's boots echoed off the stones until Leighton finally murmured something, his voice laced with heavy sorrow.

"She's gone." He looked up at Morgana with glistening eyes. "Lafreya is gone. We're too late. He killed her."

"No. Don't you dare say that." Morgana kneeled beside him and took hold of his shoulders to give him a firm shake. "Don't you dare believe she's dead. She can't be. She's the Golden Empress."

"It's over, Morgana." Leighton looked up at her, his face showing emotion for the first time in ages. "We lost. There is nothing left for me, not with *her* gone. I've got nothing to live for. I might as well just let this curse claim me."

"Stop it, Leighton. Don't be so cynical. I refuse to believe Lafreya is gone. We all hold a major arcana card; we can't lose to him, at least not so easy. There is a reason our cards are in play again, and it can't be because he wins. Surely we must be the ones who stop him."

Looking into the despair in the duke's face, Morgana, too, began to lose hope as the dream replayed itself in her mind and the demon king's words rang in her ears. As much as she wished to believe their cards would prevent the loss of Lafreya, she didn't know for sure. Even *she* had to admit that their fate was ambiguous under the best of circumstances. Last time a major arcana spread existed was right before the demon king was summoned, and all the holders of those cards perished from the Devoth, including the first Grand Duke Charmant, who raised the army against him. Shaking from fear, Morgana was starting to feel her own world collapsing under her when she heard Leopold run up to the platform.

"Morgie!" he shouted. "Leighton! You need to get up here, now."

Exchanging glances, both Morgana and the duke scrambled up to their feet and ran for the stairs. They hurdled their way up the steps and found Leo, crouched on the ground, working to untie the ropes on none other than Lafreya's brother, Prince Gabriel. The young man with curly copper hair lay on the floor, still wearing his sleeping garments, and glanced up at the three of them with his faint green eyes. Seeing the prince bound up in the tower made a lot of sense to Morgana. It was no wonder he sent the royal guard after them back when Lafreya got kidnapped—because he must have been an impostor as well. With his ropes undone, the prince sat up in his spot and looked at the three of them with a crinkled nose.

"You reek of sewage." Gabriel rubbed the red marks on his wrists. "And what took you three so long to get here? I figured you'd have come to the rescue days ago."

"We took a detour, you little snot." Morgana glared at him. "Want to tell us how you got here? Who took you?"

"You wouldn't believe me."

"Prince Gabriel." Leo frowned. "After the journey we had, I'd believe anything. Tell us who took you, and from your bed by the looks of it?"

"My father."

"King Nathaniel? But . . . that's impossible. I watched him die in battle. I was there when he was cut down by an ogre and fell."

"No, Captain," Leighton muttered. "That's just what he wanted you to believe. You never did recover his body if I recall correctly."

"No. But . . . what does this mean?"

"It means," Morgana sighed, "Nathaniel was the demon king all along. He must have killed the real Nathaniel before he married the queen, which would explain the sudden change he was said to go through. He fooled us all. Devoth are known to take on human form to play with us mortals, and it seems the demon king chose to become ruler of Perdetia so he could maintain his hold on the one province he needed to keep Dresbourn under control."

"Does that make the prince and princess—"

"Yes, Leo. It makes them half Devoth. Not that it means much, my ancestors were part Devoth too. That's how us magic-wielding creatures came to be, from humans mating with Devoth."

"Then why can't the two of them use magic like you can?"

"Just like with us, the chances for a Devoth and a human to produce a magic offspring are about fifty-fifty. Guess the demon king struck out both times."

Leo cupped his chin. "Fair enough. But then why did he pretend to die? Why would he leave Perdetia to Lafreya when he knew she was against him?"

"To make a play for the rest of Dresbourn," Leighton said, tightening his fists. "When the count of Synia refused to marry Lafreya in favor of trying to get Morgana, the demon king knew he had to take control some other way. He allowed the kingdom of Vekureth to fall to ruin with his death so only the west territories were left standing. Lafreya was powerless without a husband, and he knew his advisors would run things until she wed, which he was probably hoping would take a long time. I'm willing to bet he was going to take on a new form and go after Kalingrad or some other kingdom and then use it to form political marriage ties with Perdetia before moving on to Synia and beyond."

"Guess he didn't count on you stepping in to court Lafreya."

"That he did not, Captain. Which is why he kidnapped her. He knew I'd go after her, and this way he figured he'd get rid of me and use Lafreya as a pawn. Too bad we came too late to save her."

"You didn't come too late." Gabriel stood up. "He grabbed her this morning and dragged her down the path beyond the dunes out back. He came back an hour later and tied me up, saying he had no use for me . . . yet. I bet that if you follow the road behind the tower, you will find where he took my sister."

Leighton scrunched his forehead. "What of you? Lafreya won't be happy with me if she knew I left her baby brother here to fend for himself."

"I can fend for myself if I have a weapon, and I can come with you and fight the demon king too."

"Here." Leopold handed the prince the dagger off his waist. "There is an outpost not far from here. Go wait there for our return. You won't be much help without a sword, and we need at least one royal sibling to survive in case we don't make it back."

"Thank you, Captain Ellingham. I appreciate this, and I'll do as I'm told for now. Just get my sister back to me alive. Unlike her, I have no idea how to run a kingdom. I will go after you if you fail to return."

"We'll do our best, I give you my word. And I expect to get my dagger back. It was a gift from my lady, so I cherish it greatly."

"Your lady?" Gabe looked between Leopold and Morgana with a raised brow. "About time, I guess. I'd ask what took you two so long, but we must get out of this tower. My sister is waiting, and I don't know what the demon king's plan is for her, but I can bet it's not good."

Leo bobbed his head. "All right, let's get going."

Leaving the safety of the chamber behind them, the group made their way down the crumbling steps. Leighton walked in front with Gabriel behind him and Morgana and Leopold coming down at the rear. The four of them figured this way would be best in case they encountered any monsters coming up after them. Morgana had regained most of her mana and was ready for another round of fighting, but the battle never came. They exited the tower into an abandoned courtyard filled only with the whisper of the wind and the peel of thunder; all the monsters had retreated deeper into the barrens.

"This is where we part ways." Gabriel nodded. "I see the way out, and I think I can find your outpost. You three head over the dunes. I'm not sure what lies beyond, but I doubt it will be welcoming, so you best be careful."

"Keep out of trouble if you can, Gabe." Morgana smiled at him. "We need you alive."

"I'll do my best. You just make sure you all make it back. I can't lose my sister and my friends in the same day. I wouldn't know what to do without any of you."

Nodding her head, Morgana turned to look at the ribbon of sand leading away from them and swallowed. Whatever their fate was, she wouldn't have to wait long to find out, but all she knew was that someone was going to die today, and she sure hoped it wouldn't be any of them. Parting from the prince, she watched him walk away in the direction of the gate and vanish from sight. Looking between the two men at her side, she nodded her head, stole a glance at her quivering hands, and walked forward, taking the path away from the tower, deeper into the mounds of pitch-black sand looming in the distance.

CHAPTER 36

# The Tower of Sorrow

After scrambling up the dune of blackened sand, the three of them stopped and stood once they reached the apex, looking past the valley below at a derelict structure beyond. Of what was once a stone building, only part of a wall remained. An arch stood in the middle, its door long eaten away by the elements. Between them and the weather-torn stone, the barren floor crawled with insects the size of horses. If not for the bright red stripes on their backs, the beetles would almost blend into the darkness of the sand. Morgana looked at the bugs scrambling ahead, then at her companions.

"I think we need to be careful with them. I don't know what they are, but I'm assuming they are not your average pests."

"Agreed." Leopold nodded and drew his sword, which

glimmered in his hand. "We'll proceed with caution."

Sliding down the dune, they instantly caught the attention of a beetle, which ran over to them, its six legs leaving a trail of dust. Blocking their path, the insect hissed and drummed his legs on the ground. When the trio didn't move, its body shook violently, swelled, and released a stream of lava flowing in every direction, turning the sand into black glass. Morgana barely had enough time to put up a shielding spell as molten rock rushed toward them, scorching everything in its path. Splashing against the translucent barrier, the magma fizzled and hardened, leaving the three of them unharmed.

"Ahhh"—Leighton pulled out his sword—"guess we now know what they do."

Another beetle hissed and shook at them again, but this time Morgana reacted by encasing it in ice where it stood. Covered in a cold crystal cast, the body of the insect expanded, trying to spill its contents until its body pressed against the ice walls and exploded, the lava instantly turning to stone. Hearing the commotion, another creature jumped from the sand and landed right beside them. Spinning around, Leo cleaved it in half with the shimmering blade of his sword and leaped out of the way of the molten center spilling from its carcass. Leaving the husks behind them, the three companions ran for the ruins of the nearby abbey they had spotted in the distance.

Further down the dune, they stumbled into another group of beetles in the sand. Sensing them there, the six beetles glanced up and hissed in unison, darting around to circle them. One insect shook and ran for them, forcing Morgana to throw a spear of ice at it, piercing its center and pinning it to its spot. Hissing, the bugs charged in unison, all shaking with swelling bodies. Leopold cut down two of them at once, barely rolling away from their blistering blood. Morgana trapped another beetle in ice, then spun around and cemented the legs of another into the sand, giving Leighton a chance to take it down, leaving only one left, which buried itself in the sand.

Regrouping, the trio stood in the center and waited, and they didn't need to wait long. The sand bubbled before them, and the beetle propelled itself out, leaping over their heads. Raising his sword, Leo sliced open its belly as Morgana held up her arms, forming a barrier, which shielded them from the rain of molten magma pouring out of the wound. The shell collapsed beside them, its legs twitching as it died with a faint sizzle.

Stepping over the remains of the beetles, the three ran the rest of the way to the abbey, not daring to stop. Walking beneath the hollow arch, their eyes skimmed the ruins. Dark sand covered the shattered floor, and toppled pillars lay between them and the stone altar, which sat on a raised platform a few short steps away. Skirting around the fragments of stone, they approached the cream-colored platform and noticed the flat top was discolored by a dark rust stain that spread down the side. Instinctively, Morgana reached out her hand to touch it, and her spine shuddered as visions of human sacrifice played out behind her eyes. She yanked her hand away with a loud yelp, then held it to her chest and swiftly walked around the altar, spotting a passage hidden behind it.

The group stepped into the blinding darkness, and Morgana stopped to study the torches glowing with green flames. Her body trembled with a primitive fear, and Leo placed a hand around her, giving her shoulder a squeeze. The Heartseaker pulsed in his hand,

and she took another step down, taking care not to fall with the shifting slabs. The smooth sandstone walls crumbled around them, and chunks of stone gathered on the steps by their feet while sand rained down from the domed ceiling above. When they finally reached the bottom, the haunting chartreuse light of the torches illuminated the gloom, and a stone slab stood before them. The rough, solid-gray granite doors appeared impenetrable, if it weren't for the set of four circular dials at their center, decorated with rune carvings.

"What's this thing?" Leo reached out to touch the dials. "Another door with a strange lock?"

"Seems so." Morgana studied the runes. "The cult that summoned the Devoth was a secretive group. It's no surprise they would have locks and puzzles on every door."

"Think you can open this one as well?"

"I don't know. But I can certainly try."

Reaching her hand to the door, Morgana cast a revealing spell, and pictures of constellations glowed in a faint violet light in place of the runes: the Magician, the Rogue, the Priestess, and the Warrior. Cradling her chin in her hand, she turned the dials to match up with the constellations in the order they appeared, but nothing happened aside from the runes flashing an angry orange. Racking her brain, she studied the runes representing the stars again, and this time she tried putting them in alphabetical order according to the runes. With the last dial in place, the slab rumbled and descended into the ground, allowing them access to the chamber beyond.

After walking through the stone arch, they stopped upon reaching a crumbling platform blanketed in moss. The marble steps descended to an opening in the rock face, its mouth filled with jagged fangs of carved stone. Leighton descended the stairs first into the gaping maw. Shuffling close behind, Morgana almost bumped into him when he halted in his tracks. Taking a look ahead, she saw what had immobilized him. Their path ended abruptly in a precipice, spilling loose stone into the endless abyss of the cave. The only way to get to the other side was by a narrow stone bridge spanning a gaping chasm in the cave.

Drawing his sword, Leighton stepped onto the footpath and pressed forward, with Morgana staying close behind him. There was something about the gloom of the cave and its unnatural blue glow that unsettled her, making her skin crawl. The walls appeared to be closing in around them, and she could have sworn she saw the stones moving out of the corner of her eye. It wasn't until a pale form scurried over her head that she realized they were not alone. Her scream pierced the silence, but by then it was too late. The pale, skeletal form swung from the ceiling, grabbed the duke, and pulled him down the ravine with it.

"Leighton!" Morgana screamed and lunged after him, but a firm hand on her wrist restricted her movement.

"Stop." Leo spun her around and brought her into his chest, clinging to her back as she fought him to get away. "You'll just fall in too."

"But what about Leighton?" she protested. "We can't just leave him."

"He could already be dead, Morgie." He stroked her hair. "Although, I doubt the demon king would go through all this trouble of luring him here, only to have one of his minions kill him. I'd want a showdown if I were him."

"You're right." She pulled back and looked over her shoulder into the oblivion. "He would want to kill Leighton himself."

*Turn around, Morgana. Listen to the demon king. Take your knight and run. It's not too late.*

Furrowing her brow, Morgana looked around, wondering why her shade made a sudden appearance, but the shadow didn't show itself; she could only hear its voice. Instead she noticed the ceiling moving again and two more creatures fell onto the bridge. The slender, milk-colored humanoids stood at each end of the path, glaring at them with dark red eyes. Twitching their pointed ears, they clicked at each other, remaining in their spot. Then, with a single snap of the tongue, they charged, bounding toward them on their four knobby appendages. Swinging his sword in the air, Leo sliced a monster from belly to gullet, spilling its tangled entrails on the stones with a splash. Behind him, Morgana flashed a ball of light at the other's face, blinding it. Staggering, it pawed at its eyes, and she swiped her hand across the bridge, releasing a pulse of energy and throwing the creature off into the gulley beyond.

Not waiting for any more monsters to fall upon them, Leopold grabbed hold of Morgana's wrist and sprinted across to the other side, dragging her behind him. Clearing the other bank, he stopped and looked up at the rust-brown grate standing between them and the next room. Pressing his foot into the bars, he pushed on them, and they groaned as they gave way, falling to the ground with a deafening clang. Still holding on to Morgana, he stepped over the fallen gate, then paused on the landing to scrutinize his surroundings.

Another decaying staircase, cracked by crawling weeds, led down to a dank dirt floor covered in fog the consistency of clotted milk. A faint smell of loose soil and moss drifted up from the room, which was dotted with cracked marble sarcophagi. Half the lids from the burial boxes lay broken on the ground, the contents spilled out beside them. The ground was littered with deconstructed skeletons and tarnished jewels glistening between the tendrils of vapor. As Leo scanned the floor, he tightened his grip on the hilt of his sword and stole a look at Morgana.

"I don't like this one bit," he whispered, letting go of her wrist. "Stay behind me and move slow just in case something tries to attack us again."

Morgana raised her hand in protest, but Leo was already halfway down the steps, his sword raised to his chest. She hurried to catch up to him, even while her stomach cramped with foreboding. The heavy silence clung to the air, the sogging shadows swayed in the swirls of dense mist. They made it to the center of the room when she noticed eyes upon them. Their presence made the skin on her back crawl. Darting her head back, she stared into the layers of shadows, expecting to see someone behind her, but only a deepening haze of dark blue greeted her.

"Hello? Anyone there?" she whispered, but the shadows made no reply.

Turning back to Leo, she noticed him planted in his spot, the knuckles on his hands turning white as he twisted them on his hilt. His brow crinkled, and his eyes darted around the room. Morgana's fingers twitched uncontrollably, and the hair on her arms stood as the room filled with a cool electric energy that crackled with static as a soft wail resonated through the chamber. It was faint at first, but the melodic cry grew louder, filling the room, joined by another melancholic song. All around them, the fog churned until two shapes emerged from the milky ribbons. The sight of them made Morgana's blood run cold.

At first the specters blended into the mist. The only thing visible were their dark, black eyes and the sheet of crimson pouring out of their ragged jaws and onto their tattered white gowns. Floating closer to their victims, the phantoms revealed their grotesque nature: their flowing white hair and the clawed fingers on their four arms, stretching out as they wailed. Shooting past Leo, an apparition grabbed hold of Morgana's hair, yanking her back, dragging her across the sodden soil. Turning toward her, Leopold brought his sword down on the spirit, but as the blade came at her, the specter woman vanished, and Leo lost his balance.

Leo's ribs throbbed as he staggered to regain his footing, and the second spirit rushed him from the side. Snaring him in its claws, it dragged him into an empty sarcophagus as his sword flew out of his hand, landing on the floor with a hollow thump. Howling in horror, Morgana leaped to her feet and grabbed hold of the hilt, lifting the Heartseaker off the ground. The blade was heavier than expected, and she struggled to hold it up while the second specter flew at her with outstretched hands. Morgana swung the blade and cut through the phantom coming at her, which evaporated into the mist before her eyes. Rushing to the sarcophagus that Leo was dragged into, she peered inside but was met with blinding darkness; he was gone. Dropping to her knees, Morgana let go of the sword and wept, thick tears shattering against the blade.

"Leo . . ." she sobbed. "Not you too."

*Turn back now and save yourself. If you show the demon king you don't want to fight him, he will return your lover and your friend to you once he deals with the cursed duke.*

"No." She dug her nails into the moist soil and gritted her teeth. "I won't comply with him. He took my birth parents from me, and now he came after my friends. I will find him. I will see this to the very end, even if it kills me."

*You won't like the way this story ends.*

Ignoring the shadow, Morgana rubbed her face into her soiled sleeve and forced herself to stand up. She unwrapped the headscarf around her neck, tied it under the cross guard of the sword, and strapped it to her back. The blade hung awkwardly between her shoulder blades, and her back ached from the weight, but she didn't care. Clenching her jaw, she dug her nails into the palms of her hands and pressed forward across the rest of the burial chamber. Clambering up the partially demolished steps, she pushed through the mass of silken spiderwebs that molded together in a solid ashy mass to block the doorway.

Shaking her head and scouring her hair, she removed the sticky webs clinging to her and turned her attention to the passageway she found herself in. A narrow, brick-lined hall stretched between her and another archway with stairs leading down. Looking around her, she found nothing out of sorts, then took one step forward. When nothing moved to attack her, she continued, walking as fast as she could with the blade bouncing around on her back. Reaching the gothic arch, she took a step forward and instantly fell back when something moved in the shadows below.

A growl roared up from the stairs, and an enormous figure moved up the steps, seeming to crawl on all fours. Forcing her heart out of her throat, Morgana took a step back and waited to see what it was. The monster scampered up the stairs, filling the doorway with its massive body, and tilted its faceless head from side to side. The six-armed torso bobbed, and Morgana dared not breathe in case it could sense her, taking another slow step back. Rapping all its fingers on the ground, the monster lowered itself to the floor, and a slit opened in its taut skin to grin at her with its mouth full of tiny needle-like fangs.

The thing yowled like a wounded animal and sprinted toward her, using its fingers to propel itself along the ground. Morgana's legs refused to move, and she fell to the floor, petrified, shielding her eyes. Her body shook, and she did the only thing she could think of. She emanated a solid beam of light from her palms, cutting across the six-armed creature as it rushed across her. Squeezing her eyes shut, she pressed her face in her arm while getting showered in sticky, warm blood. When nothing else happened, she cracked open an eyelid and looked at the blood-soaked floor around her, the monster's body nowhere to be found.

She crawled along blood-slicked tiles until she found a dry patch, then staggered back to her feet. Creeping down the staircase, she kept her guard up in case something else appeared. When she reached the bottom unharmed, her shoes filled with icy water rushing up past her ankles. Creating an orb of light between her palms, she watched its reflection bounce across the mirror-like surface of the water flooding the chamber. Dark water spread between the walls, covering the floor and reaching up to the platform she stood on. Keeping the orb for guidance, she waded into the subterranean lake. By the time she reached the centermost point, the water reached up to her chest, constricting her lungs and burning her skin.

Her fingers cramped up from the cold while she clung to the stone lip and pulled herself up to the vestibule above her. Dripping wet, she looked at the options presented to her: Going left was out of the question—a rockslide shut off that entrance ages ago. To the right, a wood door let a beam of light into the chamber. Fresh air wafted through the crack. It appeared to be a way out. This left her with only the fissure in the rock before her. Gripping the sash holding the sword to her back, she walked forward into another flooded room, this time with a small path laid out in stone.

Taking her time, she hopped from one weathered platform to the next until she reached a grassy bank with a shaft of light falling from a circular, ivy-draped hole in the ceiling. Leaping onto the marshy soil, she tilted her head up toward the brass gates, which were framed on each side by two ancient oaks. A tree of green gemstone adorned the quatrefoil-carved brass. Between her and the door, a shadowy figure lingered in the gloom, looking at her with glowing red eyes. It took on a more human appearance this time, but she knew what it was, and her constant companion greeted her with an evil smirk.

*It's not too late to turn back.*

"I won't turn back when my friends need me."

*Your fate is to have no friends. That is what's in your cards.*

"You're wrong. My destiny is not up to the cards, or even the demon king. It's up to me, and"—she grabbed hold of the shadow—"I'm going to turn it around. And I'm starting with putting you back where you belong . . . back inside me."

*You sure you want your memories back? Do you really want the truth, which will destroy you? You are better off not knowing.*

"You might be right." Morgana pulled the shade closer. "But you forget one thing. For Leo, I will do just about anything, including learning what you have been hiding from me."

The shade struggled against her, thrashing and hissing while she wrapped her arms around it, absorbing it into her body. Instantly, dark and forbidden energy filled her core, seeping into her blood and spreading between her fingertips. The ground quaked, and stones toppled from the ceiling above, crashing around her. Her head flew back, her eyes rolled into her skull, and bitter memories replayed themselves in her head.

Running around the sunny field of colorful wildflowers, Morgana turned her head and looked at the pale-skinned, black-haired woman watching her from the door of a small woodland cabin. Her mother's pink eyes sparkled with the sun, and she smiled, waving to her daughter. Somewhere in the distance, the wind changed direction and brought with it a faint scent of steel. Smiling to herself, Morgana ran in the direction it was coming from before her mother ran to scoop her into her arms.

"No, Morgana."

Rushing to the cabin, her mother shut the door behind her. Puzzled—Morgana had never seen her mother react that way to her father's arrival—she looked up with a frown. Her mother didn't respond. She shoved Morgana into the old wardrobe and kneeled to the ground, stroking her daughter's hair and glancing behind her.

"I need you to do something for me, Morgana. I need you to stay in here and keep really quiet, and I don't want you to come out, no matter what happens."

"Why?"

"Because"—her mother bit her lip—"we are playing hide and seek with daddy. All right?"

"Okay."

Morgana nodded her head, and her mother shut the wardrobe door just as a knock came on the door. Standing to her feet, her mother wiped her hands on her skirt and walked up to open it. A man with pale white skin, white hair, and black horns stood on the other side, smiling. He wore a breastplate of black steel, and a black chain hung from the choker off his neck. His amber eyes surveyed the small cottage interior, and his smile faded into a frown.

"What's going on here, Evanore?" His voice was harsh but soft. "Why aren't you packed yet? And where is Morgana?"

"You don't have to do this, Abnaroth."

"It's the only way I can keep both of you safe," he growled. "Can't you see I'm doing this because I love you?"

"It's not the only way, and if you loved us, you wouldn't be asking us to give you up. You can walk away from all of this right now. Walk away from what you are trying to do, from everything. Leave it all behind and come be with us."

"Do you have any idea of what you are asking me to do? You want me to give up centuries of progress to marry you and play a doting father."

"I never asked you to marry me, and you *are* a doting father. You've been that way since she was born. Why can't you see that?"

"Because this is so much bigger than you and I. I haven't finished fulfilling my goal."

"Your goal." Evanore shook her head. "You mean your blind ambition of merging this world with the Otherworld?"

"My ambition isn't blind!" Abnaroth roared. "I want to unite our worlds so you and Morgana can live forever."

"I don't want to live forever. I just want to spend the time I have left with you."

"Enough of this foolishness." He pushed through the door and glanced about the room. "Where is Morgana? Where is my daughter?"

"She's not here. And I won't allow you to take her, to steal her memories of you. I won't have you deciding her fate for her."

"Her fate is to either kill me, or to die by my hand. Which one would you choose, Evanore?"

"Neither." She broke down crying. "It doesn't have to be either of those."

"That's what the cards dictate."

"The cards are just a guide. Their predictions are not set in stone. It's not too late to change our destiny. Come with me. Come away with me and your daughter, and I promise you, neither of you will have to die."

"You know I can't do that. I can't leave this unfinished. Not when doing so means watching you die."

"Then kill me now, Abnaroth. Kill me where I stand because I am not coming with you, nor am I letting you take our daughter. You claim you are doing this for us, so here is your chance to prove it. Kill me by your own hand or come with me."

"Very well, my love. If you wish, I see no other way to do this."

He put his arm around her and summoned a blade of black steel, driving it through her chest. A trickle of blood ran down her lip, and her head fell back. He lowered her limp body to the ground and a single tear shattered beside it. Bending down, he kissed her forehead and stroked her pale skin.

"I'm sorry it had to come to this. But I can't allow you to

endanger our daughter. I must keep her safe. And when this is all over, I promise I will bring you back to me."

"Mommy?"

Morgana had left the wardrobe and was standing behind him, looking at her mother's blood pool on the floor. She didn't understand what was going on, and she looked up at her father with tears welling up in her eyes. He turned to her, his face contorted in pain, and he made the blade vanish.

"Close your eyes, Morgana," he commanded. "You don't need to see this."

Morgana did as she was told, and he scooped her into his arms, wrapping her up in a warm, familiar hug, which always brought her comfort. She felt the cool air hit her face before he lowered her to the ground and stroked her hair. Hazarding a glance, she pried open her eyes and looked into his, which looked sad, and she reached out to wipe a tear away from his face with her small hand.

"Daddy?"

"It's all right, little one. Everything will be all right from now on. But I'm afraid I need you to forget me. All I need you to remember is what I did to your mother."

"Why?"

"I need you to fear me, baby. I need you to never want to see me again, because I never want to hurt you the way I hurt your mother. But don't worry, I will send someone to find you. You will be well taken care of."

He reached out his hand and pressed it to her forehead, and her memories faded away. A dark shadow seeped from her pores and took shape beside her. After he was done, the demon king stood up and turned his back to her. She no longer knew who the man was—only that she wanted to run after him. She took a step in his direction, but he turned to look at her and she fell back from fright. He turned his back to her once more and vanished from sight, leaving her all alone for the first time.

"The demon king . . ." She gasped and collapsed onto her knees. "He's . . . he's, my father? No"—her tears fell to the ground—"no, it can't be. He can't be my father."

She sucked in ragged breath as her nails dug into the sodden ground. Her body went numb, and she no longer knew what to do. The man she hated with every fiber of her being for the past seventeen years was also the same man she loved with all her heart and hoped to one day find. Her body shook as she replayed her stolen memories. Everything she had believed crashed down around her. She opened her mouth to scream, but the only thing to come out was a faint whimper as she realized she had come all that way to kill her own father. Sobs racked her body, and she pressed her head to the ground, shaking as her stomach turned sour.

She did not know how long she spent crying, but by the time she forced herself to get up, she had a new resolve in her. She would try to reason with her father—she would do something her mother couldn't do. Tightening the sword strap, she turned and glared at the gates separating her from the man she longed to meet. If he loved her as much as he claimed, she thought, then perhaps there was still a way she could save them all, including him. She pressed her palms against the gate and let a pulse of magic flow through her palms, toppling it with a single blast. Her breath caught in her chest. After seventeen years, she was finally going to meet her father again, with her memories intact—and this time she would get him to give up his ambitions. She could still save him, even if a part of her hated him.

CHAPTER 37

# Death

**D**ust settled around the fallen gate, the echo of it hitting the stone still resonating through the chamber. Morgana strolled down the dirt path leading down a brick hall lined in flickering flames of torches that barely illuminated the darkness. Wandering deeper into the cave, she shivered as the air grew chilly, nipping her cheeks. Her skin prickled from the ice crystals clinging to her soaked dress, and she watched the vapors of breath forming before her, hanging in front of her face. Ahead, a faint, pale blue light poured through a partially collapsed archway, from which a frigid gale whistled, wrapping her in a blanket of ice.

After climbing over the toppled stone, she stood on a balustrade covered in a sheet of snow as fine as lace. Looking beyond the cracked pillars and eroding railings, she spotted a rectangular block of ice with a familiar man in black frozen inside. Scurrying around him, a half dozen crystal-blue spiders the size of bears spun webs of fine snow threads. Their icy-blue bodies shimmered with an iridescent glimmer while they scampered across the frost-covered floor, guarding their prize.

Feeling the magic around her, Morgana drew in a sharp breath and pulled the power from the pulse lines, sucking it into her weary body. Filled with magic energy, she fluttered open her eyes, and warm flames licked her arms, dancing on the surface of her skin without burning her. Stepping forward, she ignited a path down the snow-carpeted steps, and the ice spiders took notice, rattling as they rushed for the intruder. Crawling up the steps nearer to the flames, their bodies began to melt, and she finished them off with a steady flow of fire.

When nothing but water ran down the steps, she retracted the heat back into her body, snuffing out the blaze, and walked down to face the ice block with Leighton trapped inside. She didn't know if he was still alive, but she saw his contorted face and knew she had to hold out hope, no matter how fleeting it was. Reaching up, she placed her palms on the glacial block and emitted a low, steady pulse of heat. Slowly the ice melted, dripping a stream of water by her feet, until the duke's body collapsed, convulsing on the floor as he coughed.

"Leighton." She lifted him off the floor, hugging him tight. "Are you all right?"

"I'll . . ." he gasped, holding on to her arm. "I'll be fine. Just. Freezing." He rubbed his arms, shivering, and looked up at her. "What . . . what the hell happened to you? You look a lot worse now than when I last saw you."

"It's a long story, I'm afraid. Perhaps we could save it for our trip home."

"Very well." Leighton nodded and looked around, his brow creasing. "But where is Leo? Why isn't he with you, and why do you have his sword?"

"I'm"—her voice cracked, and she fought back her tears—"I'm afraid I lost him a while back. After that thing dragged you off, we fought off the other two, but a specter dragged him off in the next room. They vanished into some type of void below the room. But I refuse to think he's dead. If I found you alive, then he must be alive too." Standing, she offered Leighton a hand up. "Are you in good enough shape to get going?"

"Indeed." Leighton bared his blade. "Let's go find Leo and finish what we started."

"All right"—she nodded, not willing to let him know her plan—"let's get going then."

Leighton led the way, and Morgana followed him up the stairs opposite the way she came. The only way forward was down a dark, musky hall filled with sweet sulfury vapor. The clouds of laurel green swirled around them, assaulting their sinuses with the bittersweet perfume. Choking on the mist thick enough to cut with a knife, she waved her hand in front of her face. Her head swam and her vision blurred with a soft white haze. A few steps ahead of her, Leighton swayed as he stumbled forward, stopping briefly to lean on the wall, gasping for breath.

"Are we walking uphill or downhill? I can't tell." He hacked and spit on the ground. "I feel like we are going down, but my eyes are telling me we are going up, and it's making my head spin."

"Neither." She pressed on her soured stomach. "We are going straight. These vapors, they smell like Dame de Mort. It's a sweet and sour fungus that's known to be a powerful hallucinogenic in small quantities, and a lethal poison in larger doses. We are feeling the effects of it now, and if we stay longer, we might not make it out. We must keep moving. Just push through it. You can be sick as soon as we are clear of this tunnel."

Grabbing hold of Leighton's stone-hard wrist, Morgana pulled him behind her, fighting the nausea in her own stomach. Breathing grew difficult, and she wheezed as she walked, her legs threatening to give out. She was starting to despair, but then she spotted a faint ray of light a short distance away. Clawing her way along, she dashed for the crack in the wall and burst through it, into an open chamber filled with clean, stale air. Gulping down the air free of vapor, she leaned over as the contents of her stomach left her, spilling on the stones by her feet. She heaved once more, and another gush of green bile splashed down. Soon the queasiness subsided, and she could see where they were.

At the center of a circular chamber lined with pillars, she spotted a ball of glowing amber light, with Leo suspended in its clutches. Leighton was already surveying the mechanism holding him in place, and she joined him. Five stone eggs, arranged in the shape of a star, emitted beams to join in the middle, forming the energy field that encased their friend. Leighton reached over to a clear, amber-colored stone to pull it out, but Morgana quickly grabbed hold of his hand, yanking it away.

"Wait," she snapped. "These are elemental crystals. It's an ancient trap I've read about in books. These things are placed in a certain order to put up a forcefield, which suspends the subject in a state of flux, and the only way to safely reverse the effects is to remove them in reverse order, or else the person inside gets torn apart."

"All right. What's the order then?"

"I don't know. It varies by trap. Let's look around and see if we can find a clue."

Splitting up, they walked around the perimeter of the wall. Morgana studied the strange carvings of people engaged in passionate sex and crude acts of violence. Men were thrusting their enormous members into women, who were being beheaded by other men. Women were on their knees, grasping firm shafts in their hands, drawing them to their lips while blades ran through their partner's chest. Lust and bloodshed all in one setting. She wondered if it was the rituals of the cult that summoned the demon king or if these were images of the Otherworld, and her spine tingled as she remembered what her father had planned: the union of the two planes.

"Hey, Morgana." Leighton's voice cut through the silence, pulling her away from the wall. "Come here. I think I found something."

She walked to where he stood before a flat slab of stone and looked up. Runes shimmered on the wall between the torch flames. Running her finger along the letters, she read the message carved in stone, speaking the words out loud:

*First, a cold, lifeless rock formed in the darkness.*
*Then a fire swept through it, warming the core.*
*Air rose from the heat, forming the clouds.*
*From the clouds came water as rain, forming the oceans.*
*And from the waves rose the spirit of man, the first beings to walk the earth.*

"Well," Leighton said, "that sounds like the creation myth of

Iatan to me. But what does this have to do with the crystals?"

"I think it tells us the order: Earth, Fire, Air, Water, and Spirit. And, if I'm correct, we need to reverse this order to free Leo."

"Fair enough. Except"—he glanced behind him— "how do we know which rock represents which element? They are not exactly labeled."

"I think . . ." —she approached a solid, marbled gray stone at the tip— "each element is a certain color. The spirit is usually gray, so this casteolite crystal must be it."

Leighton frowned, pressing his fist to his lips. "Are you sure about this? If you are wrong, you are going to murder the captain."

"Do we have another choice?"

"No," he grumbled, "I guess not."

"All right, then let me take the lead on this. I shall be the one responsible for what happens. I don't think he'll die, though. He can't. It's his job to rebuild after the tower collapses. And I already imploded before I found you, so he must live. He must help me pick up the pieces. Not to mention"—she bit her trembling lip as she looked at Leo—"I can't lose him, not when I finally have him. I won't allow it."

She turned to look back at Leighton, and he gave her a nod. Steadying her breath, she reached a shaking hand and took hold of the cool, polished stone. Squeezing her eyes shut, she yanked the egg-shaped gem out and listened for something to happen. Beside her, the duke heaved out a loud huff of relief, and she forced open an eye to see Leo still suspended in a fluctuating field of light. She'd picked the right stone. Realizing he was still alive made the blood rush from her head to her feet. Dropping the crystal to the ground, she rubbed off the sweat from her brow and turned to look at

Leighton, who stood beside her, still white as a sheet.

"All right." He shook his head with a hoarse voice. "Which one is up next?"

"Water is blue." She approached a clear cyan stone with turquoise veins. "So the arcanite is next."

Gingerly removing the stone from its metal seat, she watched the forcefield shift and drop to the floor. She gulped down the bile creeping up her throat and walked over to grab the milky white stone, unseating it—correct again. With only two crystals remaining, the light flickered, and Leo was moving inside. The amber stone was next, followed by the brown stone with green stripes. With the last of the crystals gone, the barrier broke, releasing its prisoner. Letting out a soft squeal, she untied the sword, dropping it to the ground, and ran over to his arms. He wrapped his arms around her and lifted her up, holding her tight while her body convulsed with her sobs.

"Boy, am I glad to see you both." Leo put Morgana down, kissing her on the forehead. "I've felt as if my whole life was slipping away before me in that stupid thing."

"I thought," she sniffled, "that I'd never see you again."

"Didn't I tell you that we will all get out of here in one piece?" He wiped the tears from her face. "I gave you my word as a knight. Now, what do you say we go finish what we started? This place isn't exactly growing on me."

Leighton grinned. "Captain, I say lead the way."

Picking his sword up, Leopold smirked and followed Leighton through a slit in the wall between two panels of paintings, which led them into a dark cavern. Jagged stalactites hung from the ceiling beyond their covered walkway, reaching down to a pit that glowed in an ethereal green light cast from the clear diopside crystals below. The carved-out floor was covered in thalanium, and shafts branched in every direction. Leo peered down the cavern and surmised this was an ancient mine, abandoned long before the age of the demon king.

Pressing onward, they passed empty rooms of crumbled stone and decaying shelves until they reached steps leading up to a single chamber framed by a tall set of stone doors. They raced up the stairs and into a vast room filled with jagged ruby-red stones growing out of the floor. At the far wall, a granite throne sat atop a platform, and on it sat the demon king with Lafreya at his side, her hands bound by black chains. He rested his waxen face on his clawed hand, and his white hair floated around in wisps over his horns. Upon seeing the party charge into his throne room, he perked up, waved his hand, and slammed the doors shut behind them, catching the attention of his prisoner.

"Leighton!" Lafreya shot up to her feet. "Morgana. Leopold. You finally came."

"Lafreya!" Leighton rushed for her, but a flick of the demon king's wrist produced a gust of wind that sent him tumbling back across the floor.

"So." The king stood up to greet them, his black armor reflecting no light. "You three made it this far. But let me assure you that *this* is as far as you go."

"No, father"—Morgana stepped forward—"this is where this madness stops."

"Father?" Leighton and Leo shouted in unison.

"That's right," Morgana affirmed. "The demon king is my father. And everything he did up to this point was to prevent this moment from happening."

The demon king nodded. "I see you have reclaimed the memories I took from you, little one. Then you know I did all this to keep you safe."

"Keep her safe?" Leo shouted, drawing his sword. "You tried to kill her."

"Foolish mortal," the Devoth snarled. "I never once tried to hurt my daughter. I kept her safe all these years. I even did something you couldn't. I took care of the man who violated her by hunting him down and killing him."

"Did you now? Then tell me, why plant the mana tick on her?"

"The tick was there to slow her down. I was planning to remove it once you brought her to me and I could relocate her someplace safe." Abnaroth crossed his arms. "I never expected you to take her on the run. You were never one to disobey orders, Captain. But when you did, who do you think contacted that old hag and led her to help you?"

"If that is true, then why did you try to burn her?"

"I only threatened to burn her, and I gave you a way to save her. I didn't slip up by allowing you to go to the de Laurent estate; I did that on purpose, and I even kept most of the guard away so you could escape. I thought that if I gave her what she wanted that she would settle down with you, but you allowed her to come here. Now you force my hand. I have no choice but to kill you all."

"Stop it, father." Morgana took a step forward. "You don't have to do this. Just release Lafreya and allow us to leave. Do as mother wanted and stop with this foolish quest to unite our worlds. Let it all go, and we won't have a need to fight you."

"Oh, little one, you have no idea how much I wish I could do that. But you forget one thing. You forget that your friend, the duke, won't allow me to go, not until one of us is dead."

Morgana's breath hitched. She had completely forgotten she told Leighton that the only way he could end his curse was to kill the demon king. It seemed as if she'd have to make a choice between her father and her friend—between the man she loved and hated at the same time and the friend who was always there for her, whom her half-sister loved. Darting her eyes from her father to Leighton, she noticed him give her a pained look.

"He's right, Morgana. I can't let him go. I must end this curse or die trying. But I can't ask you to help me. I won't ask you to kill your father. So you take Leo and Lafreya and you get out of here. Let us sort this out on our own."

"No." Morgana balled up her fists. "I can't do that. You are my friend, Leighton, and I'll stand by your side until the end. I'm sorry, Father." She turned to look at the demon king and swallowed the hard lump in her throat. "I'm sorry it has come to this."

"I'm sorry too, little one."

The demon king raised his hand, and a stream of black lighting left his palm, shooting straight for Morgana, striking her and flinging her across the room. Letting out a pained scream, she rolled across the floor and hit the opposite wall.

"Morgie!" Leo shouted as he lunged from his spot. Kneeling beside her, he scooped her into his arms. "Are you all right?"

"I'm fine. He's still trying not to hurt me. But, Leo"—she glanced at the red crystal lining the room—"I can't help you with the thalanium up. It doesn't have any effect on a Devoth, but it limits my abilities. You must take care of it."

Leo stood up. "Leave it to me. You just stay alive until I finish."

The Heartseaker emitted a faint glow while gently vibrating against Leo's palms, and he understood what it meant: the sword was ready to fight alongside him. He lifted the blade up and swung it around, striking a stone cluster and it shattered with ease. The demon king growled and lifted his hand to summon a whip of black electrical energy. He cracked it across the floor at the knight, who rolled out of the way, taking down another cluster of rocks. Wincing from the pain in his ribs, Leo stood back up and attacked another clump of crystals. Distracted by the thalanium crashing down around his throne room, the demon king didn't see Leighton sneak up behind him until he cracked him across the back with his blade, showering the floor in black sparks.

Roaring with frustration, the demon king turned and released a pulse of energy that slammed Leighton into a wall across from him. With a thump, the duke crumpled on the ground as Lafreya screamed his name. Grinding his teeth, the Devoth prince summoned his black steel halberd. The massive blade emitted a frightening inky glow as it swung down toward the duke's head, who was struggling to stand up. It came close to severing his head, but the shaft met with resistance as Leopold's sword came up to meet him. The knight struggled to push the weapon away, and the demon king seized the opportunity by pulling his weapon back and striking Leo across his injured ribs with the shaft. The knight crumpled to the ground in agony, and the demon king raised his blade to finish him.

The halberd came down on Leo, but it was deflected by Morgana's shield, and the battlefield crackled with black and white sparks. She stood over the knight, straining against her father, who towered almost two feet above her. Leaping from the ground,

Leighton brought his blade down on the halberd, driving its point into the ground, jamming it between the stones, away from his friends. Boiling over with frustration, the demon king unleashed a blast of dark air, blowing the trio off their feet. Then he grew bigger, gaining an extra three feet of height, filling the chamber up to the ceiling.

The demon king swooped his arm down and grabbed hold of Leighton's neck, depressing his windpipe and laughing while the duke struggled in his grip. After watching the duke's eyes roll back into his head, he tossed him aside and focused on the knight. Leo was already up on his feet, doubled over in pain, his right hand still clutching the Heartseaker. The demon king kicked Leo in the chest, sending him toppling to the floor, dropping his sword from the impact. Lying on the floor, clutching his side, Leo was unable to move. Abnaroth summoned a glowing black sword and raised it over his head.

Watching the blade come down on Leo, Morgana summoned lightning chains from the ground, winding the glowing violet links around her father's arms and legs, pulling him back before he had the chance to cut Leo in half. Twisting his body, he gave her a scolding glare, but she only held on tighter. He yanked on the chains, growling, and she stumbled forward, losing her grip. Removing the chains from his limbs, the demon king stepped toward her and released a stream of black lightning, lifting her into the air. Morgana flung her head back and screamed in pain as she felt her skin burning and the blood seizing in her veins.

Across from her, Leo forced himself to his feet. Clutching his side, he staggered to the Heartseaker and grabbed hold of the hilt. Tightening his grip on his sword, he put all his effort into covering the distance between him and the demon king. Holding his breath through the pain, he put both hands around the grip, spun around, and thrust the blade up, putting it straight through the demon king's breast plate. Dropping Morgana to the ground, Abnaroth shoved Leo out of the way and glanced down at the silver blade sticking out of his chest, his inky blood trickling to the ground by his feet, and then he looked at his daughter, who was struggling up to her feet.

"Morgana . . ." He took a step forward, reaching for her.

"Father!" Morgana screamed and ran to grab a hold of his hand as he collapsed to the ground beside her. Her hand was dwarfed by his massive palm, but she felt his grip falter. She was losing him. Her eyes trailed up to his face, and she saw a single tear leave his eye and trace its path down his ashen cheek. She reached up and wiped it away, then felt her own tears fall. As much as she hated him, she didn't want to lose him. She wasn't willing to let him go yet.

"I'm sorry . . . my little one."

"It's all right, Daddy,"—she sniffled and squeezed his hand tighter—"I forgive you."

He reached up to wipe her tears away. "Promise me you'll be happy."

"I . . . I promise."

Taking one last breath, Abnaroth closed his eyes, and his hand fell away from her face. No longer able to contain her emotions, Morgana laid her head down on his chest and sobbed uncontrollably. For seventeen years she'd waited to see the moment when the demon king would die, but that was before she knew he was the same father she missed nightly. Now that he was gone, she didn't know how to feel. Conflicting emotions surged inside her, and she convulsed from her tears.

"Oh, Morgie." Leo pulled her up into his arms, pressed her against his chest and stroked her hair. "I'm sorry. I'm so, so sorry."

"Don't be." She gripped his back and stilled her tears. "He left you no other choice."

"Morgana." Lafreya ran up to her, yanking her from Leo's arms and spinning her around to face her. "My poor, sweet friend." She stroked her wet cheek. "I . . . I can't find the words that would make this all better. But if you need to talk about it, know that I'm here for you."

"He was your father too."

"I know. But I already mourned him once. You never got that chance."

Sniffling, Morgana turned to look at Leo, who was looking at his feet as her father's body evaporated before them. Lifting her eyes, she followed the trail of smoke from the body to Leighton, who averted her gaze, his face paling at the sight of her. She could make out his upturned brows and the faint quiver of his bottom lip. Even if her father didn't die by his hand, he felt as much guilt as Leo, if not more.

"How's your hand?" Her voice cracked. "Is it cured of the curse?"

"It is." Leighton finally met her gaze and removed his glove, showing her that his hand was flesh colored and fully functional. "But I am afraid you had to pay too steep a price to cure me."

"Don't say that. I chose to help you."

"I know. But he was still your father."

"I realize this, and it's true that a part of me loved him. There is a small girl inside me who wished to meet her daddy, and she will miss him and mourn him terribly. But you forget one thing—that little girl grew up. She was raised by parents who loved her, and she grew up with friends who would do anything for her. And for them, no sacrifice is great enough. There is nothing I wouldn't do to protect you all. You are my family, and unlike my father, you never walked out on me. That's why I will always choose you. Now"—she bent over to pick up the Heartseaker and handed it to Leo—"let us not talk about these dreadful things further. Let us get out of here, regroup with Gabe, and go home. I don't know about any of you, but I don't wish to stay in this tomb any longer."

Leighton nodded. "All right. This is an old thalanium mine, so there must be an exit somewhere in those tunnels we passed. Let us get going."

Leighton took Lafreya's hand and led her through the large double doors. Morgana watched them turn the corner, then turned to look at Leo. He remained silent, his head bowed low and away from her. He gripped the Heartseaker in his hand, the blade grazing the floor, but he dared not move. It seemed he was frozen in place by what he had done, and she could sense the turmoil in him.

"Come on, Leo." She reached her hand out to him, and he glanced up to meet her gaze. "I can't sort through all these feelings on my own. I need the man who refused to give up on me to help me get through all this."

"You're . . . you're willing to burden me with your troubles?"

"As long as you are willing to listen."

"I won't only listen"—he sheathed his sword and took hold of her hand—"I'll help heal your wounds."

"Then let's go home. We both have a lot of healing to do."

Outside the chamber, they found Leighton and Lafreya waiting by the staircase leading down into the mine. Traversing the crumbling steps, they searched around the glowing green cave until they found a door leading out. They pried open the door and ambled up the sand-covered steps into a desert bathed in the amber glow of the setting sun. The old mining tunnel dropped them off a few miles from the outpost, which was visible in the distance. The reunited friends stumbled their way back, relishing in the cooling air.

Gabriel was waiting for them impatiently under the lean-to, and he rushed to embrace his sister upon seeing her alive. The group agreed to rest for the night before they would begin their journey anew and make their way slowly back to Perdetia, where a new challenge awaited them: restoring order to the kingdom. Nestled in Leo's arms on the sleeping pad in their tent, Morgana thought of her parents back home, wondering if they were safe. Knowing her mother, she was probably the one holding the kingdom together, assuring the citizens the real princess would be back soon. Her fate card no longer lingered over her, and although death did claim someone she cared about, she could sleep easy for once. The journey home would be long, but it would give her plenty of time to come to terms with her father's death—and she had Leo beside her to help. For once, the future seemed bright.

CHAPTER 38

# The Chariot of Fire

Three months had passed since they returned to their homeland and Lafreya gave the Perdetians an earful about trying to burn her sister at the stake. The princess angrily reassured everyone that Morgana would stay on as her trusted advisor despite being a witch, and she abolished the anti-witch laws on the spot. She dismissed Nathaniel's advisors, claiming, a Devoth posing as king invalidated his rein. She also assured everyone that Leopold would continue to be the captain of her guard and all the soldiers should only take orders from him. Wrapping up her passionate speech, she made it clear she would still marry Leighton because her feelings for him never changed, and she would never consider him—or anyone else close to her—a traitor to the crown.

It took the citizens a few weeks to accept what happened and welcome the three of them back into the fold, but once they did, it was as if nothing ever happened. What *did* take people a while to wrap their heads around was Morgana and Leopold's relationship. While many of the people who knew them were thrilled, some did not welcome the idea of a witch being with the captain of the royal guard. Leopold, however, was undeterred, and he angrily assured any opposition that he would not change his mind, demanding they treat Morgana with respect. Eventually, people grew to accept her for who she was, and the town quickly learned that having a witch in their ranks was beneficial for everyone.

On the day of Lafreya's wedding, Morgana stood by her friend's side, as did Leopold, and they welcomed the beginning of a new age. With Leighton crowned king, the two kingdoms became one. Sitting in the reception room, Morgana beamed as Lafreya chatted with her and enjoyed the ambience the celebration had to offer. Avoiding the wine, she picked at her food and mingled until she had enough of the chatter and clatter. Excusing herself, she got out of her seat and strolled out to the balcony for a moment of peace and quiet while the din of the party faded into the background. Breathing in the crisp autumn air, she leaned on the railing and surveyed the kingdom beyond. Behind her, the set of plated-glass doors swung open, and his scent hit her instantly, making her smile.

Softly shutting the doors behind him, Leopold stood on the threshold and watched her silently as she continued to lean on the railing. Her deep purple hair was pinned up off her shoulders for the occasion, held in place by a gold-and-malachite comb he had gifted her years earlier, the curls at her sides floating down to frame her face. His heart caught in his throat, and he smiled at how she'd kept every gift he'd given her over the years, even if she could have replaced it with something better. Dragging in a deep breath, he stepped forward and wrapped her in his arms from behind and she sighed in response, leaning her head back into his chest.

"I've finally found you." He leaned down to nuzzle her neck, fanning her with his warm breath. "What are you doing out here all by yourself? Don't you know I've been looking all over for you?"

"I just came out to get some much-needed silence. The reception room was beginning to get a tad stuffy and obnoxiously loud." She half turned to him with a smile, her pink eyes twinkling with the sun. "And what of you? Why are you here? Aren't you supposed to be on guard duty, Captain?"

"My men are more than capable of handling such a mundane task. And Leighton told me to go enjoy myself, so I thought I'd come find you. I missed you. We haven't spent much time together the last few days, with the wedding preparations and all."

"I missed you too." She turned in his embrace, standing on her toes to press her lips to his. "I'm glad you found me. I love your company, and I've been craving it lately since you haven't so much as spent the night with me the last four days."

"I know"—he planted a soft kiss on her forehead—"I'm sorry. That will all change now that we have a king and queen on the throne. I will spend all my nights with you from this day forward. And you know, it will be *our* wedding we are celebrating next, right?"

"So . . . does this mean you still intend to marry me?"

"I thought I made my intentions clear from the beginning."

"You did." She smiled at his pouting face, and her heart

drummed wildly in her chest. "I guess that's a good thing since . . ." She bit her lip, catching her breath. "Well, since you're going to be a father."

"What . . ." Leo stepped back, holding on to her shoulders, his mouth open. "Are you serious?"

"I am." She glanced up at him with a wounded gaze. "Are you upset?"

"Upset? Are you kidding me?" He flung his arms around her and lifted her off her feet, spinning her in a circle before putting her down. Pinching her chin between his fingers, he lifted her face up, and she noticed the huge grin spreading on his face. "Morgie, this is the happiest day of my life. How long have you known?"

"Just a few days. I figured it out when you left the estate this last time. I wanted to tell you sooner, but with all the chaos, I didn't get the chance."

"Does anyone else know?"

"No. You're the first one I told."

"That makes me even happier." He squeezed her tight. "But you know what would really make my day?"

"What?"

"You actually agreeing to marry me."

"How can I agree to something you never asked?"

"I thought I did by implying I was going to marry you." Leo rubbed the back of his neck, smirking. "What, did you want me to drop down on one knee and ask you with a ring and all?"

She knitted her brow. "I don't need a ring. But the other parts would be nice."

"Well," he said, beaming. "I guess today is your lucky day." Pulling a ring from the pouch on his surcoat, Leo kneeled to the ground. "Morgana de Laurent, will you marry me?"

Staring down at the small band of woven gold with a clear green stone in the center, Morgana pressed her fingers to her quivering lips as tears filled her eyes. Looking up at her from the ground, Leo's eyes searched hers for an answer. Gulping down past the lump in her throat, she took in a deep breath and pulled her hand away from her face, offering it to him, and her lips curled into a faint smile while tears dripped down her face.

"Why, Leopold, I thought you'd never ask." She nodded her head and wiped her moist cheeks. "Of course I'll marry you."

"In that case"—he took hold of her outstretched hand and slipped the ring onto her finger, then stood to lift her into his embrace—"today really is the best day of my life."

"You do know that mother will insist on you moving to the estate to live with us full time now? She won't have me, her son-in-law, or her grandchild living anywhere else."

"I can do that." He put her down, pressing his warm lips to her forehead. "When do you think she'll want me there?"

"About three months ago," Morgana giggled. "She always did fancy me ending up with you. Ever since I spoke to you first when I got here, she wanted no one else for a son-in-law, and I think knowing your fate card sealed the deal."

"All right. In that case, I'll grab some of my things from the barracks and join you at the estate tonight. You shall never have to spend the night at the barracks again."

"I have a better idea." She turned away to look down at the estate a short distance behind the wall. "Why don't we go pick up your things together and go tell her the great news as soon as the reception is over? Though, knowing her, she'll leave halfway through. She always loathed crowded spaces and small talks with the nobles."

"We can do that too. Whatever makes you happy." Planting a kiss on her head, he allowed her to return to looking over at the courtyard. Pressing her back to him, he kissed her on the head again, placing a palm over her stomach. "Say, are you worried about what fate card our child will hold? I know you put a lot of stock in those darn things, and I don't want you to be stressing over it."

"No, not anymore." She exhaled and leaned her head into his chest, looking at the clouds. "I know now that fate cards only show you a glimpse of your future. Good or bad, our destiny is up to us. If my father knew that, then we wouldn't be here now. So whatever card our child holds, it won't matter so long as they have proper guidance, which I have no doubt they will. Fate cards or not, nothing bad will happen to them."

Leaning into him, she took in a deep breath and looked at the clouds floating past them. For the first time in years, she smiled at what she saw. The colors seemed brighter and the sun warmer. The threat that had once hung over her like a dark cloud vanished, and the veil was lifted from her eyes. What she said was true. The fate cards no longer bothered her. She was free from her limited view of them, and for once she was determined to pave her own future: a future filled with the happiness and love that she had denied herself for far too long. A future with Leo. And she was looking forward to where it would take them next.

# Coming Soon

*Abnaroth and Evanore*

CPSIA information can be obtained
at www.ICGtesting.com
Printed in the USA
LVHW082004030223
738618LV00022B/615/J

9 781734 240078